JIMI AFTER DARK

A NOVEL

STEPHEN MERTZ

WOLFPACK
PUBLISHING
— EST 2013 —

Jimi After Dark
A Novel
Stephen Mertz

Paperback Edition
Copyright © 2018 (as revised) Stephen Mertz

Wolfpack Publishing
6032 Wheat Penny Avenue
Las Vegas, NV 89122

Paperback ISBN: 978-1-64119-457-0
eBook ISBN: 978-1-64119-456-3

Library of Congress Control Number: 2018962172

ALSO BY STEPHEN MERTZ

Dragon Games

Night Wind

Devil Creek

Blood Red Sun

Hank & Muddy

The Castro Directive

To Ennis Willie, the mentor I never met.

JIMI AFTER DARK

PROLOGUE

6 September 1970
Love & Peace Festival
The Isle of Fehmarn, Germany

THE BAND PLAYS A LAME VERSION OF *FOXY LADY*.

Jimi Hendrix waits for the booing to stop. The crowd is in an ugly mood and so is he. He steps up to the microphone and sneers.

"I don't give a fuck if you boo, if you boo in key."

The heckling grows worse. Someone throws a beer bottle. Near miss. Someone yells, "Go home!" This gets a cheer from the crowd.

It's a sunny afternoon but not warm enough to dry the ankle-deep mud left from the storm that shut down the festival yesterday, when he was scheduled to play. The festival turned ugly before the bad weather. A week ago he played to 700,000 people at the Isle of Wight in the U.K. Only four thousand showed up for this event on opening day and that number dwindled when the hurricane-force storm hit. A contingent of bikers has shown up and there is no one to hold them in check. Too much booze. Bad drugs. Someone has been shot. John Mayall and Joan Baez cancelled their appearances.

Jimi thinks, *They were smart. Should have known better. Should have taken the money and run.*

But he's riding the top of the charts in Europe, so this gig was booked by his manager. What hurricane? Rescheduled to play a day late? Do it, man. Can't disappoint the fans.

He looks fine in tight jeans and a wild, multi-colored jacket. A turquoise scarf for a headband, and he's given them all the stage show tricks an audience usually eats up.

But not this crowd. Miserably wet, muddy and surly.

Time to shift gears.

He nods to the drummer and bass player and they kick off the slow blues, *Red House*, from his first album. That one never grows old. He never tires of singing and playing it. Nothing but them old twelve bar blues with some Buddy Guy guitar licks thrown in, embellished with electronic pyrotechnics but it's where Jimi Hendrix came from and right now he's feeling those damn blues.

The power should be with him now. He's onstage. He should be into it. In the old days even a bummer gig like this would have ignited the raw energy in his veins, ignited from just the thrill of playing. The music was everything.

The old days. What, three years ago?

Time is a speeding silver phantom that won't slow down.

A hip Brit producer walks into a joint in the Village where Jimi's playing under the name of Jimmy James for the artsy Village crowd. The producer heard something that night. Took Jimi to England. Hooked him up with U.K. musicians and The Jimi Hendrix Experience was born. They blew the lid off the British music scene and then the whole world. Melodies and lyrics flowed from him. His guitar playing only got better. The Experience charted one hit after another.

But on this day he's only going through the motions of what then had been so fresh. So hot. So damn frenzied.

That was the word. Frenzy. Sucked his soul dry in three short years. A grueling jet speed superhighway of non-stop global touring. Fast lane rock & roll, baby. Hotels and motels, limos, airplanes, constant movement. Always something to do, somewhere to be. Dope to snort and smoke and shoot. Extreme sensation without beginning or end. The world outside the windows of cars and trains and planes became a fast-moving blur.

A too brief hiatus in New York, recording at Electric Lady Land after three nonstop years of touring. He'd poured his heart and soul, not to mention a load of financing, into the perfect studio of his own design where they spent two-and-a-half months recording even while the final phase of construction was ongoing. Then the flight to London and this tour from hell.

When did everything turn to shit?

They stretch out *Red House* into a ten minute jam.

His mind is thirteen hundred miles away. Electric Lady Land. *His* studio. His future. His dreams. When would those dreams come true? How many more tours before he can just recharge his soul and create?

He doesn't even care anymore what the music is doing chart-wise. He's come to hate the stage mannerisms, the jive tricks with the guitar that the audience expects. He's come to hate *Foxy Lady* and *Purple Haze,* having progressed musically so far beyond those little pop tunes. The goal now is to touch the people of the world spiritually with his music.

But dark forces are trying to steal his music from him.

And this afternoon on this German island, they're booing and throwing beer bottles.

The blaring banks of amplifiers vent his frustration and rage. Long, thin fingers coax improvisational blues from his guitar. His soul is screaming.

Trapped! Can't breathe. Get me out of here!

1

─────

Ten Days Later
London

Call me Soldier.

I was twenty-seven years old, six-foot-one, one-ninety in weight. No one would call me handsome, not with the shrapnel scar on the right side of my face and the bullet-nicked ear. I was wearing my Class A uniform for travel. I was in my prime and I thought I was smart.

We touched down at Heathrow on a dismal afternoon. I'd just caught my first deep sleep in thirty hours of air travel when the pilot's voice came over the PA, instructing us to extinguish our cigarettes and fasten our seatbelts. I awoke with a jolt. I was in a cold sweat. The businessman seated next to me didn't seem to notice. I'd been dreaming about, or reliving, the day Pulaski had taken point and walked into a booby trap that had splashed his middle all over the rest of us.

A time-zone shredding flight schedule, traveling east to west, had taken on its own rhythm of shifting realities morphing from the chaotic airport scene in Saigon, where the atmosphere pulsed with simmering violence, to right now with big jet engines shutting down. The airliner positioning itself for us passengers to disembark.

My uniform and its sergeant stripes got me through Customs without hassle.

Hassle.

It was part of a new language that had been born in the time I'd spent in Vietnam. I'd picked up bits and pieces in the letters from Jimi but sometimes you needed a translator from another dimension. *Crash pad. Ripped off. Shine him on. Don't Bogart that joint.* When I'd left the States for Nam, kids were listening to the Beatles but everyone over the age of twenty was getting drafted, going to college or learning a trade.

I'd seen the movie *Easy Rider* and I'd heard Jimi's music. Hell, you could not avoid hearing Jimi or the Doors or the Stones in-country. Vietnam was a rock & roll war.

A young woman of about twenty, a long-haired redhead, stood waiting for me after my duffle bag and I passed through Customs. She wore a white summery-looking dress. She had a high, smooth forehead and a thin, delicate mouth. She waited off to the side, not paying attention to any of the other debarking passengers. I did stand out. I was the only American GI on that flight.

I had the duffle bag hefted over my shoulder and

hadn't taken three steps before she eased into my path. She started to say something.

I said, "You're from Jimi?"

"I represent his management."

Her manner was brisk, self-confident. Green eyes. A cute smattering of freckles across her nose.

I said, "You're with Mike Jeffrey and his bunch?"

She blinked. Very pretty. Very sweet. I hadn't spoken with a sweet, pretty girl in years.

She said, "I'm, uh, not prepared to say."

I sidestepped her and strode on at a brisk pace. She hurried to keep up. We made our way along an arcade of gift shops, pubs and restaurants.

Jimi had been having management troubles. From the tone of the last letter I'd received from him, my buddy was having all sorts of troubles. When he found out that I had leave time coming before I reported for duty in Frankfurt, he'd invited me to look him up in London. He'd show me a good time. I'd meet some fine ladies and maybe I could help him with "a situation" he'd gotten himself involved in. I didn't have to read much between the lines to hear the plea for help from a guy who once saved my life.

I owed Jimi Hendrix my life from way back before Vietnam. I'd come to London to pay back that debt.

The redhead was practically jogging to keep up with me.

"My name is Sydney Blanchard."

"Sydney? That's a boy's name."

"No, it isn't. It's Olde English. It means wide island."

"And why would someone name you that?"

"Does it really matter?"

"I guess not."

"I was sent to meet you and apprise you of the difficult situation you're stepping into."

"I'm used to difficult situations."

"Yes, we know about Vietnam."

"We?"

"You and Jimi know each other from when Jimi was a paratrooper and you served together at Fort Campbell, Kentucky. Jimi was injured in a training jump that exempted him from service. You see? I know very well where you've been and what you've done, Sergeant."

I could see no reason to tell her that the training jump injury was a cover story.

I said, "He wrote me once that he stayed at The Cumberland when he's in London."

Intelligent green eyes narrowed, sizing me up as we walked. "Jimi's on the dodge."

"Is that how British birds talk?"

"Stop it. They haven't called us birds in years and years. At least five. You're way out of date."

I chuckled a tired chuckle. "More than you'll ever know. By the way, how did you know what flight I was arriving on?"

"The people I work for have connections."

"And you seem like such a sweet innocent young thing from a distance. Do you know where Jimi is? Can you take me to him?"

And damned if she didn't stop right there and grasp my wrist in a steel-like vise with one of her little hands. She planted herself in front of me again, slightly out of breath.

"Hold on! I'm not a bleeding marathon runner. Let me speak my piece."

I had to stop or I'd roll right over her. I looked down into those determined green eyes. I liked her.

"So you know Jimi sent for me. Then you know that I'm not in the mood to waste time. Make it good."

Narrowed eyes flared. "I don't know where Jimi is. I was hoping you'd know. That's why I came to meet you. I care about Jimi."

"But you don't know where he is?"

"He's gone to ground." Her smooth forehead creased into thin lines. "I'm worried."

"And why is that?"

"Because no one knows where he is." She spoke as if explaining to a child who wasn't overly bright. "He's dodging his solicitors, he's dodging process servers and subpoenas. This underground existence he's living has been going on for three days."

"Maybe you're one of the people he's dodging."

I sidestepped around her and continued walking.

She resumed matching me stride for stride. "You don't have to be unkind."

"I'm being realistic. I'm trying to figure how to handle you."

"Handle me?"

"You could be in this over your head. If you know anything that I need to know, brief me now."

She took a deep breath and let it out fast. She said, "The wheels are falling off. After the Isle of Wight, Jimi had a European tour. It was a nightmare. In Stockholm, he was drunk onstage. Next was the festival at Fehmarn.

Jimi was wasted. It was horrific. A riot started. The rest of the tour was cancelled."

This was all news to me. Last I'd heard from Jimi was two weeks earlier; a brief note with contact info. There had been no mention of a girl named Sydney.

I said, "So Jimi just up and disappeared?"

"That's what I've been trying to tell you. He's gone missing and this is a vital week for him to be on the scene, not to drop out of it. His ex-managers and ex-promoters are fighting over his contracts in court, basically carving up shares of his money. Stealing from him. We have to find him."

"There's that *we* again. Who's we? Who do you represent, Syd?"

"I'm, uh, not at liberty to say, I'm afraid. But I was hoping that we could work together, you and I. Pool our resources, as it were. Would that be agreeable to you?"

We were approaching a wide, busy exit bordered by broad expanses of plate glass, affording a panorama of pedestrians, taxi cabs and shuttles. A sea of executive types hurrying to make appointments. Tired tourists who looked like they only wanted a meal and a place to sleep.

A group of Hare Krishnas were chanting nearby. At least I think they were chanting. I heard the finger cymbals but their chanting was buried beneath the loud taunting of three skinheads.

Burly punks. Tattoos where hair should have been. Leather jackets, black T-shirts, denim jeans and brogans. The skinhead movement in the U.K. had managed to garner mention even in the *Stars and Stripes*.

They spotted me. They lost interest in the Hare

Krishna, who continued to chant and dance, blissfully oblivious of their surroundings.

One of the skinheads snickered. "Hey look, mates. If it ain't a Yank baby killer."

That's the first time I'd heard those words directed at me. I'd heard about guys in rotation back to the States being harassed in airports and train stations. It was an unpopular war at home and around the world. American soldiers were spat on. But I honestly hadn't given any thought to anyone ever yelling the words at me.

I once found a Viet woman having her baby, hiding alone in the high grass next to a rice paddy and somehow managing to keep it quiet. I happened upon her while dodging VC fire from a tree line. I helped deliver a little girl into the world. It was a real learning experience that I'd just as soon not ever again have to apply, but it happened sort of naturally, me holding a newborn and swatting its butt to start it crying and breathing, the little sounds of new life lost below the ferocity of combat raging around us. A clip from my ammo webbing clamped the little girl's belly button. I saw gratitude in that mother's eyes before I moved out. Baby killer?

What the hell, I wasn't going to explain any of that to these stooges. These were taunts not from sincere war protestors but from street punks who wanted to start something. They could have been triplets, that's how ugly they were. Squinting eyes, glassy and mean beneath low foreheads.

Sydney heard them, along with everyone in our immediate vicinity, but her eyes told me that we were this close to the exit, just ignore them and keep walking.

I heard myself mumble, "Welcome to London. I'm starting to miss Saigon."

Then one of the skinheads spat at me. His phlegm glittered like a gray pearl on my uniform.

"We're talking to you, Yank." A heavy cockney accent. "So where have you been, soldier boy? Killing babies over in Vietnam and raping their mamas for Uncle Sam?"

In combat, you react instantly to any sign of aggression. Pure survival reflex. You don't even stop to think about it. Every part of me except my body was still back on patrol with the guys in my squad—Doc, Stookey, Ponch and the rest of those jackoffs.

I brought the duffle bag around with enough force to double up the spitter with the big mouth. He made an *ooooof!* noise when the heavy bag caught him in the gut.

His two pals threw themselves at me, snarling like they were ferocious or something. I met the nearest one with my left elbow to the side or his head, intending to crush his temple but I missed and caught him behind the ear, rendering him unconscious on his feet instead of dead. The other one tackled me, toppling us both down onto the marble floor. Gasps of civilized dismay surrounded us. This guy made a dumb mistake in taking me down to ground level with him. I was on the wrestling team in high school. I slid around on the floor's smooth surface and vised his neck between my spit-shined black combat boots. I could apply pressure to the throat that could crush his larynx or a sharp twist would break his neck. I cracked his head on the floor. I didn't kill him, don't ask me why, but it was a hard enough tap to render him an unconscious dead weight across my legs, pinning them.

The third one, the spitter who started it all, had recovered from my duffel bag to his gut and took this opportunity to throw himself at me, pinning me to the floor before I could shove the unconscious lump of his partner off my legs. This one's beefy hands went for my throat. He thought he was going to bash my brains out on that marble floor but I surprised him by not resisting, instead drawing his head down toward me. I steadied my grip on his head and I bit off his ear. It's not something that's particularly difficult. You're biting through tissue and gristle, not bone. A child could do it. I've done it before. He squealed like you'd expect someone to after he's lost a body part.

I spat out the damn thing. The punk was screaming his lungs out but I've heard worse. I scrambled to my feet. The entire incident had gone down in less than thirty seconds.

Sydney stared, wide-eyed, her jaw gaping.

I retrieved my duffel bag. I snagged her wrist and we started away from there. People gave us a wide berth. There was no sign yet of security or police but there would be soon enough. I threw a glance along our backtrack.

The guy had found his ear and was screaming louder than before.

We made our way outside.

Sydney managed to say, "But . . . but—"

I said, "Stop it, you sound like a motor boat."

I felt great. My adrenaline was pumping. The action had revived me from the lethargy of travel.

I drew her over to the nearest taxi.

The driver was reading a newspaper, oblivious to what had just happened inside. I swung open the rear door and steered Sydney into the back seat. I slapped the roof of the cab with the palm of my hand hard, three times.

"Take the lady wherever she wants to go."

The driver must have been an old military man. He responded automatically to a tone of command. The taxi bolted away from the curb.

I shouldered the duffle bag and started walking.

2

A TAXI WAS EASY ENOUGH TO FIND ONCE I'D PUT SOME distance between me and the action inside the terminal. I had to refer to that last note from Jimi, the one I carried in its envelope folded in my pocket, before I could give the driver the address. Then I leaned back in the airy black London cab and listened to the driver, a good-natured geezer in a wool cap, tell me about all the fine Americans soldiers he'd served with during the war. They were good joes, is how he put it.

I let this new environment that I'd dropped into wash over me, the old salt reminiscing behind the steering wheel while images sped past beyond the taxi's rain-streaked windows. Everyone drove with their lights on because the middle of the afternoon was like dusk, steady showers, nothing like the monsoon season in Nam but with a low cloud ceiling that made dismal and depressing the row houses with their chimney pots and brick walls and the severe postwar commercial architecture.

The cabbie dropped me off in the middle of the block

on Fulham Road. Traffic on the rain-slick pavement whispered sibilantly. I wanted to approach the corner pharmacy on foot. No pedestrians were in sight. I hugged the storefronts, staying relatively dry under awnings.

The double glass doors were right where Jimi's letter said they would be, just short of the pharmacy. I eased one of the doors open and stepped inside.

Jimi stood with his back to me, at a payphone attached to a yellow wall at the foot of a wide and worn set of stairs to the second level.

He was busy yammering into the phone. "Don't tell me I'm high, like that means you don't have to listen to what I'm saying!" He gesticulated with a free hand that held a smoking cigarette. "Hell yeah, I'm high. Couldn't find me no hash so I bagged me some heavy reefer. Got a couple of hippie chicks waiting on me upstairs soon as I hang up. So don't be acting like your time is more valuable than mine. No, I ain't going to tell you where I am. Ain't none of your boys going to hunt me down, so don't come at me like it's all groovy because I know damn well it ain't. Okay, okay. I'm listening." He remained unaware of my presence. He was jittery and angry.

I set my duffle bag down next to the doorway. I leaned back so it cushioned my butt and crossed my arms to wait. I'd come a long way. I was here. Now I could wait.

From on high a woman's voice yelled, "Hey you!"

Since Jimi and I were the only two in sight, I figured that the "you" she was addressing was me.

A woman near my age stood at the top of those stairs. She had a pleasant face with an expression of good humor. She wore a white peasant blouse with cleavage trimmed in lace, and an ankle-length, tie-dyed skirt and sandals. She had a dusky complexion and was built up front, with nicely rounded hips, a wild mane of midnight black hair and an animated disposition. She wore a great deal of jewelry: necklace, rings, bracelets, earrings.

She came down the stairs.

Jimi was consumed by his telephone conversation, his back still to me. His hand with the cigarette continued to wave about while he spoke. Smoke left grey zig zags in the air.

He interrupted whoever was speaking on the other end. "Look man, I can't stay on if you're just going to jive me. I've been working this damn phone all day."

Peasant Blouse reached the bottom step. She eased past Jimi and said to me, "That's God's truth. Jimi's about to take root with that phone to his ear."

She smelled of patchouli oil perfume. There were fine lines around her eyes. She exuded a sense of life and purpose and amusement.

Jimi raked fingers through his hair. "Damn, my managers are totally screwed up! I'm looking down the barrel of financial ruin and all you want is another piece of me. Dude, I talk to spaceships in the sky so I'll talk to you, dig? But damn, I need me some help and understanding."

Peasant Blouse said to me, "Don't tell me the U.S. Army is after Jimi. That would be just too dadblasted much."

Since my jet had lifted off from Saigon, I'd been surrounded by nothing but Australian and British accents.

I said, "Dadblast back at you, girl. You're from Texas."

"Everyone's from somewhere," she said. She placed a hand on one of my elbows in an attempt to guide me and my duffle bag toward the street door. "Sorry. No room at the inn for you, Sergeant. We're strictly peaceniks under this roof. Now if you'll just—"

Jimi shouted into the phone, "Hey, I said don't worry about it!" He slammed the receiver back onto its hook. He turned and started to say with petulance, "Now how's a dude supposed to do business on the phone when—" He stopped talking when he saw me. His eyes grew wide.

I said, "Hey, Jimi."

The anger and whatever else I saw in his eyes gave way to the kind of unfettered joy a kid gets when he finds exactly the present he wants sitting under the Christmas tree.

"Well my my," he said in that smoky, laid-back voice that I remembered. "Look what the cat dragged in."

I said, "Long time no see, buddy."

We shook hands and braced each other on the shoulder.

The patchouli gal stood back to allow us the space there in the vestibule for that little display of male bonding, watching us with keen, uncertain eyes.

Jimi said, "Angel McGuire, I want you to meet—"

I stuck out my hand.

"Soldier."

Jimi didn't miss a beat. "Soldier here, me and him go back. I mean way back to like Fort Campbell, Kentucky. Soldier, this is Angel's place. Sort of a commune, you might say."

Angel said with a pleasant laugh, "Call it what it is, Jimi. It's a sanctuary for runaways and sometimes I think that includes you." Her handshake was brief, but firm enough to be sincere. "Welcome, uh, Soldier. Sorry about the rude reception."

Jimi draped his arm around her waist with a nonchalance that was more affectionate than possessive. "Angel here is my angel of mercy."

Angel said, "Jimi, let's get you upstairs and away from this street door. Monika knows about this place, right? She'll come here looking for you."

Jimi's cigarette waved. "Aw, she's just another someone who wants a piece of me. Now this man," he told Angel with one of his arms around Angel's waist and the other draped over my shoulder, "this cat came from the other side of the planet to help out a brother."

He needed a little help getting up the wide stairs. I braced him from his left, with the duffle back over my free shoulder, while Angel helped guide him from the right.

He was the same Jimi that I'd known at Fort Campbell in some ways and a whole different piece of work in most other ways. He wore tight black jeans, a white silk shirt worn open at the collar, a necklace of multicolored beads and a short jacket that matched the jeans, a hippy getup that wouldn't have lasted a minute back in the barracks without severe harassment. His hair was worn long and frizzy but not as well-tended as the album covers and publicity photos I'd seen. His eyelids drooped in a stoner gaze. The eyes are something you remember about an unusual guy like Jimi. He was stoned to the gills, sure, but back when I'd known him at Fort C, whether he was on duty or hanging out with the guys at the NCO club, Jimi always had that faraway look, like he was waiting for something to show itself way off on the horizon or gazing somehow into another world.

As we made it up the stairway of the old building, to the level above the corner pharmacy, the stairwell walls began to resemble more and more a museum of modern art. Pale blank yellow gave way to swirls of colorful rainbows and butterflies and unicorns everywhere I looked. Heavy acid rock blared from the top of the stairs.

Angel had to raise her voice to be heard above the racket of Iron Butterfly.

"Welcome to what I prefer to call my playground of expression. Are you around for awhile?"

"For a few days, on my way to Germany."

"Do you need a place to crash?"

"Crash?"

That was a new one. I was jolted by the mental image, sparked by the word crash, of a Huey gunship exploding into a fireball and going down with the shouting and screams of everyone left alive to burn when it crashed to the ground.

Jimi translated. "She means a place to spend the night"

I said, "I'm improvising."

Angel nodded her approval. "That's the best way to live."

The strains of *In-A-Gadda-Da-Vida* engulfed us when we reached the landing at the top of the stairs.

"I'm intruding on your party."

She laughed. "It's not a party. It's a crash pad. My crash pad."

From below a woman's voice suddenly screamed, *"Jimi!"*

The three of us turned as one to see a tall blonde step

into the vestibule from the street below; a beauty with long blonde hair, in her mid twenties, wearing a stylish outfit that consisted of an abbreviated top and bell bottom pants, bisected by a six-inch span of flat midriff.

Jimi managed to regain his balance.

"Oh shit! I don't want to deal with this."

The blonde started up the stairs toward us.

"Jimi, we must talk." She spoke in what sounded like a German accent. "I have been looking everywhere for you."

Angel whispered, "Jimi, you know the back way out. Take it." She started down the stairs to intercept the blonde. "I'll divert Monika as long as I can. Git, and take this soldier with you. See you again, solider man."

I said, "Uh, sure."

With an ally now initiating action on his behalf, Jimi came to life. He left the landing like a deer leaping off a dark road and back into the forest to escape the headlights.

It was my turn to hurry to keep up.

From below, a shrewish Germanic voice shrilled up the stairwell after us.

"Jimi! Come back, you coward! Don't you walk away from me in the middle of a fight. Come back here, I say!"

Angel McGuire could be heard speaking in a placating tone of voice. I imagined her standing in the center of the stairway, impeding Monkia's progress.

I followed Jimi through my first crash pad.

A modest but artfully furnished loft. Walls knocked out so that only a few rooms (one of which had to be Angel's) were walled off to themselves, making everything else an open communal area of polished wood flooring and a high ceiling. A dozen or so kids, there couldn't have been anyone I saw over the age of twenty, singles and couples, lounged here and there about large throw pillows and on sofas and chairs amid tasteful furnishings, everything from psychedelic wall posters advertising the Jefferson Airplane and Jimi Hendrix playing at the San Francisco Fillmore to iconic figures of Eastern religions, some of the icons serving as holders for sticks of incense that emitted smoke that mingled with the scent of hash being smoked.

As I passed through, tagging along behind Jimi, schlepping the duffle bag over my shoulder, only about half of those we passed seemed to notice. Long haired boys and girls, the male faces smooth, each still with the blush of youth. Untested. Not like the forty-yard stare of twenty-year-old Corporal Hicks, who'd been the only one of his squad to survive a VC ambush. After that, Hicks' expression was a mask of stone until the day he died a month later in a firefight.

Jimi took us past two guys holding hands while they smoked a joint. I passed a couch where a couple of girls were making out, kissing and touching each other's hair. I'd never seen anything like that before except in dirty pictures but here it somehow looked perfectly natural.

Someone said, after I'd passed, "Uh oh, we're being invaded."

Another wit chortled. "We're the next Vietnam!"

A pretty girl of about eighteen stood leaning against a wall. Long chestnut hair, all nubile and fresh. Her nipples poked out from beneath a Freak Brothers t-shirt. She offered me the joint she was smoking.

She giggled. "Do I salute or offer a toke? I haven't

experimented with a soldier yet. Want to get it on, big man?"

Jimi disappeared through an archway.

I gritted my teeth and told the girl, "Another time, sweetheart."

I hated to say no, but Jimi came first. I followed Jimi through the archway, into a large kitchen where several young men and women, all clad in the hippie regalia of tie-dye and denim, worked at a big stove, filling the air with the aromas of baking bread and stove top stew.

Jimi was just stepping through a doorway at the far end of the kitchen. I caught up with him halfway down a narrow flight of stairs. Then we emerged from the building into the daylight. The rain had stopped but the low sky remained gloomy.

I'm a country boy, born and raised, and the jungle had become my home. But I'd done enough time in big towns. The stench and sounds of an urban alley are universal: that closed-in feeling of a canyon of towering walls, the stink in a dumpster and the smell of urine fouled the air. The alley was noisy with the nearby passing traffic.

A man stood in the alley, waiting for us. Smoking a cigarette. Feet squarely planted. A big bruiser of a man, something over two hundred pounds, pushing forty. He wore a tan trench coat and a fedora. A hard face was pockmarked from childhood acne. His eyes were cold. When we drew up several paces from him, he flicked away his cigarette.

"Well hullo there, Jim."

Jimi tensed. His nonchalant demeanor evaporated. He nodded and said in a wary voice, "Inspector."

I didn't need anyone to tell me that the guy was a cop. The type is as universal as the smell of an alley. I never had much use for cops. I was raised to handle my own trouble. I had a good raising. I don't need the law to keep me in line.

The cop said, "It occurred to me that perhaps I should keep an eye on Angel's little nest of misfits. When I saw an angry blonde arrive a minute ago in such a, shall we say dither just now, shouting your name, I somehow thought there could be a chance that I might encounter you exiting via the back way. A real backdoor man, eh, Jim?"

Jimi said, "I don't know why you want to talk to me, Inspector. I haven't done anything."

"Oh come come, Jimbo. Lots of people want to talk to you, or so I'm told. Managers and record companies breaking out their high-priced legal teams. Millions of dollars at stake."

"Yeah, my millions and the vultures are trying to pick off every penny of it."

"Vultures only go after the dead, Jim. You look alive to me."

"Yeah well, sometimes I don't feel alive. Sometimes death don't sound so bad."

"You've been keeping the wrong sort of friends, Jim."

"Aw, Angel's okay—"

"I'm not talking about Angel McGuire and you bloody well know it. I'm talking about two brothers named Kray."

"Inspector, last I heard they were doing thirty years apiece in prison and you put them there."

"True enough but I don't have to tell you, Jimbo, that what's left of their old crowd is still actively trying to pick up the pieces. You know I like you, Jim. My teenage daughter buys all of your records."

"Then you know my name isn't Jim or Jimbo. It's Jimi."

"Don't get smart with me, lad."

"I'm no criminal," Jimi said quietly.

The cold cop eyes shifted to me. "Who's your friend?"

"Just a friend." Jimi said to me, "This is Inspector Hudberry."

I said, "People around here call me Soldier."

"Seeing as you're wearing a U.S. Army uniform, I can see why. Well around here is my bailiwick, Soldier, and I don't much like Yanks that play it smart. What's your name?"

Jimi said in a reasonable voice, "Come on, Inspector. We ain't broke no laws. Let us pass."

"I'll let you pass when I'm damn good and ready," said Hudberry. His eyes stayed on me. Mean eyes. "Soldier is *what* you are, Yank, not *who* you are. Soldier. Seems I caught a radio alert on a scuffle out at Heathrow. Rough stuff involving a U.S. serviceman. Three men down, one in a coma. You wouldn't be that serviceman, would you, laddie?"

"It wasn't me."

"Well that's mighty interesting because you know what? I think it *was* you. I think I should be placing you under arrest right now for what happened at the airport. You see, Jim. I told you. You're running with the wrong crowd."

The moment held.

Hudberry and I were different in every respect except for what I saw in those mean eyes. He was a mean ass, tenacious bulldog and once he clamped down on something he wasn't likely to let go. My hope was that he would see the same thing in my eyes and be smart enough to let us pass. But no, he wasn't the type to back down. He reached out with his right hand and grasped my arm above the elbow.

"Let's you and me take a little trip, Yank, and have us a chat."

I don't like being manhandled. My right hand seized his wrist. My left leg straightened. With a shove I took him down and stood over him with my boot at his throat.

He stared up at me in a feral rage, grasping and tugging at my ankle with both hands, trying to shake loose the boot that pinned him to the damp, smelly pavement.

He glared at Jimi.

"Call this mad dog off me, you hippie son of a bitch."

I said, "You know, Hudberry, all I'd have to do is twist my boot and lean in at an angle with the slightest amount of pressure and you're dead."

Jimi said to me, "Brother, you've got a short fuse!" He winked. "Don't hurt him, man. He's got a family. You're already in deep shit. Let's get gone."

Hudberry said, "Hendrix, you're dead if you don't get this maniac off me. I'll get you both for this."

No, not the type to back down even when he was down.

I said, "Jimi."

"Yeah, what?"

"The cops don't pack heat in England, isn't that true?"

"That's right."

"Not even plainclothes inspectors?

"Not even them."

I removed my boot from his throat.

Hudberry lifted his head from the dank pavement and

started to sit up. He reached around to the small of his back. That's how a lot of plainclothes cops in the U.S. carry their handcuffs.

He said, "Soldier, I'm placing you under—"

Before he could say "arrest," I leaned in and punched him a short right jab that caught him right in the face. He fell back to the pavement with the whites of his eyes showing. I gave him a quick frisk. Jimi was right. No gun.

When I stood, Jimi met me with a worried frown. "Dude, we're in some deep shit now."

"You sent for me, Jimi. I can't do much if I'm arrested and in jail. What the hell's going on? Who are the Krays? I can understand lawyers giving you a hard time but why the cops?"

"Screw that." He glanced around. "We've got to split. You didn't kill him, did you?"

"Do you want me to?"

"Jesus Christ, no! Are you crazy?"

"That's debatable. Relax, I'm jerking your chain." I nudged the side of Hudberry's head back and forth with the toe of my boot. He sputtered. "Your inspector will be awake soon enough."

The shrill squeal of brakes sounded on wet pavement. A sporty red-and-white Austin Healy four-seater skidded to a stop on the wet pavement at the mouth of the alley.

Sydney Blanchard sat behind the steering wheel. Her red hair framed an expression that was equal parts concern and youthful enthusiasm.

"Looks like you boys could use a ride. Hop in." She was not oblivious to Hudberry's prone form. "And make it snappy."

3

WE SAT WITH SYDNEY IN A BOOTH AT A WIMPY'S.

I'd noted several of these fast food hamburger joints since arriving in London; sterile little chain franchises like the White Castles and McDonalds back home, the name inspired by Popeye's pal ("I'd gladly pay you tomorrow for a hamburger today"). The four-lane scene of passing traffic beyond the windows could have been any Grease Row in any American city except of course that everyone was driving on the opposite side of the street, I mean road.

Sydney had ordered for us at the counter. A Coke for me, Coke and hamburgers and fries—chips—for each of them. Sydney and I sat side by side. Jimi took up his side of the booth, sitting sideways with his legs stretched across the bench, his back to the wall.

Jimi said, "I miss soul food."

I said, "I miss knowing what I'm dealing with. At least over in Nam you know they're out there waiting for you. I thought swinging London would be more, well, civilized."

The first thing I'd done while Sydney ordered was to dip into the gents room and make quick work of swapping my uniform for a pair of denim jeans, a dark t-shirt and a light jacket. I still wore my combat boots. The duffel bag now resided in the trunk—I mean boot—of Sydney's Austin Healy.

Jimi was drawn and lethargic, obviously high on drugs. He'd spotted the Wimpy's and insisted on us going in and now he was not touching his food.

He said, "Was Hudberry right? Did you get in a scuffle out at the airport?"

Sydney nudged his unwrapped, untouched meal toward him. "Eat your food, Jimi," she said between bites of her burger and fries. "And yes, he did."

Jimi said, "I ain't hungry."

I said, "Sydney met me at the airport. Apparently she hasn't gotten around to reporting to you yet what with everyone dodging here and there."

Sydney nodded. "I met you and after your impressive demonstration of arse kicking, you deserted me. I shouldn't forgive you for that so easily."

I said, "Just out of curiosity, Jimi, was Sydney meeting me at the airport your idea or hers?"

Jimi avoided my eyes, preferring to watch the traffic beyond the window. "It wasn't my idea," he mumbled, "but she told me what she was up to."

Sydney said, "For your information, Soldier, this girl does not require other people to give her ideas. I get plenty of them all by myself, thank you. I thought it would be in Jimi's best interests if I, well, sized you up, to put it frankly. He told me you were coming and what flight you'd be on. I just thought it prudent, given the state of

Jimi's affairs and everything that's going on. I was going to call ahead and warn him if you weren't, well, as advertised. It's been years since the two of you last saw each other. People can change."

Jimi continued to gaze out the window. "And there are tabloid photogs trolling Heathrow. You see what it's like with me right now. No disrespect, Soldier. I'm damn glad you're here, even after what you did to that cop. It's good to have someone like you on my side."

I said to Sydney, "You told me you didn't know where Jimi was."

Her small shoulders gave a slight shrug. One of her pinkies dabbed away a spot of ketchup from the corner of her mouth. "I'm an aspiring actress, among other things. How did I do?"

"Okay, I guess. You knew where he was all the time. I should be ticked off about that."

She paused in lifting her half-finished hamburger for another bite. "And are you?"

"I guess not. You seem okay."

"Seem?"

"I'm still getting the lay of the land."

Sydney smiled sweetly. "Of course you're referring to Angel McGuire?"

Jimi said, "Aw Sydney, don't be like that. You're good people and so is Angel. You know that."

Sydney finished her hamburger. "All right, all right. I was being catty. I love Angel more than you know." She added as an aside to me, "It's hard to be a woman and want Jimi to jump your bones, and you want to mother him at the same time."

Seemed like people couldn't stop saying things that I didn't know how to respond to.

The best I could manage was, "Uh, I'll take your word on that."

Jimi turned his attention to contemplating the empty row of booths along the opposite wall. There was sparse business at Wimpy's this time of day and every time he sensed a new customer entering the establishment, he would glance around nervously until, satisfied by the sight of an ordinary customer, he'd resume staring off into the distance the way I remembered all those years ago at Fort Campbell.

I said, "So Jimi, tell me about Hudberry. His daughter buys your records but his job is to bust you?"

Jimi sat up straight, turned to face me and lit a fresh cigarette, his elbows resting on the table. "I'm not really the target."

"I'm glad to hear that."

"A few years ago Scotland Yard launched this big sweep to rid the world of rock and roll. People were having too much fun and the man didn't dig it."

Sydney crumpled the wrappings of her hamburger into a ball and took a noisy slurp of her Coke through a straw. "They bugged telephones," she said. "They bought snitches and whatnot so they could frame famous people in the music business. The tabloids were behind it for all the sensational dirt it provided them to sell their filthy rags."

Jimi said, "The Stones almost went down. I knew Brian Jones. He died way too young. A messed up cat but it was stress from the drug bust hassles that did him in.

They almost put Mick and Keith in prison. Others went down too. The cops were like mad dogs."

"But the tables turned," said Sydney. *"The London Times* ran an editorial denouncing the authorities for squandering their resources on otherwise law-abiding citizens who happened to be rock stars."

Jimi reached across the table and tickled her under the chin with his index finger. He'd always been a lady's man and obviously still filled that bill even when baked out of his skull.

"Damn you talk so right, girl, I ought to put you through law school. There's an idea! I need me a lawyer who cares about *me* instead of those bloodsuckers in suits so busy carving up the bread I earned 'em while I'm left to live on the run."

Sydney said, "Jimi was supposed to meet today with legal consul in two separate actions pending in court. He's been summoned to appear but as you can see, that was pretty much out of the question given the state he's in."

I said, "Let's get back to Hudberry. How much is he part of the trouble we're having?"

"I wasn't lying to him," said Jimi. "I ain't broke no laws except for getting high. After they got their hands slapped for trying to frame rock stars they started going after the bad cats like the Krays that they should have been trying to take down in the first place."

"Who are the Krays?"

Sydney said, "A more precisely phrased question would be who *were* the Krays. They're a couple of East End hooligans currently serving thirty years to life for numerous organized crimes including murder. They ran a nasty loan shark racket and now that they've been put away, their former associates are jockeying to see who gets what."

I couldn't hold down a quick grin. "You sound like a crime reporter."

"I'm happy being what I am," she said tartly.

Jimi said, "Hudberry's after a loanshark named Tobe Gearson and some of his boys. Gearson's the main former associate that Sydney's talking about." He regarded his cigarette as he tapped it on the plastic Wimpy's ash tray. "I know Gearson so I guess Hudberry thinks he can lean on me as a way of getting to Gearson. That's a crock. I don't know nothing about the hood games in this town."

"How do you know Gearson? Drugs?"

He waved a dismissive hand. "Naw, man. I owe him some money and I'm late paying off, so he's giving me heat. That's him I was talking to on the phone when you showed up. I got people heaping all the smoke and pills on me that I can take. Naw. I'm a musician, man, I ain't no drug dealer. There's a cat named Mike Jeffrey."

I nodded. "Your manager. You mentioned him in your letters."

"Yeah well, make that ex-manager. Jeffrey's one of the guys that's suing me. Hudberry thinks he can tie Tobe Gearson to Jeffrey, but he won't. I'm just a pawn, Soldier. I'm everybody's pawn."

"So you're in a bind between your manager and some hoods?"

"Bingo. I hired a private accountant and found out that Mike Jeffrey has been robbing me blind, skimming off my concert tour earnings. I'm talking big money. So I fired his ass. Jeffrey hates my guts. So I've got him and Gearson and Hudberry and a mess of lawyers all out to get me."

He put out his half-smoked cigarette, lit another and resumed leaning against the wall with his eyes closed.

Sydney said, "Jeffrey is a rough customer. The word on the street is that when he was in the military, he was stationed in the Middle East. He speaks Russian. There have been rumors that he worked undercover against the Russians, rumors about mayhem and torture and murder in foreign lands. Of course there are those skeptics who say Michael Jeffrey created this mysterioso image as a form of self-protection and to pique public interest. Jimi should never have gotten involved with the guy, but he needed a quick infusion of startup capital when he first arrived here. Jeffrey provided those funds and he's been taking his pound of flesh ever since."

I said, "A journalist. That's what you'll be when you grow up, Sydney. A journalist writing about the pop music scene."

She made a face. "Stop teasing me. I'll always be what I am today. A shop girl on Carnaby Street. That is, until I'm discovered and become a famous actress. And I'm Jimi's friend."

Impatience that had been building in me broke to the surface.

"I need more."

She blinked. "More?"

"Jimi, you and I were always able to talk straight, man to man."

His eyes cracked open. "That's telling the stone truth, brother." The cigarette dangled from the corner of his mouth as he spoke. "That's why I wrote you to come help me out."

"Right, and that's what I'm here to do. But Jimi, you're higher than shit."

He gave that throaty chuckle of his and smiled his big toothy smile. "Don't let that stand in your way. What about you? You're all wound up like a time bomb ready to explode. And you know what? That's just what these namby pamby punks need. Jeffrey, Gearson, the whole lot of them. These limey dicks need a taste of some real American ass kicking. That's the best way I can put it. That's the long and short of it. That's all the words I got, man. I'm standing at the cross-roads is the best way I can put it. You know that song?"

"It's on Cream's *Wheels of Fire* album," I said. "It's an old blues song by Robert Johnson."

Jimi chuckled and said to Sydney, "Ask him what time it is and he tells you how a watch works."

I said, "Save it, Jimi, and we can talk music later. Point me in the right direction and I'll take care of business. I owe you that and I'm glad to be here to help you out. So what's going on that I can fix? Give me a point of entry into this. You owe me the straight line."

Sydney spoke up. "I can help. What do you mean, point of entry?"

Jimi said, "Stay out of this, Syd."

I said, "I need the big picture. You two are feeding me bits and pieces of a puzzle and I'm late to the party. It's like you're the ones with something to hide."

Jimi drew back. "Don't turn on me, man. I don't need that. I need you to be on my side."

I said, "You're too damn high to even be on your own side. Jimi, if you need to stay this loaded to handle what-ever you've gotten yourself into, okay, we'll see about you later but for now that's part of the scenario that I have to roll with. Now tell me how it got to be this bad. Hell, there's more GI's back in Nam baked on weed and almost as many hooked on smack than anyone will ever cop to. I don't like, it but I get it. But I need you to sharpen it up for me, Jimi."

He diverted his eyes back to the business of fumbling to relight his cigarette.

"That's just it. If I could get my head around this whole thing, maybe I could get straight and I wouldn't need any help. But I can't."

"Jimi, I'm a soldier. I need a mission. You are frustrating the hell out of me."

"Yeah? Well, take that and multiply it by a couple thousand and you've got some idea where I'm coming from. Ever since I left New York and came to London, what with the lawsuits and the tour getting shut down and these hoods and that fucking Hudberry, it's like the whole world is closing in on me and sucking me dry." He turned to Sydney. "You should've heard that pig. Jimbo this and Jim that. Soldier, I ain't into violence but I admit I like what you did to him."

"I'm asking you again, Jimi, straight up. What do you want me to do?"

Averted eyes. Throaty, self-conscious chuckle.

"I don't know. Uh, I'm thinking that maybe just having your energy around will get this shit to back off. There's energy to everything, you know. Me, you, the cosmos, it's all energy."

"Okay, I'll do what I can with the time I've got. We've got to set up a defense perimeter around you."

Jimi nodded. "A defense perimeter. I like it. That's

exactly what I need. I'm sorry, man. I know it's a drag getting you involved in this. I wouldn't blame you if you told me to fuck off and just walked away."

"There's our friendship," I said, "but there's this too: you can't make it through a day in Vietnam without hearing *Purple Haze* or *Foxy Lady* over the radio or on somebody's stereo on base. When I think of the sound-track you've provided to make life bearable by providing some relief to the men serving over there, I figure I'm doing this for them too."

Jimi said, "Shucks, man, I'm just playing rock and roll and writing songs."

I said, "We digress. Tell me about Monika."

Sydney chimed in with, "She's trouble."

Jimi said nothing.

I said to Sydney. "You don't think much of your Jimi's taste in women, I take it."

"I want what's best for Jimi." She gave me a Mona Lisa smile and reached across the table to lightly touch Jimi's arm. "He's not wrong all the time. I'm sure you've sussed out about Jimi and me. We're not a couple but, well, we have balled."

I looked to Jimi. "And you and Monika *are* a couple?"

He shrugged. "She thinks so. I don't know. Monika's an artist. She's attentive and warm. She takes good care of me when we're alone. She has a sweet side down deep and she can be pleasant company when she wants to be. But yeah, uh, there are problems, you know? Everything coming down, it's a heavy scene. A bad scene."

Sydney saw something across the hamburger shop that caused her expression to freeze.

"Uh oh," she said. "Here comes trouble."

4

A PAIR OF OVERSIZED GUYS IN WORKMAN'S CLOTHES entered the place, one through each of the glass doors situated to either side of the counter that faced the booths. The two bruisers could have been exactly what they looked like, hulking construction workers dropping in for a quick burger on their lunch break. Except for their synchronized entrance and the fact that, upon entering, they started for our booth.

Jimi sprinted from the booth without a word, transformed from stoned repose into a human blur with the physical agility I'd seen in that clip from that movie, *Monterey Pop*, where Jimi does a somersault while he's playing a wild guitar solo.

I came to my feet, ready for anything.

Jimi was darting for the food prep area, passing the pair of startled teenage girls stationed at twin cash registers behind the counter, disappearing from sight beyond the wall separating the restaurant from the prep area in back

The two men angled off, running after Jimi.

I pursued them, wishing I had a gun.

I hustled past the startled counter girls, into the extended, narrow prep area. Black tile floors. Plain white walls. Fluorescent lighting. Grill and other stations to the right, storage lockers and office cubicle to the left. A pair of husky teenage boys in Wimpy uniforms stood with stunned expressions, looking after the two guys who had just dashed past them toward the back door that yawned wide at the far end of the prep area.

Jimi had left the building.

One of the guys bolted through the doorway in hot pursuit. The second one looked over his shoulder and when he saw me, he pivoted, grabbed hold of one of the kids by the back of his trousers and the scruff of his neck and pitched him in my direction.

I waltzed the kid past me, wheeling him out of my way like we were a pair of ballroom dancers. He smelled of hamburger grease. I caught a glimpse of Sydney, drawn up just short of the prep area, her expression fearful, her hands clasped before her. The move hardly slowed me down but it accomplished its purpose and gave the second guy time to make it through the doorway.

I followed him out, into another alley.

Jimi had already reached the top of a fire escape that ran up the side of the three-story building that housed the Wimpy's on its ground floor. The fire escape ended at the line of windows along the top level but it was an easy reach from its top rung up to the flat roof. The first of the two guys was scrambling up the fire escape, closing in fast on Jimi. Another bulky hardguy, positioned at the mouth of this alley, stood with his legs spread, hands on his hips.

As an evasion tactic, it's generally best not to go up unless you're seeking a defensive position in which case hell yeah, take the high ground. But going up can often limit your options. Your pursuers can wait below, leaving you nowhere to go. Jimi was improvising because they'd left him no choice, and this roof offered an advantage, an escape route with buildings of similar height, one to either side, practically abutting. Not bad improvising.

The guy who had tried to block my way in the prep area reached the bottom rung of the fire escape, raised both arms and drew down the ladder. He started up but his foot slid out from under him because the metal was slick from the rain. He jarred sideways but managed to maintain his grip. He steadied himself and started climbing more carefully.

That false first step gave me the seconds I needed. I barreled into him, knocking him off the fire escape. We slammed into a dumpster and I bounced his head off its side. He collapsed. KO-ed or dead, I couldn't tell.

I frisked him. His jacket pocket yielded a snub-nosed .38 revolver. I had me a gun. I looked up. The first guy was following Jimi onto the rooftop, which put them both beyond my line of vision. I took a running start, caught the ladder at its third or forth rung and started climbing like a monkey up a coconut tree. I reached the top of the fire escape. I paused there with an index finger curled around the .38's trigger. I stole a look over the parapet.

The bruiser must have made me as just some innocent bystander at the table, yakking with Jimi when they first came in, and considered me taken care of by the clown I'd left unconscious or dead next to the dumpster. He stood in the middle of the roof, a towering slab of humanity facing away from me, his uplifted arms, thick as tree trunks, hoisting Jimi Hendrix high in the air like an offering.

Jimi's wiry form struggled in vain, panicky.

"Damn, don't do this, man! Whoever you are, I can pay you!"

The over-sized human meat slab advanced inexorably toward the far parapet with the obvious intention of dropping Jimi over the edge.

I scrambled onto the roof and edged in a few feet, drawing a bead with the .38.

I said, "Hold it right there. Turn around and set him down."

He turned and grunted. He wasn't prepared to commit murder with a witness present. I'd caught him off-guard. He said, *"Schiese!"* and threw Jimmy aside like an oversized child discarding a toy. He started toward me.

I aimed the .38 at his forehead.

"Hold it right there, ton of fun."

Sydney's voice echoed up, calling something distorted by the canyon of the alley walls, making her words indiscernible.

Jimi sprang away from the big guy with that lithe grace of his and started toward me.

"Thanks, bro!"

Then he saw something over my shoulder. Alarmed, he started to speak and at the same time I realized that the bruiser I had drawn a bead on was wearing a small, knowing smile.

I started to pivot, knowing even as I did so that I was too late. One of the guys from the alley below had come up to join the party. That's what Sydney had been shouting about.

The blow caught me on the side of the head and the only thing in my world then was an explosion of pain and then a bottomless hole of blackness that opened and swallowed me.

5

_____

It was a pool hall not far from the main gate.

Jimi sat in to jam with the house band whenever he could, and one night he invited me to drop in and listen. I went on in alone. Late. The band's last set of the night.

I was the only white person in a crowded, dim, smoky dive. I didn't think anything of it.

A miniscule stage occupied one corner. The band—piano, bass, drums and sax—were playing a funky soul groove. Six pool tables, three to either side, faced the bar.

Jimi stood over in the corner of the stage, lost in deep concentration, playing tastefully intricate guitar licks. The band wasn't playing loud. Their droning groove cast a hypnotic spell over a handful of dancers near the bandstand who were bumping and grinding to every nuance of a slinky instrumental.

I made my way to the bar. Glances swept over me. Maybe it was my imagination but it seemed like conversations in the place tapered off for the handful of seconds it took for my presence to be noted. I wondered what the hell. Had I made a mistake? Then the conversations resumed, my presence collectively accepted by patrons who went back to enjoying themselves.

The barmaid must have weighed three hundred pounds. She had a sassy countenance, a severely stylish coiffure and a gold tooth smile.

"What'll it be, sugar?"

"Beer."

Friendly and bouncy, she placed it before me. I added a tip. She scooped it up and went off to wait on someone else.

Onstage, the band closed out the instrumental number. Jimi had noticed me from the stage while I was ordering my beer. His left hand lifted in a brief wave. I lifted my beer bottle in a return salute.

The bandleader called off the next tune. Jimi's grin got wide. He kicked off the funky guitar riff of *Mustang Sally*. That was a popular song back then. People left their tables and crowded the dance floor.

About a minute into the song, I became aware of some guy shouting into my left ear. I couldn't hear him over the loud music. Chunky black dude. Drunk and mean. I couldn't place his ugly mug from on base but that didn't mean anything.

He was snarling. "You know what would happen if I showed up at a rodeo with all you offay white breads? You'd stomp my ass. That's right. Maybe try and lynch me." Noxious alcohol fumes. His spittle sprayed. "So what right you got coming into this place, huh? You white bread peckerwood."

The barmaid stopped beaming. She scowled in his direction.

"This ain't your bar, TJ. You ain't nothing but a customer and right now you're a customer fixing to get hisself eighty-sixed if you don't hush your fuss."

He swung in her direction. I had to sidestep to keep from being knocked by one of his massive shoulders.

"What're you saying, Thelma Lou? You saying you're going to let this offay patronize your establishment after what his people been doing to us for two hundred years?"

I said, "I haven't done anything to your people."

The music from the stage tapered off.

Jimi's voice, reasonable and calm, came over the house PA system. "Aw, leave him alone, dude. The man's a soldier serving his country, and he's a friend of mine. Let him be."

The drunk tilted the bottom of his beer bottle at the ceiling. With the band no longer playing, the electronic hum of their amplifiers was the only sound in the joint, underscoring a taut ripple of anticipation; that collective holding of the breath that can precede violence.

Thelma Lou said, "TJ, you haul your drunken ass out of here. Ain't going to be no scrapping in here tonight."

TJ said, "Like hell there ain't. I don't care who this offay is." He twisted the beer bottle in his grip and brought it down on the bar, smashing glass. He wavered on his feet, holding the bottle like a knife. "I'm cutting me some white meat tonight."

I eased back a pace, bending my knees, readying myself for the onslaught.

Thelma Lou said from behind the bar, "TJ," and this time there was a cold edge to the steady voice.

She held a sawed-off shotgun, aimed at TJ's chest.

TJ considered his options, shifting his bleary eyes

45

between me and the shotgun. Then he said, "Aw hell." He flung aside the broken beer bottle. "This ain't over, white bread. Count on that." He stomped out of the pool hall.

Folks stepped aside to give him a clear path.

Thelma Lou returned the shotgun to its shelf under the bar. She glared at the gaping musicians onstage.

"Well, what are you waiting for? I ain't paying you boys to stand up there looking like dummies."

The band resumed playing *Mustang Sally* and people went back to dancing as if nothing had happened.

Thelma Lou reached across the bar and tapped me on the shoulder. "Sonny, you watch your back. That TJ's a mean son of a bitch."

I said, "Thanks for the warning, and for taking the heat off me." I tapped the bar with the bottom of my bottle to indicate the unseen shotgun. "Ever kill anybody with that thing?"

"Yes, I have."

She returned to tending the bar.

I sat on my stool and attended to sipping my beer and listening to Jimi, who played guitar that night like a long-time regular member of the band, the rest of their set comprised of a mixture of instrumentals and slow ballads as the evening started to wind down.

After the set, Jimi had me meet the guys in the band. We had a beer at a table near the stage as Thelma Lou announced last call. The musicians were local black guys who were married and worked during the week but picked up spare change playing on the weekends.

Jimi packed his guitar in its case.

By that time Thelma Lou was telling folks they didn't

have to go home but they did have to leave the bar. The patrons started filing out.

I got a hug from Thelma Lou. "You come back anytime, sugar. This here pool hall is not segregated."

I appreciated that and I told her so.

Then Jimi and I were out in the parking lot where his ride awaited us, a raggedy ass old Chevy Impala that had seen better days. The night was alive with engines coming to life and departing vehicles, while some folks milled around the dirt parking lot. It was late Fall. The night air nipped at the lungs after the closeness of the pool hall. I stood on the passenger side of the white Impala, waiting while Jimi went to messing with his keys.

TJ stepped out from the shadows. The pistol he held reflected the pool hall's neon sign. He snarled something drunken and incomprehensible, and then the pistol barked flame.

The bullet caught me high in the left shoulder like the kick of a mule. Slammed me backwards against the car. I dropped to one knee. It hurt like hell.

TJ towered over me. He pressed the muzzle of the pistol against my forehead.

"So long, offay."

Jimi sailed into him from the side in a flying tackle, toppling TJ.

My shoulder throbbed, spurting blood. I drew myself up and leaned against the Impala. One step and I'd fall flat on my face. Survival instinct and training kicked in. Reflexive action. Find something to use as a tourniquet. Stop the bleeding. I peeled off my shirt. I started wrapping it around my arm to stem the flow of blood that looked like oil in the light from the pool hall. My knees turned to butter and I sank back into a sitting position against the car.

Jimi and TJ each regained their footing at the same time, Jimi having hit the ground in a loose roll, coming up from the tackle to assume a limber, combative stance.

TJ swayed on his feet, the pistol still in his hand. He started to track the piece in Jimi's direction. All I could do was watch. Hell, I couldn't even stand. Jimi kicked TJ in the nuts. TJ screamed like a woman. He dropped the gun. His knees buckled. Holding his groin with both hands, he fell forward onto his face and started making burbling noises into the dirt.

Jimi snorted his contempt.

"Dumb ass racist."

Jimi picked up the pistol, broke open the chamber and the shells fell free. They made distinct, small clinking sounds upon the ground. Jimi drew back his left arm and pitched, sending the gun sailing off into the night beyond the parking lot.

Onlookers who had been holding back started calling out to each other and began cautiously advancing for a better look at what had happened.

Jimi snapped a branch from a nearby tree, ran over to me, knelt down on one knee and went about making it into a tourniquet. He took off his shirt, a snazzy satin stage number, and used it to plug up the hole made by the bullet.

Sirens were closing in, drawing closer by the second.

Jimi said, "Looks like the bullet went clear through. You'll be okay."

"Jimi?"

"Yeah, man?"

"Thanks. You saved my life."

He nodded at the sound of the approaching sirens.

"We'd best be gone."

I learned later that when the police arrived, the pool hall was closed and the parking lot was empty.

6

___

When I started coming around, a world of pain was there to greet me, coursing through me like liquid fire.

I forced my eyelids to open. A wavering haze like the fog of combat accompanied the pain. Then, very slowly, details of my surroundings began to take shape.

The living room of a house or apartment. Apartment, I decided, looking out a window across the room at the plain brick wall of the building next door. The décor was lavender and lace. Feminine. Sky blue walls, decorated with prints. A comfortable ambiance that soothed the pounding at my temples, reducing the pain of regaining consciousness to a low-grade but constant ache.

A thin stream of white smoke snaked past my nostrils. Delicately caressed my senses with a trace of musk. Incense. The pain notched itself down. Perceptions cleared.

Sydney was gazing down at me with those soft green eyes. We were on her couch. She sat with me stretched out, my head resting on her slender, shapely lap. Her fingertips ever so gently grazed across my temples. She made gentle cooing sounds as if to a baby.

I remembered getting conked from behind on the roof, probably with a professional leather sap. I tried to sit up. Pain walloped through me like catching a haymaker to the jaw. My head sank back down on her lap. I groaned. It didn't sound like me.

She purred, "Easy does it, big man. It's not your nature to just lay down and let life happen, is it?"

I propped myself on my elbows. The room tilted around me for maybe twenty seconds before settling itself.

"Let me try again."

"Slowly," she admonished. "You must loathe the banal, so I'll spare you having to say 'where am I?' We're in my flat. You're safe here."

This time I managed to sit up. I leaned back against the cushions and massaged the back of my neck, avoiding the tender, throbbing area behind my right ear where the sap had connected.

"How the hell did I get here?"

"Would you care for a cup of tea?"

"No coffee?"

"Afraid not. I have a bottle of Zinfandel in the refrigerator."

"Green tea, if you have it. Thanks."

She actually patted my knee, efficient and bright-eyed. "Coming right up."

I hadn't been touched tenderly by a woman since I couldn't remember when. She glided smoothly off the couch and walked to a small kitchenette. She was barefoot. I watched the way her hips and bottom moved under the fabric of the linen skirt. Yeah, I was going to be all right.

She commenced preparing our tea.

I said, "So what happened?"

"It was the one of the men you left down in the alley. I tried to call up to you but I guess you didn't hear."

"I was busy."

"Yes, Jimi told me. He told me how you stopped a man from throwing him off the roof."

"They wanted it to look like suicide or a drug-induced accident. Once I made it onto the roof, there was a witness so that wouldn't work."

A comfortable silence settled in between us while I sorted out my mental cobwebs. She got the tea together, and then she served me and sat down beside me. We sipped our tea. Steaming hot, needing to be breathed over to cool it for sipping, the way I like it.

I said, "How did you get me down from that roof?"

"I didn't. You can thank those two young chaps who were working the grill. Turned out they were both Jimi Hendrix fans. They recognized Jimi when we first walked in but were too cool to make a big deal out of it or say anything. London's a hip town that way."

I set down my teacup. I placed the palm against the back of my head where I'd been sapped.

I said, "Yeah, real hip."

"Anyway, we got you down and into my car. When we got here, my gay neighbors, Glenn and Bruce, helped me get you inside. Glenn and Bruce and I have sort of a mutual coexistence pact where nobody bothers with anybody else's business. But they're both weight lifters and were happy to help. They didn't even ask any embarrassing questions. I trust them not to say anything to anyone about you being here."

"You're a strange one, Sydney. I wish I could get a handle on you."

She smiled a pretty smile. "Am I an enigma to the worldly Soldier? My feminine mystique, perhaps?"

"That's part of it. But see, I know Jimi. I even know types like that crew at the Wimpy's and cops like Hudberry."

"And me? What type am I?"

"In this scenario? You're the FNG."

"FNG?"

I finished the tea in with a long slurp from the cup.

"We call them FNG's when they first report for duty. Fucking New Guy. He's the FNG until another new guy transfers in the unit or until he buys the farm."

"Buys--?"

"Gets himself killed. See, you never know how the FNG is going to act or react."

"And it's that way with me?"

"That's the way it is with you. I appreciate you bringing me back here, but you're a bogie. An unidentified blip on the radar. You seem to be a spirited, intelligent, efficient young woman. But we've just been up against some damn competent bad guys who were bad enough to lay me out. And here you sit, cool and mellow as you please. You're a piece of work, Sydney. You intrigue me."

"And you intrigue me, soldier man."

"So where's Jimi?"

"He was worried about you but I told him to split after we got you down off that roof and loaded into my car.

Jimi can't afford to be involved in something like this, not with all of his legal problems. He said he was going to Monika's."

"Then that's where I should be if there are people out to hurt Jimi. I'm here to prevent that."

I started to stand.

She checked my movement with a feather-light touch to my sleeve. "He told me he'd see you tonight."

"Tonight? What's wrong with right now?"

"He said he was going down to Ronnie Scott's Club on Frith Street tonight, and that we should meet him there. He needs to relax and regroup."

"What about those guys who jumped us at the burger joint? Any idea who they were?"

"No, I'm afraid not. Could they have been connected with that bunch of ruffians at the airport?"

"Too soon to tell. When I surprised that lug on the roof who was about to throw Jimi over, he said 'shit' in German."

She frowned a pretty frown. "German? Then that would be Monika."

"Why don't you tell me about Monika."

Sydney sighed. "More tea?"

"I'm fine, thanks."

"Monika and Jimi have a tempestuous relationship."

"I noticed. She showed up at Angel McGuire's looking for him. We got out of there in the nick of time, but we ran into that salty cop and then you reappeared."

"I drove to Angel's straight from the airport," she said," but traffic tied me up and you beat me there by a few minutes. When I saw Monika's car double parked in front,

I just naturally went to the alley. I knew Jimi would be coming out the back way."

I massaged the back of my neck some more. "I feel like I've jumped into a whirlpool."

"As a soldier rotating out of a combat zone, shouldn't you be relaxing, recuperating, enjoying life on a beach somewhere?"

"I wouldn't know how. Jimi sent me an SOS, so here I am."

"When's the last time you saw Jimi before today?"

That one came out of left field.

I said, "Uh, let me see. Maybe four years? We stayed in touch with a letter every six months or so. We became buddies at Fort Campbell. See, I played guitar in a high school rock and roll band when I was growing up. Jimi left the army for a career in music. I left behind playing in garage bands for carrying a rifle in Vietnam. I guess we see in each other the path not taken."

"I'm glad you answered his SOS. Somebody needs to keep a protective eye on our Jimi. He's walking around in the middle of a nervous breakdown. There's a strong bond between the two of you, isn't there, Soldier?"

I said, "Monika. I need BG on Monika."

She blinked. "BG?"

Like I suspected, Miss Sydney Blanchard was traveling in fast and rough company but she herself was not a player, even if she wanted to be and had pretended to be one. I read her as a good kid with a good heart.

Kid?

Hell.

She was a fine specimen of female pulchritude, and I'd been without for too damn long.

7

I said, "BG is background. I need background on Monika. That could help in keeping Jimi out of harm's way. Tell me about her. Full name. Where she's from. Anything that comes to mind. If you want to help Jimi, help me."

Sydney said, "Monika Dannemann. Honestly when I first met her I thought she was sweet. She draws and she writes poetry. She's exhibited her photographs in galleries. She's been on the scene for awhile. Bohemian would be the word."

"How did they meet?"

"I honestly don't know. Monika was a skating instructor in Germany. She's from one of the richest families in Düsseldorf. She's always worrying that her family will interfere in her life. Her family is prominent in the business world and her dad has made statements about not being terribly happy that his daughter is consorting with a Negro rock and roll musician. I've had maybe a dozen conversations with Monika in a variety of settings and at least once every time she mentions being paranoid about her family name being linked to drugs."

"Is it a fling, her and Jimi? My buddy always had a way with the women even back in our service days. "

"Monika's been flashing a snake ring Jimi gave her. She's telling whoever will listen that she's his fiancée."

I said, "Maybe those German goons were brought in from Düsseldorf to make a permanent split between Monika and the Negro rock and roll musician."

Sydney shook her head. "Not her family. From what Monika says, they're stern but they do genuinely care about her. They'd never resort to something like sending ruffians to interfere with her life, and certainly not have someone thrown off a building. The Dannemanns are a respected, law-abiding family." She flicked errant strands of long red hair back across her shoulder. "There's another questions, isn't there?"

I nodded. "How did they find us at a Wimpy's? They could only have followed us there from Angel McGuire's. Everyone seems to know that's the place to find Jimi. That cop, Hudberry knew. I knew. You knew it even if you pretended not to."

"I am sorry about that, really, Soldier."

"And Monika knew," I said. "My point is that everyone knew except the process servers."

She nodded. "He rents rooms at the Cumberland Hotel for cover to lose the suits. Most nights he's with Monika. She rents a suite at a residence hotel in Notting Hill. The suits haven't found out about her yet. She'll be with Jimi at the club tonight. You can make your own assessment."

"I will. Right now I think I'll concentrate on assessing you."

"Goodness. Are you coming on to me, Soldier?"

"Not yet."

"Not yet?"

"A little BG on you wouldn't hurt."

That brought me a small good-natured chuckle with a smile to match.

"I bring a helpless man to my apartment. I nurse him back to life. And he wants top know *my* BG? Well if it's pedigree you want, Daddy is in plastics. He owns three factories in Manchester and one in Liverpool. I have two older siblings, both married. I was a surprise baby, you see. The unexpected one. I'm the accident. Mother is always busy with a myriad of worthy social causes and civic affairs, always tending to humanity's ills as long as the human isn't related to her. I got my mother stoned once."

That brought a laugh out of me.

"You're a spoiled brat."

She pouted. It was cute as hell and the thing was I didn't know if she was putting me on or it was for real.

"That's not very nice."

"Sorry, kid. I'm not a very nice guy."

"Oh yes, you are. You flew halfway around the world to help a friend." The pout went away. "You can stop being such a tough guy when you're with me, you know."

"Maybe I can, maybe I can't. Why should I try?"

She settled back against the cushions, lifted her right hand and let her index finger idly trace the shrapnel scar on the side of my face.

"Because I may be a spoiled brat from Manchester who left a life of privilege to become a shop girl in Carnaby Street and an aspiring actress, and maybe I'm more like Monika than I'd like to admit, but I want to be part of something that's exciting. I freely admit to being an idealist. The world needs more of us! But that does not necessarily mean that I am naïve and shallow. It doesn't mean I don't know things about life that you don't know."

"You're kidding, right? You say that after knowing where I've been?"

The fingertips' feathery caress traveled south from the scar, along my chin, to continue on a slow straight line down over my throat and slowly, inexorably further south.

She said, "You did what you did as a soldier performing his duty. I think that is a noble thing in the fields of fire. But perception is reality, Mr. Soldier, and our perceptions can change. You're not in Vietnam anymore, are you? You're in the heart of one of the largest cities in the world." No sarcasm. No bite. Empathy radiated from her, making me feel uneasy. She said, "You think you know more about life than I do because you've been in battle."

"Something like that."

"Would you let me inside the walls you've built around you?"

"You wouldn't like what you'd find."

"You don't scare me."

"That's because you don't know me."

She said, "You've been wounded."

"Yeah, a couple of times."

Her eyes held mine as her hand rested over the region of my heart, her touch warm through the material of my shirt. "No, I mean here, and in your soul. You've been wounded and scarred as real as that scar on your face."

"You could say the same of any soldier from any war. I'm no different from any man who's survived combat."

She didn't remove her hand. "I know that, but I'm saying it about you. I've seen you in action firsthand. And I have something that can restore a wounded heart and soul."

"Peace, love and flowers?"

"You're patronizing me."

"I'm sorry."

"Stop patronizing me. Stop mocking me. What is your BG, soldier man? I don't mean where have you been. I mean, what do you think?"

"Nothing that matters."

"It matters to me. What do you believe in?"

"I believe in what I know. Peace through superior firepower."

"And that's it?"

"I read *Rolling Stone*." I chuckled. "The hippie free love business sounds all right."

Her essence brightened. That's the only way I can put it. She sat up straighter and her smile became wider. A healthy, fresh, toothy smile.

"There, you see? Love." Her hand gracefully drifted further down my chest. "It's the strongest force in the world, Soldier. It's not about who's got the biggest gun. Who's got the biggest heart?" Those feathery warm fingers traveled south of my belt line and came to rest over the front of my slacks. Sydney said, "Love unites. Love heals," and she began caressing and kneading what she found there.

I caught her wrist and guided those knowing little

fingers away from what should have been growing rigid under her touch…but wasn't.

I said, "I was kidding about the free love business."

"I don't kid about love." Her fingers squeezed a little tighter. A mischievous grin. "Don't tell me you lost it in the war."

"And wouldn't you be embarrassed if I had."

Her eyes widened. "Oh—"

My turn to smile. "Relax. Everything's intact, in working order and I like girls."

She looked down at my hold on her wrist. "Then?"

The hurt at the back of my head where I'd taken the hit from a sap was forgotten. I'd been roughhousing literally since my plane had touched down but this was more unnerving than any of it.

I gave her her wrist back. "Time and place, kid. This ain't either."

"I wish you wouldn't call me kid. I happen to be a grown woman. There can't be more than a two- or three-year age difference between us."

"It's how we spent those years."

"Fear," she said. "You're afraid of me. You fought the Viet Cong and survived. In the jungles, in a war zone, you're fearless. But you're afraid of the Carnaby Street shop girl."

I managed to stand from the couch, already feeling better. I extended my hand to her in the best approximation of gallantry that I could muster. "Let me take you out to dinner."

She hesitated. "And you'll know the right time and place." It was a statement, not a question.

I said, "Show me your favorite restaurant. Then you can show me Soho."

She rose and I drew her to me. I looped my free arm around her slender waist and the kiss that flowed between us then was gentle, tentative. When we loosened the clinch I was grinning an alpha-male grin and she was flushed and a little out of breath.

"Bastard," she said. "Give me five minutes to pretty myself up."

8

Soho turned out to be Greenwich Village with a British accent. A world of the young. Energetic bohemian types, crowding sidewalks that fronted block after block of artsy shops, restaurants and chic nightclubs.

The skies had cleared and dusk had brought on a pleasant summer evening. We strolled along the crowded sidewalks. We passed a house of prostitution where the hookers, posing on a balcony and leaning from windows in the provocative attire of their profession, beckoned invitingly to unattached males passing by. We walked past The Marquee Club on Oxford Street, where everyone from the Rolling Stones to Cream had gotten their start.

While the males of this night world dressed casually, female fashion had taken to being more revealing in the leg department than I had ever seen before. Lots of baubles and bangles. Dresses so short that it was sometimes hard to tell if they had one on. Gorgeous legs everywhere I looked. I almost got run down a few times when I couldn't help doing a double take on a pair of pretty legs just as I was about to step off a curb to cross a street, forgetting that the traffic traveled in the opposite direction as back home. This happened three times.

Sydney thought it was funny and teased me about it. I did my best to explain that it was general culture shock on my part, not rudeness toward her because Miss Sydney Blanchard looked finer than fine for a night on the town. High-heeled black leather boots. Tight black leather slacks. Thin white silk blouse. With her read hair cascading onto her shoulders and with her bright smile, she was radiant.

She chose a little, out-of-the-way Indian restaurant. Tasteful décor, pleasant staff and excellent curry. Sydney and I got along fine. If I hadn't spent the last couple of years killing people and watching people getting killed, I might have felt like a high school kid out on a date. She carried the conversation naturally, commenting to me in a whisper on what the people around us were wearing. This made sense since she worked in the fashion trend center of London, at least according to what I'd read in *Rolling Stone*. She had a keen eye, and always included something nice to say in any fashion critique of our unsuspecting fellow patrons. By the time we left, I felt okay for a guy who'd spent part of the day unconscious.

At Ronnie Scott's Club, a line of fashionable hipsters were queuing up but the doormen recognized Sydney with a bawdy welcome and allowed us access to a noisy, dim, smoky place. Onstage, a band played funky jazz in front of a crowded dance floor and tables. On the far side of the club a low wall, topped with potted plants, separated the dance room from the bar, which was about half full.

I did my best to keep up with Sydney. She took hold of one of my hands when we reached a long corner table where everyone seemed happy to see her. I was introduced around and folks were gracious to me.

Then I ordered drinks. Sydney, a gin and tonic. I stayed with my Coca Cola.

I was accepted and considered okay because I was with Sydney. Everyone liked Sydney. She laughed at their jokes and made droll comments that fed the busy chatter of several conversations going on at once, back and forth around me. I wondered where Jimi was.

A couple sitting near me decided that they wanted to civilly discuss global politics with the Yank. I kept remembering why I was there and pretty much kept my mouth shut. They'd deduced that I was a GI from my haircut. They were against the war and wanted to know what I thought about the National Guard shooting down and killing four anti-war protestors at Kent State U in Ohio a few months earlier. Campus demonstrations were raging across the U.S. in the wake of Nixon's escalation of the war. Nixon had called the student demonstrators "bums".

"Did you think about that while you were in Vietnam?" asked the guy pleasantly enough.

His wife or girlfriend chimed in with, "Did you as a soldier ever question the politics behind why you were over there?"

I said, "A soldier obeys orders. He doesn't question them."

The woman muttered, "That's what Eichman said at Nuremburg."

At least that's what I think she said. With the

surrounding chatter, the band playing and the general background noise of the club, I couldn't be sure so I let it pass.

Her husband/boyfriend was more clear-spoken. "Isn't that called being brainwashed?" he said from behind his oh so civil smile.

To him this was little more than a frank intellectual exchange, so I restrained the impulse to break his face and leave him half-dead.

I said, "It's called military discipline."

They started to respond together but everyone's attention suddenly became sidetracked by a shift in the atmosphere of the club that rippled through the smoky air.

Sydney reached over and touched my wrist.

"It's Jimi. He's here."

9

A TALL FIGURE MATERIALIZED AND APPROACHED OUR TABLE. Jimi wore a cape, stylishly draped over his shoulders. He moved slowly, as if in a daze. He was high. Monika Dannemann's face glowed. She clutched Jimi's arm. Expensively dressed. A little too much makeup. Everyone at our table called out a greeting with the deference accorded a king. Sydney guided Jimi and Monika next to where I sat.

"This is Monika," Jimi introduced needlessly. "Baby, this is my friend from long ago and far away. These days we call him Soldier."

She made a point of seating herself between me and Jimi so that we would have to talk across her. Her handshake was strong. So was her perfume. I don't know anything about women's perfume, but I know what I like and this wasn't it. Jimi went about ordering drinks for them and for everyone else at the table.

Monika said, "It is a pleasure to meet you, Soldier." Precise English. German accent.

"Miss Dannemann."

She did not seem to recognize me from when she'd been shouting up the staircase at Jimi at Angel McGuire's crash pad. I must have been no more that a peripheral presence at Jimi's side when that was happening. If she did recognize me, she gave no indication.

She said, "Jimi told me that he asked you to come to London. He does not speak to me often of his life before he became a rock and roll star."

I said, "Then I'll follow his good example."

Jimi finished giving his order to our waitress. Seen up close, his face was ashen. Exhaustion. Completely undone.

He said, "It's good to see you up and around, man, after what happened on that roof."

Monika said, without hesitation, "What happened on what roof?"

I said, "Jimi, you'll laugh when I tell you what flashed across my mind just now when I saw the buzz you caused, walking in with this beautiful blonde at your side."

The tactical maneuver worked.

Monika liked what I said and beamed with pleasure, her interrogation momentarily forgotten.

Jimi said, "So make me laugh. I could use a laugh."

Monika said, "Jimi spent the afternoon in our flat tripping on acid, or so he claims." Her tone indicated not so subtle disapproval. "I call it his bat routine when he just sits in the room with the curtains drawn and the lights down, feeling weird."

Jimi said to me, "Go on, man. Make me laugh."

Individual, independent conversations continued to prattle on around us.

I said, "I thought of you in morning formation with

Sergeant Hines. The company got so sick of him bitching at you about your gig line, the whole outfit started making jokes about it." I added for Monika, "The gig line meant that the buttons of your tunic had to be properly aligned with your belt buckle."

Jimi chuckled vaguely. "I think Top was hip to me not being soldier material. Damn, man. Seems a long time ago, don't it?" He gestured at the surrounding noisy atmosphere of the club. "So what do think of my scene nowadays? A lot more laughs than we had back in the barracks, eh?"

Monika said, "Jimi and I are engaged."

"I heard. Congratulations."

Jimi pitched his voice low. "Shine it on, Monika. This ain't the time."

Her expression morphed into one of hurt feelings. "Why should I not speak of this? Why should I not tell the world? Are you going to change your mind, Jimi? Are you ashamed of me?"

Jimi said, "Aw, stop being so sensitive."

She turned to me. "I have a right to be sensitive if I am to be his wife, is that not so? A wife needs to trust her husband. Soldier, you must tell your friend this."

Across the table, Sydney must have picked up a trace of our conversation. She'd heard Monika, and she was watching me for my reaction.

I said, "I make it SOP to stay out of my friends' personal affairs."

She frowned. "SOP?"

Jimi said, "Standard operating procedure. Look Monika, you've got to stop bird dogging me, all right?" His exhausted brown eyes connected with mine and he said, as if she was not seated next to him, "Now you know the kind of shit I'm dealing with. I'm sorry I had to split so fast after what happened, but the heat's on me. I'm glad they got you back to Sydney's in one piece."

Monika's back straightened. Her steely gaze skewered Sydney, who made a point of becoming engaged in a conversation with the couple who had been pestering me, as if she hadn't been paying attention to our conversation.

Monika's said, "I do not like Sydney. I told you to stay away from that bitch." Steely German eyes shifted to me. "Should I be worried about your friend? Soldier arrives and things happen."

Jimi gave a nervous laugh. "Things always happen around a guy like Soldier." He said to me, "Sorry, man. Monika's kind of possessive."

"I am not possessive. I know about you and Sydney. You are through with those tarts, Jimi Hendrix."

"Aw, baby—"

"You said you wanted to marry me. You gave me a ring—"

Jimi said to me, "Soldier, did you ever want to be someone else?"

I considered this for a few seconds.

"No, but there are times I wished I was somewhere else and this is beginning to be one of them."

Monika arched both eyebrows. "So! What has Jimi told you about me?"

Jimi lit another cigarette. "That's enough, sugar. You talk too much."

She pretended not to hear him. "I want to hear Soldier talk. Tell me about yourself, Soldier. How do you like London? What do you think?"

I glanced around. Scores of healthy young men making passes at healthy young women and vice versa to the throbbing pulse of live music.

I said, "I come from another world. Until a couple days ago my life was a firebase in Quang Ngai Province, north of Saigon. Pulaski stepped on a land mine last week. The bottom half of him just wasn't there any more and all the guys were splattered with him. He screamed for his mother and for us to kill him with a mercy round but that only lasted for a minute or two and then he was nothing but a dead guy. I still see that happening every time I close my eyes. He was a hell of a poker player and he had a nice little wife back home. For the ones who die, it's over. The survivors are the ones who go on living in hell. Pulaski's wife, or in-country. Have you ever seen a cluster of starving, ten-year-old orphans, alone and squatting outside a burnt-down village, going through their own feces for chunks of undigested food to eat?"

Monika cringed. "Please. Do not speak of such horrible things."

Jimi's eyes were steady. "You asked. Let the man speak."

I looked around us and said, "This is a pleasure scene fueled on drugs and sex. I won't take issue with fun and games and letting off steam. But if we were in the States, half the men in this place would be drafted and on their way to Nam."

The waitress brought our drinks. Monika threw hers back and held out her empty glass for another. The waitress took her glass and Jimi's money and left us.

Jimi said, "That's a good thing about living in exile over here, man. There's heavy shit going down where you've been but there's heavy shit going down in the old U.S. of A. too, coming from every side. Over here in England I might miss my soul food and my crib in NYC, but I sure as hell don't miss all the bad vibe that's going down. Nixon and his bunch are Nazis, man."

Someone overheard us and said, "Tell it like it is, Jimi."

Jimi said, "That's why I stood up and endorsed the Black Panther party. Nixon and his guys would like to wipe out anyone who opposes them in America or anywhere else. Lock away anyone who speaks out of turn. I'm an American. I love my country. But a whole lot of what's happening in America right now, man, it is a heavy scene. A stone drag." He lowered his voice to me. But I'm going back. I'm getting the hell out of London. I've got to clear things up in my head and in my life. Stress is making me a wreck. I can't sleep. I can't focus to write any songs. I've got studio time booked at Electric Lady Land in New York for next week."

Monika clutched his arm with both hands. "Jimi, no! I thought we had discussed this."

I said, "Sounds like a good idea, Jimi." I could have added that at least in New York guys weren't trying to throw him off roofs, but I didn't honestly know if that was the case or not so I just said, "How can I help?"

He started to answer when Sydney said, "Jimi, the band is calling you onstage to jam."

His name could be heard booming over the PA.

Someone at our table said, "Do it, Jimi," and everyone in the place picked up the chant.

Jimi extinguished his cigarette in an overfull ashtray and said, "Seems like music is my only escape." He ambled away from the table, standing taller than when he'd come in.

The crowd erupted in wild applause. After a little tuning up, the band and Jimi lit into a smoldering version of *Tobacco Road* and the place went crazy.

Everyone at our table, including Sydney, leapt to their feet and poured onto the dance floor. Everyone except Monika, who remained seated next to me, the two of us alone at the table. She did not speak while the band played, which was all right with me. *Tobacco Road* has always been one of my favorite songs, probably something to do with my own upbringing under rural, shall we say modest, circumstances.

It was interesting to see Jimi working as a sideman behind the band's singer, like he had when starting out in the road bands. When his turn came to solo, Jimi played with restraint and with the taste of jazz guitarists like Wes Montgomery. They finished that number and applause rattled the walls. Everyone was on their feet, cheering. I'd lost sight of Sydney and the others from our table who were part of the compressed crowd mobbing the dance floor at the front of the stage.

Monika brushed away an errant tendril of blonde hair and leaned toward me.

"I would like to speak to you."

"Please do."

"I am good for Jimi. It is very difficult for him right now. The week before last, they cancelled his tour. It was in Germany. The audience was abusive. A very bad scene. When he got to London, Jimi came to me. He was near collapse. I am healing him. I love Jimi. He tells me that I am his muse and I choose to believe him. So should you. I do not *take* from your friend. I *give* to him. I give him inspiration."

"Are you going with Jimi to New York?"

"But course. Jimi would never leave London without me."

"That's good."

"You don't believe me."

I shrugged. "Don't let it bother you. Tell me about your quarrel with Jimi today; why you were hunting all over London for him and why was he so intent on dodging you?"

"And why should I tell you anything?"

"Because I care about Jimi too, and I want to help."

She drew a fresh cigarette to her red lips and waited for me to light it, which I did. She sharply exhaled a twin stream of gray smoke.

"Have you never had a lovers' quarrel with a woman? How can one explain such a quarrel to another and not sound like a childish idiot? I am like every woman. I can love and nurture. I can be a jealous bitch. It is not something I am proud of. But Jimi thinks I'm worth it and I choose to believe him."

"If he's going to be staying with you, I'd like to have your address and phone number."

She nodded. "Yes, Jimi said I should do that and so I will." She opened her purse and withdrew a small spiral notebook that had an attached pen. She used the pen to jot in the notebook. She tore free the piece of paper with a brisk flick of her wrist. She handed me the paper. "You are welcome anytime. I'm sorry if you do not like me, Soldier. Many people do not."

I glanced at the information, then folded the paper once and slipped it into my wallet.

"Thanks."

Jimi and the band started playing another number. I didn't recognize this one. A few bars into the song, before Jimi had a chance to step out and start playing, Monika leaned in closer to me. I caught the scent of a less than subtle perfume.

She said, closer to my ear so I could hear above the music and the crowd, "I would like us to be friends."

I took a sip of my Coke. "Let's take it one step at a time."

"Why do you dislike me?"

"I don't dislike you. I barely know you. For now as far as I'm concerned, you're Jimi's girlfriend and that's good enough for me."

"I am not his girlfriend. I am his fiancée."

She drew away from me. She sat with her back held erect, her eyes riveted on the bandstand.

When the second number ended, the club again went nuts. Applause. Whistling. Cheering. The band's lead vocalist onstage acknowledged the applause and thanked Jimi for sitting in. He informed the audience that the band would be taking a short break. The crush on the dance floor slowly dispersed amid much good cheer. Those who had been sharing the long table with us returned, laughing and chirping among themselves.

Monika's expression grew tight. She started looking around.

"Where is Jimi?"

One of the guys said, "He's chatting up the chaps in the band. He'll be right along."

A saucy brunette, who wore a red dress and high heels and lots of bangles and beads, told the guy, "Don't lie to the poor girl." She spoke with a faintly drunken slur, and addressed Monika. "We just heard Jimi say that he was leaving for the night. He was acting awfully chummy with that Sydney Blanchard chick."

Monika bolted to her feet as if she'd received a severe electrical jolt. She spat something in German, and then she lifted an arm and pointed toward the stage.

"There he is with the little whore now!"

That brought me to my feet.

Through the haze of the club and the thinning crowd around the front of the bandstand, Jimi and Sydney could be seen striding briskly together toward a door next to the stage.

Monika shouted after them.

"Jimi!"

Jimi and Sydney were already leaving through the outside door, which closed after them. Monika began frantically working her way in that direction through the dense, drunken club crowd.

I had another idea.

The front entrance was a mass of people coming and going after the band's first set of the evening while the late crowd was arriving to replace them for the midnight show. Noisy. Pushy. The press of laughing, shouting, well-lubricated citizens having a good time.

I brought my elbow and as many "pardon me's" and "excuse me's" into play as I could in order to make a way through the hubbub. I reined in the impulse to just toss aside a few people. When I finally broke free in front of the club, I took off at a brisk walking pace, practically jogging but not fast enough to draw attention, that got me to within sight of the Indian restaurant, where Sydney and I had dinner, on a side street that was shadowy because the nearest street light was at a far corner where a pair of taxi cabs idled in front of a small hotel, opposite a subway—I mean tube—station. I wanted to reach the parking lot on the far side of the restaurant, to see if Sydney's Austin Healy was still parked where we'd left it.

When I still a half block away, the sports car wheeled out of the lot, its headlights swinging in their arc as the car turned in the opposite direction, passing under a street light.

Sydney drove. Jimi was slumped in the passenger seat. I couldn't make out if he was awake or passed out. Then they were gone.

I hustled over to the first black London taxi in front of the hotel. I flung myself inside. I pointed after the Austin Healy.

I said to the driver, "Follow that car."

A stoplight at the other end of the block changed. The tail lights of Sydney's car indicated that she had braked for the light. Her left turn blinker flashed.

The cab driver glanced around to inspect me. A crusty old salt with lively eyes and a bright red drinker's nose. "Here now, Yank. That's a cliché, is what that is. Are we filming a movie?"

I reached for my wallet, pawed out some paper money. I'm not sure how much. My eyes were on the tail lights of the Austin Healy.

I said, "Lights, camera, action."

He took the bills and practically licked his chops. It must have been a handsome sum. It went into his wallet.

"Yes sir, guvnor."

The taxi leapt away from the curb just as the Austin Healy turned the corner up the block. We made the corner before the stoplight could change again, less than thirty seconds behind them.

My driver locked in behind Sydney and Jimi at a comfortable distance.

10

Sydney was a proper, law abiding motorist and once or twice my cabbie had to fall back but for my money his maneuvers in the moderate nighttime traffic were deft enough to avoid detection by those we were tailing.

I settled into the comfortable leather of the cab's spacious interior and watched the flow of night traffic and the neighborhoods we drove through without really seeing a thing. I had no idea what parts of the city we passed through.

Random thoughts passed through my mind, the way they will at a time like that.

Listening to the radio in Nam and hearing *Purple Haze* and the rest of his hits on a daily basis, we got the impression in country that back in the world a guy like Jimi Hendrix had it made. He should be sitting on top of the world, riding high. Well, my buddy from Fort Campbell was high as hell, all right. But everything else about his life looked ready to crash and burn.

The Austin Healy found a parking space near the well-lighted front entrance of Sydney's apartment building on its quiet, tree-lined street. Jimi and Sydney disembarked. My driver drew to a stop about half a block away. In the still night in this residential neighborhood, the sounds of the city were muffled and distant. Jimi and Sydney, engaged in conversation but with no physical contact between them, entered the building.

I started to slide out of the taxi.

"Thanks. I'll take it from here."

His eyes caught mine in the rearview mirror.

"Uh, if that's the missus, mate, perhaps you'd best think this out. Take a deep breath and all that. I hate to see a bloke get in trouble after I drops him off. Be a good sort and let me take you home."

I closed the door after me.

"Don't worry," I said. "I'm just going to watch."

He muttered something derogatory under his breath and drove away.

The neighborhood slept. The houses lining both sides of the street, less than ten feet apart from each other, were bulky dark shadows in gloom that owned the night beyond the ring of illumination around the front entrance.

A light went on midway back on the ground floor.

Sydney's flat.

A narrow service passage between her building and the brick building next to it led directly beneath that window. The brick building stood as silent and dark as all of the other structures on the block. I hoped it stayed that way. It would be hell to be caught as a peeping tom. But that's exactly what I intended to do. If things got steamy and intimate in there, I'd be more than happy to withdraw and give them all the privacy they wanted. But I needed to gather intel if I could and that could only be accomplished at this point by eavesdropping.

I advanced on the square of illumination that was Sydney's window. The window ledge was even with my line of vision. The bottom of the shade stopped half an inch short of the sill. I couldn't see much. I saw the couch where Sydney had cooed me back into consciousness with my head in her lap not that many hours ago.

Why hadn't I gotten hard when she had fondled my lap while we sat on that couch? I'd never had the problem before of not being able to get it up. Men are funny. Everything else going on today and tonight and I have to think about something like that. I derailed that train of thought.

The window was open about four inches, allowing me to hear the conversation from within.

Sydney was saying, from somewhere beyond my line of vision, "Jimi, put on a record if you want to hear some music."

Jimi was patting his pockets. "In a sec, babe. Want to do a line of coke with me?"

"No, and I wish you wouldn't either. We need to talk and it's serious."

He flopped onto the couch and produced a vial from his shirt pocket.

"Well in that case, a little bump should help."

He tapped white powder onto the back of one hand. He inhaled the powder through one nostril with a quick sniff.

I shifted sideways as far as I could, peering around. It would be a hell of a note if Jimi found me spying on them.

Or maybe he wouldn't mind. I'd assured him that he could depend on me to look out for him. I told myself again that's what I was doing.

Inside the flat, Sydney stepped into my line of vision and handed Jimi a cup of ea. She held one for herself.

She sat beside him.

"Cheers," she said with a little smile of irony.

They clinked tea cups.

Jimi said, "So what's up, hon? What is it you couldn't tell me at the club or on the drive over here?"

Sydney said, "It's complicated. It isn't really so much that I have something to tell you as I simply want to get you away from influences that are doing you in. I'm like Soldier that way, don't you see? I really care about you, Jimi."

"Influences that are doing me harm? You mean like Monika?"

"I'm not sure about Monika but I do mean drink and drugs."

"Don't start, Sydney. You mean you brought me home for *that*? Damn."

"You may think I'm just a spoiled rich brat," she said, "but I can make things happen in your life, Jimi. Good things. I can steer you to my family's physician. With treatment—"

The door buzzer buzzed.

Sydney got a look in her eyes like prey when it knows it's been caught in the sights but doesn't know what to do or which way to jump.

She said, "Shit."

Jimi said, "Now what the hell."

"Let's pretend we're not here," said Sydney. "Whoever it is, they'll go away."

The person at the door gave up on the buzzer and started hammering on the door with a fist.

"Jimi! Jimi, open up for chrissake. It's Bandy. I've got to talk to you, mate."

Jimi and Sydney exchanged a glance.

Jimi called, "Not now, Bandy. I'm busy."

Bandy, whoever he was, thumped hard on the door again. "But Jimi, I've got something that won't wait. Let me in! I've got to talk to you."

Jimi sighed. He touched Sydney on the leg. "Let him in, baby."

Sydney made a face. "But Jimi--"

"Let him in. Wonder what's so damn important."

"Bloody hell if I know!" Sydney left my range of vision. When she returned, she stood behind the couch where I could see her. She placed a hand on Jimi's shoulder.

Bandy remained beyond my line of vision. From what I remembered of the layout, he probably stood just inside the door where a square of tiles and a mounted mirror created a small entranceway.

Jimi said, "Hey, Bandy," in that lazy drawl of his. "What's up? Bummer to be bugging people at this hour of the night, don't you think?"

"Don't kid with me, Jimi," a raspy, Cockney voice said. "You're a creature of the night, you are."

"So what's up?"

"I've got news, I have. News you've gotta hear."

"So let me hear it."

Bandy said, "Uh."

Sydney removed her hand from Jimi's shoulder. "Oh, I see. You don't want me to hear the exciting news."

Bandy said, "Uh," again. And then, "Uh, Jimi …"

Jimi said, "Bandy, get out of here, man. I'll call you tomorrow."

"I'd like that, mate. I surely would. And, Sydney, I'm sorry, darlin', but I need to speak with Jimi alone."

Sydney said, "Well then you can both bloody well haul your arses out of my domicile and talk until you're blue in the face for all I care."

Jimi said, as if thinking aloud, "Y'know, I'd sure like to find me some fucking peace and quiet for just five minutes."

Sydney laid both hands on Jimi's shoulders. "That's why I brought you here." Then her hands dropped to her hips. "Damn you, Bandy. It's not a very nice thing to say but damn you to hell. You don't care a twig about Jimi, so stop pretending that you do."

Jimi drew himself to his feet. "It's cool, Syd. Okay, Bandy. Let's you and me step out into the hallway. Go out there and wait for me."

Bandy said, "Right you are, Jimi."

I could hear his footsteps leaving the flat.

When they were alone, Jimi eased around the couch, toward Sydney.

She crossed her arms and took a step back. "Don't touch me, Jimi. I don't like your friends."

"I'll give him one minute, not a second more. Promise."

"You can't talk in front of me? I can't be trusted in my own bloody home?"

Jimi slid his left arm around her waist. His right index finger tilted her chin so she had to peer up at him.

"Look, I'll give him thirty seconds. Then he's gone and we won't answer the door no matter who comes knocking."

"I can help you, Jimi. I want to help you."

"I know that, Syd." He kissed her forehead. "Don't unlock the door for anyone but me."

He stepped out of my frame of vision.

When the door closed after him, Sydney mumbled something and lit a cigarette. She paced out of my line of sight in the direction of the kitchenette. Ice cubes clinked into a glass.

Something was wrong. I felt a tightening in my gut like when you're on night patrol and your senses pick up some sort of anomaly in the atmosphere but you can't quite tell if it's just the jungle night or your nerves. I had that feeling.

Once Jimi and this Bandy were out of the flat, I figured they could stand in the hallway and talk. On the other hand, if Jimi was serious about giving the guy only thirty seconds, he might listen while he was escorting Bandy out of the building. I could track Bandy. A conversation with him could be helpful. Counting on Jimi to supply me with information hadn't worked out so well.

Someone rushed me from my blind side.

I heard the blow before it struck me from behind, catching me behind the right ear and for the second time that day.

Only this time it was different. I wasn't completely KO-ed. I felt like a guy shooting Niagara Falls in a barrel, my reality a tumbling, disjointed and dizzying haze. I had the impression of being physically carried. Of words being spoken over me. Then everything faded away.

11

————

THE JUNGLE REEKS OF DEATH. THE STENCH OF DEAD vegetation and animal rot permeate often impassible undergrowth. A claustrophobic steam bath, noisy with chattering birds and insects. Visibility in any direction is restricted to no more than a few yards. A blistering sun commands a washed-out blue sky.

We're locked and loaded.

Much death has gone down in this sector in the very recent past which is why our squad, plus the four Monts with us, are filing at combat intervals just inside the line that borders a network of dikes and rice paddies.

We're an hour into the patrol after having watched the chopper that brought us in lift off from the LZ and rotor out of sight beyond the treetops. We're to rendezvous with a chopper at a different LZ at 1900 hours, so we're outfitted for light, combat-ready travel: camou fatigues, soft camou hats and field webbing.

The Montagnards are small-boned, fierce mountain tribesmen. Stoic. Supplied by Uncle Sugar with weapons, ammunition and training because they hate the communists who have tried to eradicate the Montagnard's cultivation of the poppy which is then sold to Chinese gangs for processing and shipment to Europe and the West. The Viet Cong terrorize the mountain hamlets and sabotage the fields of poppies with the aim of destabilizing the Monts' control of the region.

The Montgagnards are scouts. Like us they carry M-16s and like us they eye the jungle warily as we follow a winding game trail. This is their land. They know every inch, every trail. Their leader, Hoa, has taken point. One of his men is next in line behind him, then our squad and two more Monts bringing up the tail end.

Our top kick is Master Sergeant Chug Brown, a hulking black bear of a man.

I'm four days into my first tour of combat duty in country and this is my first patrol.

The full might of the 1st US Infantry Division swept through during the preceding five days. Operation Hellfire, they called it. The objective: locate and destroy a sizeable, well dug-in VC force. By the end of the operation, the enemy body count was one of the highest yet. Then J-2 Intelligence sends in a handful of A-teams like ours to verify the strength and location of any remaining VC in the area.

We track deep into the bush, through tall grass along a narrow stream. There's water under the grass, and our boots are soaked. We catch glimpses of open country, of tiered rice paddies through breaks in the tree line, but nothing appears to live or move out there except for the occasional water buffalo baking lazily in the sunshine.

It's as if Operation Hellfire purged the area of all

human life. Charlie has been cleared out, or at least driven underground. The civilian population is lying low, holding its collective breath, waiting to see what will happen next.

I know just how they feel.

"All right, take five," Chug Brown instructs in a low voice. "Keep your eyes and ears open and a finger on the trigger."

Hoa translates for his men. The Monts fade away into the bush to form a loose defensive perimeter.

Sergeant Brown finds himself a raised, dry patch of ground and parks himself. Takes a swig from his canteen.

Me and the other guys of our squad squat near Top and wolf down our delicious lunch: a couple handfuls of rice, vitamins and salt tablets, all washed down with warm water from our canteens.

Our radioman, Rick Chavez, says, "Miracle of miracles, could be the Big Red One got the job done." Chavez totes a compact HT-1 radio along with the rest of his gear. He grins at me and Moore. "You cherries drew a walk through the park your first time out."

"Suits me," says Moore, an E-4 like me. "I told my girl back home to pray for me, so maybe she is."

Chavez chuckles, experience in eyes that are dark like polished black marbles. He looks at me.

"What about you, cherry?" he asks with a grin. "Ready for your first firefight?"

I tell them, "That's what I'm here for."

A few more minutes of small talk and swatting mosquitoes, and then Sergeant Brown heaves himself to his feet.

"Break's over. Let's see what we find around the next bend in life's highway."

Chavez says, "Me, I'd rather be on the highway out of town."

Hoa signals his Monts, who start to reform the column.

The sharp report of a rifle, muffled by the heavy jungle foliage but not that far off, catches everyone's attention.

Moore assumes a combat crouch. "What the hell—"

Chavez chuckles. "You didn't really think Charlie was cleaned out? Don't let a little rifle fire throw you. That's one of Charlie's favorite tricks, right, Top?"

Sergeant Brown nods. "They'll peg a round or two in the air. See if that draws return fire. If it does, they've pinpointed our position. But they may have done that already. Stay sharp.""

I notice an abrupt silence. The jungle which moments earlier had been noisy with chattering insects and birds. Now, nothing.

Chug starts to say something.

The angry chatter of automatic rifle-fire! Saffron flashes from twin angles of attack! Two of the Monts spin, whirling dervishes, blood spewing.

We scatter for cover in the deep brush that borders either side of the trail, automatic rifle fire tracking us.

Jumbled sensations and images. Moore has not sought cover fast enough. Horror on his face when he realizes he's fallen behind, then a determination to pick up the pace and reach us. His face is blown away in a smear of blood. Hoa and the remaining Mont are dead on their feet before they can fire a shot. A whistling round sizzles past my right ear. Me, Chavez and Sergeant Brown return fire on full auto, backpedaling deeper into the jungle. I've fired off a whole clip! A flurry of movement comes from where the incoming fire is originating. A body tumbles to the ground from the underbrush. I reach for another magazine and palm it into the M-16. Did one of my rounds drop the son of a bitch? Was that my first kill?

Searing white-hot flame lances the upper left side of my body. In a crazily disjointed flash of tangential lucidity, I remember the time as a kid when an ornery mule back on the farm kicked me in the ass. My face plunges into the muck of the jungle floor. *Am I dying?* This can't be. Not like Moore, greased my first time out. No, goddamn it, *no!*

Without a word, Chavez slings his M-16 over his shoulder and hoists my lower half while Sergeant Brown wraps a thick bear-like arm under my arm. They hustle me along, barely slacking their pace with my added weight. Top braces the butt of his rifle against one hip and hammers out a steady stream of fire, raking the thorn brush and fronds that conceal the bastards. We reach a point where a dip in the terrain provides better cover.

My senses are stabilizing. I've lost my rifle back there on the trail. The left side of my body is numb, cold, tingling like when your foot falls asleep. Shock. The pain will hit me soon enough unless unconsciousness or worse gets me. I twist my head for a better look at myself.

An ugly hole near my left shoulder, pumping thick red blood.

Sergeant Brown slaps a fresh magazine into his carbine.

"Hang tight, son. You'll make it."

I can hear in his voice that he isn't so sure.

Further up the trail, our ambushers reveal themselves. A pair of men and one woman in the Viet Cong uniform of black pajamas and conical straw hats. They advance with their AK-47s blazing. Projectiles zip and ping from the earth and rocks near us.

A hard-wet *slap!*

"Ugh!"

Chavez stumbles beside me as if tripping over something and he goes down, his spurting blood splattering across my face.

Sergeant Brown squeezes off another short burst. Then I hear another hard-wet *slap!*

"Mother*humper,*" he gasps in a strange voice. "I'm hit!"

12

A PAIR OF WIDE GREEN EYES STARED BACK AT ME. THE green eyes did not blink. Did not move. Did not register any sort of emotion. Two blank staring eyes, less than ten inches from my own. They could only be the eyes of a dead person.

I sat up.

I was on a rug and I recognized its pattern. This was the second time I'd regained consciousness here. I was in Sydney's flat. I glanced at the window. There was the blank brick wall of the next building.

Sydney's dead body had been stretched out on the floor, alongside me.

Deep purple bruises encircled her throat. Someone had choked Sydney and smashed her head repeatedly against the floor. The carpet around her head was soaked with a pool of her blood making a sort of halo, but this was no medieval painting of the Madonna. The poor kid's red hair was tangled and smeared with strawberry jelly that matched the goo that covered the business end of a black sap on the floor next to her body.

If I was a gambling man, I would have bet every cent (or shilling) I had that the grip of that sap held my fingerprints.

I came close to retching. My chin dropped to my chest and I drew in some deep breaths, then forced myself to stand. My knees wanted to buckle. I steadied myself with a two-handed hold on the back of the couch. I tried to grope at memory, veiled in a half-light of awareness, receding away from me. I'd been too single-minded. Too intent on eavesdropping outside of the flat to be as careful as I should have been. Write it off to fatigue.

A bright, pretty, energetic young woman who had, I suppose, cast me under her spell. With a good family behind her and a heart full of dreams, a bright future before her, to savor and conquer.

I'd seen plenty of dead guys in Vietnam. Guys I'd gotten a chance to know and like. Every one of them took a little piece of your soul with them when you stared down into their face before the body bag was zippered shut and the remains of what had been a good person were loaded with the other body bags onto the evac chopper.

Looking down at Sydney filled me with a different kind of ache. What could be so important that this young woman had to die like this?

Sydney kept a clean flat, but clutter now topped the small end table next to the couch. A bent spoon. A gutted candle. Vials. A kit for shooting up. Multicolored pills, like beads spilt across floor and furniture.

Suddenly a heavy fist pounded on the door.

"Miss Blanchard, are you there? Miss Blanchard, open up please. It's the police. Hullo in there?"

I knew that voice. Officious. Demanding.

Inspector Hudberry.

And he wasn't alone. Through the narrow crack of the open window, where I had been eavesdropping, through the stillness of the night, came the static crackle of a police car radio and then footfalls slapping the pavement of the service way between the buildings.

First things first.

I used one of my own shirt tails to wipe clean any fingerprints on the sap, taking a few seconds longer than I should have because I had to be extremely careful not to get my shirt smeared with the bloody hair and body tissue that covered the weighted end of the sap. My fingerprints would be around the flat from my previous visit so that I could explain, if pressed, but not prints on a murder weapon.

I took a final moment to pause, standing over Sydney.

I said, "I'll get them, kid. Whoever they are, I'll get them in my sights personally and I'll be thinking of you when I squeeze the trigger."

The thump came of Hudberry bodily heaving himself against the door. The Inspector was a big man. He'd break it down in another try or two.

I whispered, "Rest in peace, Sydney."

I looked past the archway that was hung with a beaded curtain. Sydney's bedroom was feminine in the extreme. Soft lighting. A made bed with a blue nightgown spread across the coverlet. A draped window over the head of the bed.

There was another thump at the door and the first cracking of wood. One more try and Hudberry would be in.

I glanced at the kitchenette. A back door let outside. I eased myself out into the darkness. Then I ran like hell for the narrow service way that would take me to the street. My duffle bag was still in the trunk (I mean, boot) of Sydney's Austin Healy from when she had rescued Jimi and me behind Angel McGuire's commune. No time now to retrieve that. I almost reached the sidewalk fronting the building when the bobby who'd gone behind the house yelled after me, his voice amplified by the confines of the service way.

"Stop! In the name of the law!"

I guess that was supposed to get people's attention in civilized Olde England.

I just kept running.

I reached the sidewalk. I sprinted away in a dead heat. I rounded the next corner, into another sleepy residential street lined with automobiles.

When the bobby emerged from the service way, he wouldn't know which direction I'd taken. Footfalls receded in the opposite direction in the still of the night. He'd made the wrong choice, buying me a little time but not much.

I tried the door handle of every car I walked past. It took me almost to the next corner before I found the vehicle of some unfortunate trusting or absentminded soul who had neglected to lock his or her car after parking it.

A late model Toyota. I did time in juvie for hot-wiring

cars, so I could have done it blindfolded. Less than twenty seconds for the little engine to turn over.

I caught a main artery and kept my speed down, cruising with the sparse night traffic.

The cold, calculating impulse to formulate a strategy for survival fell on me with the same clarity as if Charlie was out there in the bush and we had to make our way back to the firebase before dark. Here I was back in "the world," and nearly every action I took and every thought I had felt rooted in Vietnam as surely as my heart was rooted in my chest.

At the first intersection, I had to brake for a stoplight. I reached into the glove box and found a street map of London. I pulled over and spent a few minutes figuring out how to reach the address Monika Dannemann had given me.

I made it to the Notting Hill Secton without difficulty. Traffic was sparse at this hour and so was any police presence. I passed one bobby walking his night rounds on a road of closed shops. On the surface, London sure was civilized and law-abiding.

The address in Notting Hill was a flat with its own street entrance. A single-story residential hotel. I cruised past slowly. Monika's windows were dark but that didn't mean anything at this hour. I found the nearest parking space, turned off the engine, wiped clean the steering wheel and any other part of the car that I remembered touching and left the stolen Toyota, taking only the street map with me.

I knocked on Monika's door and waited, trying to calm a pulse that wouldn't stop racing. I knocked some more. Waited a little more. Knocking any louder or calling a name to see if anyone was home would risk drawing attention. I didn't want that.

I started walking toward a cluster of lights that marked a tube station down the block.

I knew what I needed.

I needed me an angel.

13

My phone call yanked a groggy Angel McGuire from a sound sleep, but she woke up fast once she knew it was me. I made it short and sweet. Told her I needed to see her. It couldn't wait. She gave me directions to an all-night restaurant and told me she'd meet me there.

The gray of a false dawn had just started delineating the London skyline when I emerged onto the sidewalk from the Charring Cross tube station. The restaurant was a five minute walk from the station, a modest little café, located on a side street, which did a moderate pre-dawn business. The all-nighters were starting to wind down before heading home and the early-to-work trade was starting to filter in.

Angel sat waiting for me in a booth toward the back and if I had awakened her from a sound sleep less than thirty minutes ago, it sure didn't show. Her wild mane of midnight hair had a healthy, brushed sheen, her animated nature muted out of respect for the early hour and those around us while her eyes were lively and inquisitive. She managed to look great in a faded pair of jeans, a suede jacket thrown over a T-shirt adorned with the Grateful Dead logo and pair of Converse sneakers.

I slid in across the table from her in the booth.

"Thanks for meeting me. Sorry about the hour."

She appraised me with inquisitive eyes. She winced at what she saw. "You've had a rough night."

"Tex, you don't know the half of it."

A stout waitress, far too cheery and effusive for the hour, took our orders—salad for Angel, a ham and cheese omelet for me. Coffee, black.

Angel waited until I'd been served the coffee and the waitress had withdrawn. The murmur of conversations and the clinking of silverware from nearby tables provided a degree of privacy.

Angel said, "When you and Jimi left my place yesterday, you sure left me with a mess on my hands what with beating up a cop on my back doorstep. They raided my place good and proper after you guys left. A lot of the kids who show up at my place are runaways. They hauled off a couple in from the States who weren't fast enough at getting rid of their stash. Oh, there's a warrant out for your arrest. I've been wondering whatever happened to you, Soldier."

"Maybe I shouldn't have been so rough on that cop."

"Yeah, maybe so. The medics had to work on him. Inspector Hudberry's a proud man with a strong rep on the streets. You busted his nose and his image."

"A tactical error. But he shouldn't have laid a hand on me. I'm sort of wound up."

"I've noticed. Jimi told me about you. You went to

Vietnam and he broke his ankle and was discharged from the Army."

"That's the cover story, yeah."

"You mean you didn't go to Vietnam?"

"I meant about Jimi's ankle. He liked the army well enough when he first signed up because he was born a wild child and he thought a dose of military discipline was what he needed. It wasn't, he found out soon enough. He psyched out the shrinks, told them what they wanted to hear so they'd determine that he wasn't emotionally fit for military service, which was true enough, and they were glad to see him go."

The hint of a smile touched the corners of her mouth and her eyes. "And the world's a better place for it. I don't see Jimi as a soldier."

I said, "Jimi soldiers on. He's just fighting another kind of war on another front. But this is all history. I need to know more about his world today. How much do you know about that world, Angel?"

She sighed.

A brief intermission while the waitress served the food. She again waited until after the waitress left.

Then Angel said, "You've seen the shape Jimi's in. It's been getting worse by the day. I've known Jimi since Chas Chandler debuted him over here three years ago. On this visit Jimi's been dropping by my place at least once a day. As you saw, it's sort of a relaxed atmosphere. Jimi feels comfortable there, and there's a phone for him to use."

"He was jittery as hell yesterday when I showed up."

"I know. Going a mile a minute on that pay tele-phone, tying it up for hours at a time. Before that he was sitting alone upstairs in a dark corner, listening to a

Ravi Shankar album with his eyes closed like he was meditating, drawn into himself. When he caught me watching him he told me I was his best friend in London. Then he's off on another ninety-minute telephone jag."

I said, "I've got to trust you."

She registered a slight frown. "Trust me with what? What's going on? I'm dragged out of bed before the sun comes up to meet a man I barely know. He looks like hell, no offense, and he wants to interrogate me about a dear friend. So I repeat, what's going on? Why all the questions?"

"Have you seen Jimi since he and I left your place? Has he had any contact with you?"

She rolled her eyes. "Still with the questions. No, not since you and Jimi lit out on the run from Monika. Did she ever track him down, by the way?"

"They were lovebirds last night at Ronnie Scott's."

"Figures." She exhaled a plume of smoke, tapped her cigarette on the table ashtray and stared at the ashtray as if it was going to do something.

I said, "Then he left Monika and took off with Sydney Blanchard."

She snubbed out her cigarette. "I adore Jimi but he's a fool."

"Are he and Monika really engaged like Monika says?"

"You'd have to ask Jimi about that."

"I'm asking you."

"Listen to me, Soldier. Rule number one, I leave other people's personal business alone."

I finished the omelet, pushed away the plate and fired up a cig.

"So Monika is just a delusional girlfriend with personal ambition, is that it?"

"You have a way with words, I'll say that for you. Ever think about becoming a writer?"

"Maybe someday. I've written some stories."

"You still haven't told me why you're asking me all these questions. Why do you need anyone to trust, especially me? You're a loner, big man, and you like it that way."

"Any pilot flying a Huey over in Nam will tell you that the hotter the LZ, the more cover fire you need."

"What's an LZ?"

"Landing zone. That's what this whole damn city is for me and I don't have a soul I can trust to give me cover and support except for Jimi and he's MIA."

She thought for a moment, and then nodded her comprehension. "Missing in action." And when I nodded, she reached across the table and rested a hand on mine. "You can count on me."

The waitress returned, cleared away our plates, asked us if we wanted anything else and waddled off after a single shake of my head, and during that time the moment held between me and Angel, her hand remaining on mine, infusing me with warmth that brought clarity.

I said, "Let's get out of here."

Outside, a damp morning chill was in the air. A gray blanket hung over the city. Vehicles drove with their lights on. In a small park across the way, birds sang from the trees.

We started walking.

Angel said, "So are you going to tell me what happened last night? What's this about?"

"It's about Sydney Blanchard. You know her, right?"

"I do indeed. Sydney is part of the scene. She's sweet."

"She's dead."

She registered a blank stare. "What?"

"Someone killed her in her flat. No one knows about it yet."

She stopped walking. She appraised me all over again. She bit her lip.

"Did you--?"

"What do you think?"

What followed between us could only be described as a pregnant silence. Then her manner relaxed. We resumed walking.

"Okay, I trust you too. I'm a Texas gal who follows her heart. Sydney. My God. Who did it?"

"I don't know. Not yet. Someone tried to make it look like I killed her."

"Tell me what happened."

So I told her how I'd followed Sydney and Jimi to Sydney's place from the club.

"I thought I was looking out for Jimi. I was eavesdropping outside her flat when someone conked me and when I came to I was inside the flat and it had been made to look like I'd beaten Sydney to death with a sap. I came to with your friend Hudberry trying to beat the door down. I got away by the skin of my teeth."

"My God. Poor little Sydney, zipping around in her sporty little car while she chattered about music and fashion and acting. She had so much life in her. It's hard to believe."

"She intercepted me at the airport yesterday. Tried to be clever about it. I still don't know if she was a sweet rich kid with a lot of what my old man would have called moxie, or if she was into something over her head."

"Could have been both, poor kid." Angel blinked away a visible surge of emotion. She arched an eyebrow. "Can the police tie you to with what happened?"

"That's the nail in my coffin."

"So how bad is it?"

"Sydney was driving around with my duffel bag in the boot of her car. Hudberry will know that by now. My transit orders were in that duffel bag, along with everything else I own. Scotland Yard now knows who I am, how long I'll be in London, where I'm bound and when I'm due there."

"Jeez, Soldier…"

"Yeah, I know. I've stepped in it big time."

"What about Jimi? Where's he in all this?"

"Now that's a damn good question, Tex. Your wide circle of friends and acquaintances wouldn't happen to include anyone named Bandy, by any chance?"

"And why would you ask that?"

"Just curious."

She made a face. "Yeah, right."

"Well?"

She sighed deeply. "You're talking about Bandy McGuire. I was married to the no good son of a bitch for the worst eighteen months of my life."

Talk about a curve I didn't see coming.

I found myself saying, "Ah," as a way of processing unexpected data.

"And what is that supposed to mean?"

"Tell me about Bandy."

She opened her purse as we walked, tapped a cigarette from its pack and paused so I could light it for her.

She said, "It was a Yardbirds tour through Texas. My groupie days. Bandy and me, we did a one-night stand after a concert in Austin and, well, we just sort of hooked up, I guess you could say. He'd come over to the States as a roadie or a hanger-on traveling with the road crew, I never did quite get that part straight. The Brit accent is what got little ol' me. That and of course traveling with a rock & roll band, even if we never actually got anywhere near the guys in the band. But I was naïve and too hung up on Bandy to notice or think it mattered. When the tour ended Bandy asked me to fly back to London and marry him, which sounded like a cool idea at the time. After we were married, I started finding out more about him and the life I'd married into. Whatever the roadie deal was, that was only a one-shot. Over here, Bandy picks up pocket money sometimes loading gear for a couple of London pub bands but that is just for a few quid and getting in without having to pay the cover charge."

"So how does he support himself?"

"From the rackets that Hudberry is trying to bust. Loan sharking. Dope peddling and protection. Pimping. I knew Bandy was a rough boy back home when I met him. That was part of his charm, you might say. But enough about me. Why do you want to know about Bandy?"

I told her about me not being able to see Bandy from my vantage point outside Sydney Blanchard's flat, and about Jimi leaving the flat with Bandy just before I was slugged.

She said, "Jimi's been scrambling for bread since his tour fell apart. Staying on the dodge from lawyers can't be cheap. If Jimi's into loan sharks, that could be a connection with Bandy. He provides muscle when people need a reminder to pay up."

"Would he lean on Jimi?"

She didn't pause to consider. She nodded.

"I married a thug. Worse mistake of my life."

"Could Bandy be tied up with a pack of German hoods? I stopped them from trying to throw Jimi off a roof yesterday afternoon."

"My, you are having an eventful stay in London."

"Well?"

She said, "Bandy hates Germans. When he was a boy he idolized his older brother who was a prize fighter or something. The brother was killed in the blitz. Bandy never forgave the Germans for that."

"I want to talk with this ex-husband of yours."

"That might take some doing. Bandy McGuire is not an easy man to track down."

"You know London, right?"

"Three years' worth. I've been enjoying my expatriate life. They make it a little easier over here to be a free spirit than the good old boys back in Texas."

"Last I saw of Jimi, Sydney was still alive and he was heading out the door of her flat with your ex-husband. Let's find your ex-husband."

She touched a hand to my sleeve. "Wait. There's something else. You've had so much to tell me, I haven't had a chance to tell you."

"Does it concern Jimi?"

"It sure does. It concerns keeping him alive. There's someone you have to meet right away."

14

WE HAD PICKED UP A TAIL.

There are things you can't intellectualize that are linked back to our primal source. The instinctual sensory response that cats and dogs still have but that civilization has bred out of us humans except for those rare, weird times when you reach for the phone a split second before it rings or you look up because you sense someone looking at you from across the restaurant or from the next car over at a stoplight.

I could feel our shadow's eyes on my back.

I didn't mention the sensation to Angel. We strode arm-in-arm and for the heck of it I let her set the pace; a quick, determined pace.

The city's working stiffs were out in force, flooding the streets and the double-decker busses and the subways on their way to serve the great god of commerce in the busy stores at street level or high in the skyscrapers that loomed overhead, monolithic towers rising so high that their upper floors disappeared into the hovering gray.

I was curious as hell about where Angel was taking me and about whoever who was tailing us. Someone on foot. Had to be. Vehicular traffic was too dense for someone to be shadowing us that way.

Someone on foot, tracking from behind.

Angel resisted slightly when I paused a couple of times to study plate glass windows of stores we passed. I made an act of gazing at display items before relenting to the whims of my partner and continuing on. Each time I made a careful scan of our backtrack, eyeballing the sidewalk scene behind us that was reflected in those plate glass windows. I detected no hesitation on the part of any pedestrian in our wake, or any anomaly in the crowd's fluidity that would suggest someone trying to avoid detection. Whoever followed us was good enough to keep their cool and not give himself away.

Or was I delusional, paranoid, and no one was following us?

I said, "Angel, did you tell anyone that you were going to meet me?"

"No. Why?"

"No reason."

How had the tail picked up our scent?

Angel steered us into a pub near Trafalgar Square. A working man's pub, smoky and noisy even at this hour. Someone was playing a squeeze box in back, accompanied by a chorus of inebriated out-of-tune voices raised in merry song. A spirited dart game was in progress. The crowd was sprinkled with guys in suits, some even in homburgs with the requisite closed umbrella, ducking in for a quick snort before popping a peppermint and reporting for their day's labor, rubbing shoulders with all night merrymakers and sulking loners having one for the road to cork the evening.

Angel subtly took the lead. I let her navigate us through the cigarette and cigar smoke and the spirited conversations, a few of which paused momentarily as we passed. She possessed an earthy beauty any man would be proud to be seen with. Angel was that type of a woman and the eyes that followed the mane of flowing black hair, the strong chin held high, the shining of bracelets and the sway of hips were filled with envy. I saw unconcealed desire in the eyes of the businessmen, the nighttimers and the old duffers alike.

We reached a table where a solidly built guy in his thirties sat waiting, nursing a pint of dark ale. Casual slacks. Open-necked shirt. His sport jacket looked slept in. There was a harried look about his features and demeanor. He did not rise at the approach of a lady to his table, the way many gentlemen still did in those days. We settled into chairs across from him.

A middle-aged barmaid had seen us come in and was waiting to take our orders. Angel ordered a Coke. I ordered a cup of coffee.

Angel said, "Chet Daly, this is Soldier."

There are those who have seen too much of the dark side. I'm one of them and so was this guy. It's in the eyes. I recognized in him what he would plainly see in me.

He said, "Soldier? What the hell kind of name is that?"

Angel picked up on it real quick. Growing up surrounded by good old boys in Texas had left its mark. She may have spent her time running a crash pad for spoiled runaways or doped out artists but this woman also knew something about handling a pair of alpha dogs sizing each other up.

She said, "Soldier, Chet has something incredible to tell us. He's one of us. He showed up at my doorstep just like you did, looking for Jimi . He's not working for the law."

Daly snorted. "That's a laugh. I was the law, then I got religion."

I said, "Why are you looking for Jimi?"

"To warn him"

"Warn him? Warn him about what?"

He took a gulp of his ale. "You know what I am, don't you, Soldier?"

"I know the type. Hard guy. Field op. You're overseas so that makes you CIA."

He said, "Leave the alphabet out of it. The only thing that matters is that you buy who I am and what I'm here in London to do."

"We take orders from you guys in Vietnam. Then you board a chopper and get somewhere else fast before the shooting starts."

"Soldier, I've contributed to the rise of at least a third of the regimes in the Third World. Assassinations, coups d'etat, psy wars, rigging elections." He spoke with a raspy Midwestern accent. I would have guessed Chicago.

I said, "Dirty tricks."

His wary eyes darted here and there, trying to watch everyone and everything at once. "As a soldier, I don't suppose you have an interest in politics."

"I serve my country," I said, "not the idiots who think they run it."

"Then we're in agreement."

"Is that right? Convince me, why don't you?"

"Okay, I'll try. I'm *ex*-CIA."

"Prove it."

Angel said, "Soldier—"

"It's okay," he assured her. "He has no reason to like or trust me."

"Yes, he does. Because I want him to."

Daly said, "I'm recently retired from government service. I was subsequently offered an off-the-record deal from my former associates. With the years of dirty work I've done for them, they thought they could trust me with anything. They were wrong. I declined their offer. Consequently there's a shoot-on-site order out for me as we speak."

Angel exhaled a stream of cigarette smoke at the ceiling, then caught my eye. "I told you. Chet showed up at my place just before you called. He needs to find Jimi. I told him the last time I saw Jimi, he was with you. I asked him to wait for us here."

Daly said, "Soldier, if you're a true friend of Jimi's, you need to help me. I came to London to save Jimi's life. Where is he?"

15

I said, "Show me yours first. What if Jimi doesn't want to be found?"

Daly took another gulp of his ale. He didn't look drunk. He looked edgy.

He said, "Okay here it is straight and I don't care who hears it. I'll be going to the TV and newspapers with what I've got as soon as I know Jimi's safe. If I went public with I've got before that, it could speed up their timetable and Jimi will be dead, probably from an 'accidental' drug overdose."

"What the hell are you talking about? Who wants Jimi dead?"

"The United States government, that's who. President Nixon and his Gestapo cronies want to prevent the communist menace from infiltrating the United States. Keep the black power and the anti-war movements in their place, powerless and discredited. They're out to obliterate the opposition by any means at their command. They wanted to enlist me but what they were up to sickened me to my soul. So I've turned on them. I'm blowing the whistle. That's why they want me dead."

I said, "You didn't mind fermenting that kind of political unrest in other countries for Uncle Sam, by your own admission. You don't look like an idealist to me."

He said, "And you don't look stupid enough to look a gift horse in the mouth."

Angel rested one hand on Daly's wrist and her other hand on one of mine.

"Boys, boys. Let's be nice. Soldier, jeez, let him tell us what he knows."

Daly sat forward, his shoulders hunched. "They wanted me to run a deep-cover black-ops unit sanctioned to assassinate selected targets in the entertainment industry, starting with musicians like Jimi Hendrix."

Angel gasped. She said in a small voice, mostly to herself, "Oh no…"

I said, "A death squad under sanction of the executive branch?"

"You heard me. Some brain in the White House sub-sub-sub basement came up with it, and there are enough nuts in the White House today who think like that, they managed to slide it through under the radar of everyone."

"And you turned it down?"

"That's right. If you don't believe me, you have nothing to work with."

Angel said, "I believe you." Her voice and eyes were dull with sadness.

"Political assassination of American citizens by their own government because they're cultural leaders who are deemed subversive by the administration. That's the bomb I'm going to drop in the media's lap after I leave here. I was shown the hit list. Jimi's at the top of the list."

Angel said, "But why, for pete's sake? Jimi Hendrix is a great musician. He is a pure artist. He plays rock and roll guitar. Frankly, he's above politics. It's a whole different realm of reality."

"He's made public statements in support of the Black Panthers and the defendants in the Chicago Seven trial who happen to advocate an armed struggle between the races in America."

I said, "Who else is on the list?"

"The ones who are stirring up the most rabble. The ones those dead kids at Kent State probably had posters of on their dorm room walls. Jimi. Janis Joplin. Jim Morrison. John Lennon. Last year Jimi was placed on the Federal Security Index."

Angel said, "The what?"

"A list of subversives who are to be rounded up and placed in detainment camps in the event of a national emergency."

Angel seemed to have trouble finding her voice. She cleared her throat.

"But that's outrageous. The United States government wouldn't do such a thing."

"Wouldn't they? Maybe you never heard of the prison camps for Japanese American citizens during World War II."

"But what about free speech, for heaven's sake?"

"Don't ask me," said Daly. "I was a part of it but I never figured that part out."

I said, "So you're telling us that you've come to London to warn Jimi that assassins working for the U.S.

government have been sent here to kill him?"

"Right on the money, Soldier. They'll most likely use a hit team. A spotter and the one who drops the hammer. Mercenaries not traceable to our government."

"How long have you known about this?"

"Three days ago. I confirmed it yesterday. We don't have to go into that now. Not with the clock ticking. They've been keeping tabs on Hendrix for awhile. What do you know about Michael Jeffrey?"

I said, "Not much, but I think I should. Jimi's manager. Likes to talk up having been an intelligence agent with a Mafia tie-in. Mysterioso."

Angel said, "If the creeps Chet is talking about wanted to keep tabs on Jimi, they couldn't pick a better man for the job than Mike Jeffrey."

Daly used a napkin to dab at perspiration that sparkled on his forehead. He said, "That's my theory. Jeffrey fits the bill to a T. He did serve as a professional soldier in the Intelligence Corps; a very obscure phase of his life. He was stationed in Egypt. He does speak Russian. The perfect profile for an imbedded resource."

"Jimi obsesses all the time about the troubles Jeffrey has brought into his life and career," said Angel.

Daly nodded. "That would be his objective. My reading is that Jeffrey is a pro. Jimi is being played. He's being pushed to unravel so his death will look like suicide or a drug overdose." He finished off his ale and set the glass down with a clunk. He burped.

I said to Angel, with a nod in Daly's direction. "What if this guy's one of the hit team? He's the spotter. That's why he wants us to find Jimi for him."

"I served my country," said Daly, "not the idiots who

think they run it. I like the sound of that, Soldier, because it's exactly how I've come to feel. I saw the photograph of the young woman student at Kent State, crying out her anguish over the spilled blood of another student gunned down by the National Guard. One day I'll face judgment in the here and in the hereafter for the things I've done, but I won't be part of a conspiracy to murder U.S. citizens who happen to be entertainers who happen to disagree with an administration's policies. They thought they had me in their pocket after all those years in the field but they don't, and I have enough hard information to shut down the whole thing. But first I've got to do the right thing by Jimi. I want to make sure he's safe before I blow the whistle."

Angel glanced my way with uncertain eyes. "Soldier, what should we do?"

Daly said, "Jimi's life depends on your decision. Trust me, both of you. Help me, please. Help Jimi. Where is he?"

I said to Angel, "We need to find your ex-husband and I need to find me a piece."

Daly said, "Yeah, funny about guns, these limeys. Even the cops don't carry them. But that doesn't mean a fella feels safer without one." He eased aside the left lapel of his sport coat enough to reveal the butt of a pistol that rode in a concealed holster sling under his left arm. The jacket lapel fell back into place. He said, "Tell you what. I've got a spare piece where I'm staying. It's yours if you think you need it. Just get me to Jimi. He needs protection."

I said, "I know. That's why I'm here, even though I've done a pretty piss poor job so far."

Angel touched my wrist. "It would be foolish to blame yourself, Soldier, so don't."

Daly frowned. "What are you talking about?"

There was no reason at this point to tell him about Sydney Blanchard and about the police looking for me. No reason to tell him that Jimi had gone missing. We'd do better to find out what else he knew and then cut him loose. But I wanted that gun he'd offered.

I said, "Is your place near here?"

He caught my drift. He wiped suds from his lips with the back of his hand.

"Close enough. Let's go. We'll fix you up in the hardware department."

The three of us had reached the entrance when the pretty barmaid caught up with us.

"Sir," she was calling after Daly. "Sir, you forgot your hat."

It was a battered fedora to match the rumpled condition of his slacks, shirt and jacket. He tipped her.

"Thank you, gorgeous."

She grinned wide at the size of the tip. "Why, thank *you*, sir."

She turned back into the pub, pocketing the tip.

We started out of the pub.

The booming report of a rifle shot split apart the mundane morning sounds of the city. The pretty barmaid pitched uncontrollably forward into those patrons lining the bar, the back quarter of her skull violently, bloodily blown away.

Daly said, "Holy shit!" He went into an instinctive crouch. Reaching for his gun.

I pounced on Angel, sending us into the pub for cover.

Then the rifle boomed again.

Daly drew up short in the open double doorway. He

said, "Oh." It sounded like a cough. His pistol clattered to the floor. That's how quiet it became in the immediate, stunned wake of the barmaid being shot. That sliver of time before collective reactions sets in. Daly took a step backwards, and then another before his knees buckled and he fell onto his back.

Another heartbeat of silence. Then a woman screamed. A flurry of reaction erupted in the pub, people frantically diving for cover.

I scrambled low over to Daly's body. Grabbed an arm. Pulled the body into the pub, out of the line of fire, and retrieved his pistol, a hefty .45 Colt automatic. I scampered back to Angel, who had regained her footing.

A weird silence after the echoes of the gunfire rolled away down the canyon of the city street.

Sensing that the killing was done, people were starting to edge forward to view the carnage. The pretty barmaid had been collateral damage and once he'd corrected his aim, the shooter had taken out his intended target.

I scanned the rooftops directly across the street from the pub. Something on the periphery of my vision caught my attention. A blur of movement, three buildings down, vanished behind the parapet of the narrow five-story brownstone; an antique nestled in among towering modern buildings of glass and steel.

"Keep your head down," I said to Angel, "and your eyes open."

I concealed the .45 under my jacket, so that it rode under the belt at my hip, and I took off running. Pedestrians either saw me coming or found themselves brushed aside. A chorus of "I say" and "Bloody fool" sputtered in my wake. When I saw an opening, I angled across four lanes of traffic.

Brakes squealed. Tires shrieked on slick pavement. The thump of a fender bender. Someone started cussing.

I gained the front stoop of the brownstone and entered the small vestibule of a sedate, carpeted, well-lit hallway adorned with frosted glass doors, office waiting rooms of the white-collar businesses listed on a directory posted on the wall next to a stairway leading upstairs. A delicate wrought iron stand supported a vase of flowers beneath a mirror where you could make one last inspection before punching in for work or chatting up a business associate.

The office doors remained closed. Soundproofed tombs of white-collar industry. The existence of a world outside barely intruded in here. If the gunshots had been heard they would likely have been dismissed as an automobile backfiring, so unlikely was the notion of rifle fire in central London.

He came down the stairs, into the vestibule, and drew up short when he saw me. No sign of the rifle. He'd left it on the roof. It would be untraceable. He'd taken his sweet time, strolling down the flight of stairs from five levels up while I dashed like a crazy man through traffic. Except for eyes that flared with surprise, his face remained frozen as if carved in stone.

Businessman, American version. Sturdy build, around forty. Caucasian Everyman. Stylish black raincoat. Brooks Brothers in a city where the uniform of the business executive was a bowler hat, umbrella and crisply folded copy of the *Times*, closely clipped moustache optional.

He whirled and hustled back up the stairs, reaching under his jacket.

I approached the bottom of the stairs. No sounds from above. No fleeing footfalls. Was he up there on the second-floor landing, waiting for me to show myself?

I flung the vase of flowers.

Three rapid gunshots shattered the vase and the sedate atmosphere, punching three holes in the wall where I would have been, had I gone rushing after him in hot pursuit. Now came the scrambling of receding footfalls. I cautiously started up the stairs, hugging the wall, moving sideways in case he tried to fake me out again by tiptoeing back to catch an easy target. I made myself as thin a target as a man my size possibly could, the .45 up and ready on full cock.

The loud, bright sound of shattering glass brought me around the corner of the first floor landing, slow and careful at first. Then I over rushed to the window without glass at the end of the hallway.

He was straightening up from where he'd landed on the upper level of one of those British red double-decker buses that you everywhere in London. This was a tourist bus, not one of the standard public double-deck conveyances, and had been converted with an open air upper deck that had no roof. He'd landed there in the aisle near the front of the bus. No sign of a gun. The passengers seated around him displayed that mixture of interest and a disdain for getting involved with a man who had just leapt into their midst from a second floor window.

I still had a chance. It was slow going for the bus because of the fender bender I'd caused out front. Traffic was funneling into a single lane. I bolted back down the steps and across the vestibule, toward the street door.

Frosted glass office doors inched open. Curious faces peered out, now that gunfire and shattering of glass had breeched the walls of their sedate world.

I stormed back onto the busy sidewalk and caught up with the double decker just as it started picking up speed where the traffic again widened into twin lanes. I boarded the bus on the run. A quick glance down the rows of seats told me that he was still on the upper deck. I started up the winding steps.

The kick from above lashed out fast. I only had time to bring up an elbow to block my face. The blow sent me back and I reached out to grasp the hand rails at my either side to keep from tumbling off the bus. I started hoisting myself back in.

He dropped down from the top level, braced himself on the same rails I was holding onto and lashed out with another kick aimed at my head. I knew if he connected, the blow would either cave in my skull or send me falling into the traffic where I'd be ground into hamburger. I dodged to the side and the kick missed by a fraction of an inch.

The upper half of my body stretched out of the bus, but my grip on the rails kept my lower half inside from the hips on down. My assailant hadn't released his hold on the safety rails, either. He drew back his right foot for another kick.

The driver announced the next stop over the public address system, unaware of what was happening in the rear of his bus.

I gained traction with my butt on the floor and

pivoted my legs in an attempt to bring Brooks Brothers down, but he saw it coming. He laughed and stepped out of my range. He drew his pistol.

People around us started diving for cover. Awareness that someone had a drawn gun rippled down the aisles. Cries of alarm.

I couldn't allow him to start shooting. I heaved myself into the bus, the momentum carrying me into the dive I took at him. The bus driver, finally realizing what was going on, hit the brakes. The abrupt stop, combined with the impact of my dive, sent me and the shooter tumbling to the floor, landing with me on top.

My right hand went for his throat, pinning him to the floor. His left hand went for my throat, clamping hard. My left hand gripped his right wrist. I slammed his gun hand against the floor. The pistol loosened in his grip but I hadn't broken his wrist and made him drop the piece like I'd intended. He tightened his grip on my throat, cutting off my air supply just like I was doing to him. I had to disarm him.

A gunshot hammered my eardrums.

At the front of the bus, the driver collapsed forward onto the steering wheel. His foot fell heavy on the accelerator, and the double decker lurched forward. Then a powerful jolt when the bus collided with something, sending passengers tumbling like bowling pins. The bus veered away from whatever we'd collided with and continued on, picking up speed.

I used my grip on the man's throat to draw his head up six inches off the floor, then hit the back of his head against the floor twice, hard as I could. The clamping hand dropped away from my throat. His eyes had rolled back in their sockets. The pistol left his hand. I brushed it away. The gun skittered along the floor and fell out of the bus.

I flung myself to the front of the bus, placed my hand at the back of the driver's collar and hauled him aside. I dropped into the driver's seat, took the steering wheel and worked the brakes. The bus drew to a stop some thirty paces short of a red light at a busy intersection. I left the driver's seat, staying low.

The man in the black raincoat had either made a fast recovery or he'd been faking. He was on his feet, taking aim at me with another pistol.

I threw myself to the floor. Another gunshot. I heard the round pierce the front windshield of the bus. When I looked up, he was gone.

Someone had propped the driver up against a seat. Someone else started applying pressure to a shoulder wound that darkened the front of the driver's uniform with a red stain.

The driver managed a weak smile. "Thanks, mister."

A sort of orderly confusion reigned. Passengers starting to pick themselves up. Checking themselves for injuries. Looking about. Staring at me with eyes that said thanks for saving our bus but now please get the hell away from us!

I was happy to oblige.

I catapulted from the bus no more than twenty seconds behind Brooks Brothers. I caught a glimpse of the tails of his raincoat flapping behind him like a cape, and then he vanished into the crowd of curious onlookers gathering near the bus. I blended in easily enough, rubber-necking with the best of them, but my man had already been absorbed by the morning rush hour that swirled around us.

I managed to put enough distance between myself and the double decker so that no one paid attention to me when I leaned against a storefront to catch my breath and get my bearings. Then I started walking back in the direction of the pub.

I could still feel the icy fingers clamped around my throat.

Angel was waiting for me a block shy of the pub.

Angel came up close to me and said, "What now, Soldier?"

I said, "Let's get the hell out of here."

16

Jimi is tied up, bound to a low-backed wooden kitchen chair, his wrists and ankles lashed to the chair with what feels like rubberized clothesline. He lifts his head and looks around.

Nothing has changed since he fell asleep, tied to the chair.

A large, open room with deep blue carpeting, open-beam cathedral ceiling. Sliding glass doors cover one wall that opens onto a patio. A small foyer over his shoulder. An archway leading to a dining and kitchen area on the other side of him.

Bandy McGuire is sprawled across an expensive leather couch, nursing a bottle of beer and watching the telly. Sprawled was the only way Bandy could sit, given that his six-foot-four and two hundred pounds usually spilled over from any furniture he utilized. Some of that two hundred pounds was fat, put on since his divorce from Angel, but most of Bandy was a broad slab of muscle. His hair is over his collar and unwashed. An extreme Fu Manchu moustache droops down past his chin.

Jimi pretends to remain asleep, which is not difficult at all. His senses are hazed from drug withdrawal, hangover and lack of sleep. He wills his mind to drift away on the magic carpet of dreams. His mind shifts. He doesn't know if he's in a dream or if he's having a flashback real enough to see, touch and feel.

Before he became Jimi Hendrix...

He is Maurice James, the guitar player in Little Richard's band, aptly named The Upsetters.

Since the Army he's been playing guitar on the road, working as a sideman first for The Isley Brothers, then for Wilson Pickett and even for The Ike & Tina Turner Revue. And he's been fired from every one of these bands for being "too flashy." The flash, the spotlight, belongs to the star, he's been told again and again. Backup musicians supply the music that allows the star to shine. Period.

This gig in Richard's band has lasted longer than most.

Little Richard Penniman. The self-proclaimed Georgia Peach. The Bronze Liberace. The King of Rock & Roll is another self-bestowed title and the name of one of his albums. Elvis who?

But Richard's career is in a funny place. A long fall from headlining Alan Freed's stage shows at the Paramount Theater in the 1950s or on national TV shows like Dick Clark's *American Bandstand*. Those were the days of Richard's hits. *Long Tall Sally. Tutti Fruity. The Girl Can't Help It. Lucille. Good Golly Miss Molly.* With an insanely high pompadour, hot boogie piano playing, showmanship to spare and his gospel influenced delivery, Little Richard is one of the architects of rock & roll, and in high school Jimi had rocked to Richard's records when they were big.

Then at the height of his career, Little Richard gave up the Devil's music to become a fire and brimstone Pentecostal preacher. It seemed that his days as a rocker were over. Eventually, though, God (or Richard's accountant, or both) had guided the Georgia Peach back to rock & roll. On a British tour, just before Jimi joined the band, Richard's opening act had been a new group calling themselves The Rolling Stones.

But none of that European star power has translated to the States. The present "tour" has been endless one-nighters, playing cheap whiskey-and-switchblade chitlin joints in the Deep South with an occasional excursion to the North to play the teen beer bar circuit that wasn't much better.

At first it was a stone gas playing behind Richard. Jimi is too shy to tell the bombastic little showman that when Jimi was thirteen his father had taken him to church to hear a fiery sermon from the Reverend Penniman or that when he was fifteen, he and his buddies had gone to a Seattle theater to see Little Richard perform rock & roll. Not only that, but they sat in the front row! They found a way backstage and met Richard. He had laughed then, in high good spirits, and had actually commented on their dance moves. This made Jimi and his pals the coolest guys in high school for at least a week.

But there was little opportunity to bring up any of that personal history because before long, Jimi found himself going out of his way to avoid his employer, as did the other cats in the band.

Richard is a control freak. He tells his backing musicians where to stand on stage when he makes his grand entrance and he tells them exactly what and how to play even though his only instrument is the piano. As a performer, Little Richard is still at the top of his game but this awareness only fuels his dictatorial ways. He regularly fines his musicians if they don't do exactly what he tells them to do, both onstage and off.

For Jimi, as with Ike & Tina, the Isleys and others, there is little challenge in repeating these same none-for-note arrangements night after night. He cannot resist throwing a little something extra into the signature standards that Richard serves up in identical fashion every night. Jimi creates his own guitar licks, his own way of stretching out notes and solos. He's working up killer stage moves to go with the guitar solos. At first just for fun, clowning around to keep from being bored out of his skull, and the audience response surprises him. Chicks and their fellas all go crazy when he plays a blistering guitar solo with his teeth or holding the guitar behind his head, practiced tricks that went back to the old blues cats like T-Bone Walker and Guitar Slim. Jimi would play solos with his guitar held out in front of him from the waist, humping his hips so the guitar was like a big hard dick in action. That always brought the house down. A look from Richard the boss usually shuts down such embellishments and more and more, Jimi has started to chafe under the muzzling. He finds himself thinking and talking more and more about moving on, but…moving on to what? A steady gig is a steady gig.

Maurice James is onstage. He's playing guitar while the tenor sax man takes as many rides as he can before Richard gives him the nod and resumes the vocal.

It's a Friday night and the place is jumping. It doesn't matter where. Neon beer signs glow through the blue haze. Packed. Hot. Sweaty. Richard gives his nod, and the sax player steps back to his assigned position with the others band members, riffing slightly behind the piano that is provided by the promoter at each venue.

But before the next verse of *Lucille* can spew from Richard's lip-stick red mouth, Jimi rips into a solo he'd put together in the motel room the night before, sort of a cross between B.B. King and Hubert Sumlin that is amped up with a distorted tone and use of the guitar's whammy bar. And he doesn't stop playing. He brings out all of his stage tricks, using the guitar as a playful prop. When he finally finishes, he steps back to take his place with the other guys, who have been chuckling among themselves during his extended solo, avoiding eye contact with Jimi, who studiously avoids the burning embers that is Richard's glare.

After the show, Richard corners Jimi backstage. Richard's eyes are red. Displeasure animates the diva's features.

"Oooh my soul, child, what are you wearing tonight?" is Little Richard's opening shot. He bats his long eyelashes. "You are very pretty this evening, Maurice."

Jimi's wearing a loud woman's print blouse and a bolero hat.

"Had a girl I met in the last town curl my hair."

Little Richard is the most sexually charged person Jimi has ever known. Flagrantly homosexual and obsessed with everything about sex from role playing to voyeurism. Another reason Jimi wants out.

Richard says, "Trouble is, you're prettier than me and,

honey, that doggie just had its last hunt. I am Little Richard." He is shouting and Jimi remembers again when his father took him to see Richard preach at the Pentecostal church. "I am the *only* Little Richard by the bountiful grace of my Lord God Jehovah. I am the *only* one allowed to be pretty on *my* stage."

Down deep Jimi wants to retreat under the verbal assault, but he stands straight, packing away his guitar in its case. "Thought we was here to show the people a good time. That's all I was doing." Softly spoken, hardly audible through the music from a loud jukebox that has started playing out front now that the show is over.

Richard's voice grows shrill. "You ain't getting paid for tonight. I ain't paying you to steal my stage. I been carrying your sweet young ass but you ain't been nothing but trouble." Richard leers at the other band members who are hovering nearby. "Sweet sugar here thinks he's too good for the Georgia Peach. Won't even let me watch him and his girlfriends make love like I asked him to. You ain't nothing but a stuck up sideman, Maurice James."

The guys in the band busy themselves with personal tasks. They are on Jimi's side but they won't say so.

Jimi says, "I keep my sex life to myself."

Richard cackles. "You close the door of your room, sure enough, but you and them sweet little things that crowd you after my show raise a hell of a racket. All that Richard wants is to take him a peek. Ain't no harm in that."

Jimi says, "If you're going to fire me, fire me."

"What the hell do you think I'm doing?" Richard shakes his head. "You're a damn fine guitar player, brown sugar, but you're always late. Always holding up the bus, waiting on your ass. Always trifling with the girls and stuff like that."

"Am I supposed to be trifling with you?"

"Wouldn't have hurt you none. But it's too late now, Maurice. Get your gear off my bus. You're fired, hotshot."

Jimi snaps his guitar case shut. "That's the best news since I got hired. Find yourself another step 'n fetchit, Mr. Penniman. I'm out of here."

And he was.

Gone from Richard's band. Back to New York, playing for the hip white folks in the Village when the Brit producer walks in one night and it starts happening for him.

Then he is gone from his dream too.

He is tied to a wooden chair, listening to Bandy's snoring grow louder from the couch.

He must organize his thoughts.

Sydney told him at Ronnie Scott's that he looked terrible, that she needed to speak with him. She suggested her flat. Jimi went with her because what the hell. Monika was becoming more and more of a drag to be around. She could be sweet and tender when she wanted to be, but she knew that women threw themselves at Jimi and he did love the ladies. Pretty soon she'd find out that he'd only booked one ticket for the flight to New York.

He'd always had a good feeling about Sydney. Smart and pretty, she had soul. How many educated Brit chicks did you meet who knew the name of Howlin' Wolf's guitar player or even the Wolf's real name, or the label that Jimmy Reed recorded his classic blues sides on? She had an incredible collection of jazz and blues LPs, and there were books lying around about everything from reading tarot cards to fashion magazines. But it went even deeper than that. Sydney draws from a deep well. She understands the flow of spiritual energy connecting everyone and everything that he wants to put into the words of his songs.

Sydney has taken it upon herself to sort of looked out for him. She calls him when she holds back some new clothing item at the shop where she works, where they first met. Everyone else, including Monika, wants something from him. Compared to them, Sydney comes from a pure, giving place. She already had everything money could buy. She loves the arts and when she saw an artist adrift, in need of finding his inner karmic compass, she listened when he needed to unload his mind, never judgmental, conversations with gently probing questions rather than opinion. He tells her about Soldier flying in and Sydney takes the initiative to meet his flight, to check Soldier out and make sure he isn't some useless burnout come to further complicate Jimi's life. You had to love a friend who would do something like that.

He wanted to be with Sydney. He would deal with the fury that would be Monika when the time came. Sydney was right; he needed peace and quiet to get himself together.

That's when Bandy McGuire came rap-rapping at her door. Stepping into the hallway outside the flat with Bandy had been a big mistake. Bandy had a gun. At first Jimi thought he was kidding. A sharp jab in the kidneys made the point that Bandy was not kidding.

A black car waited at the curb out front. A guy he couldn't make out sat behind the steering wheel, waiting. The rear door at the curb yawned open. Bandy gave Jimi a shove that sent Jimi into the rear of the car. Bandy followed him in while the other man threw the car into gear and they were off.

When Jimi spoke, wanting to know what was going on, no one answered him. He lay face down with Bandy's knee pressing into the base of his spine. After awhile he gave up on conversation. He'd been doing dope all day and all night and that's why he fell asleep. Or maybe passed out.

And here he is now.

Tied to the chair.

Wondering what crazy shit is going to happen next.

17

We walked briskly to put distance between ourselves and the pub where Chet Daly and a pretty barmaid had bought the farm. I again let Angel determine our direction and destination. She strode with her eyes straight ahead, saying nothing. Tension tightened her features. We withdrew with dispatch but, to avoid drawing attention to ourselves, slowed our pace by unspoken mutual consent after rounding a couple of corners.

Her arms swung straight at her sides, her fists clenched. Our shoulders brushed as we negotiated the dense pedestrian traffic of the morning rush hour. From time to time her leg brushed against mine and I felt stirrings inside me that were wholly inappropriate for time, place and circumstance.

Angel McGuire was the sort of woman I'd always found attractive and been drawn to. Earthy. Sensual. A good, generous heart. An honest, forthright nature. And she was easy on the eyes. Meet Soldier's dream woman.

We found a bench in Trafalgar Square, near four

monumental bronze lion statues that guard the base of Lord Nelson's Column. At this hour on this overcast morning, most of the other benches were occupied by retirees feeding the pigeons, which suited me. The open area would allow me to hopefully spot trouble before it reached us.

Angel began shivering spasmodically the instant we sat down. My arm encircled her shoulders as if it had a mind of its own. I drew her to me and she did not resist, resting her head on my shoulder. Soon the shivering ceased, replaced by a half minute or so of subtle shoulder movement that told me she was quietly shedding tears. Then she lifted her head so that her back was again held straight. She sniffled twice and quickly brushed away one last pearled tear from her cheek.

"I'm sorry. I've never seen anyone die...like that before. Chet and, oh that poor barmaid. That poor woman, to die like that."

I said, "Doesn't matter how many times you've seen it. It's always ugly as hell."

Her gaze settled on a particularly forward pigeon whose goofy waddle drew him closer and closer to us, begging for peanuts. I didn't see any reason to remove my arm from around Angel, and she made no indication that she wanted me to.

"So that's what war is like? One moment a person is alive, healthy, vital as you or me and the next...oh God, seeing people killed like that day after day for how long?"

I said, "We've got to regroup. You have a decision to make."

"I know."

"You were a witness to what just happened but no one can tie you to what happened to Sydney."

A brief nod of agreement against my shoulder. "Now's the time for me to bail if I'm aiming to."

"That's what you should do," I said. "It's been nice getting to know you, Angel, but yeah, it's decision time. What's it going to be, Tex?"

She raised her eyes to mine.

"I'm with you, Soldier, come hell or high water."

"Are you sure?"

Hell yes, I'm sure. If they killed that Chet guy, does that confirm all that wild stuff he was talking about?"

"I don't know. But if we want to help Jimi, it sounds like a good place to start would be to locate your ex-husband."

"Damn."

"So where do we start?"

Her eyes followed the pigeon that had given up on us and was waddling off in search of better prospects.

"He calls me every couple of months and even drops by the pad now and then like a beaten dog hoping I'll take him back in. He takes it when I show him the door, the idiot. It's been a couple of months. I've been hoping he finally got the message that I never want to see him again."

"You don't know where he is?"

"Not a clue."

"Hudberry could be at the pub given that it's a double homicide right on the heels of the Blanchard murder. Let's go talk to him."

She leaned forward far enough to shrug off my arm from her shoulders. She stared at me.

"Jumpin' Jesus, Soldier, are you out of your cotton picking mind?'

"I've prefer the direct approach."

"I can tell." She got a cigarette going, and said after her first puff, "First off, what makes you so sure he's going to show up at the pub? I mean, the police will be there already. But why Hudberry?"

"He'll learn quick enough that we didn't shoot anybody, but Jimi is Hudberry's handle on busting some loan shark."

"Tobe Gearson."

"Right. Since your ex- works for Gearson, Hudberry might know where we can find Bandy."

She took a last drag on the cigarette, dropped it to the pavement and snubbed it out with the tip of her shoe. "Believe it or not, I'm the kind of girl who likes to stay out of trouble."

"And yet here you sit in Trafalgar Square, watching the pidgies with a man the cops want for murder."

She nodded. "And now you want to go see the cops. You're stone crazy, cowboy."

"Cowboy was in another life a long, long time ago."

She smiled a smile that made me wish I still had my arm around her.

"It was just a figure of speech but I should have known. All right, it'll be Cowboy after this is done, but you're Soldier until it's cleared up. I don't care what you call yourself but you're crazy to want to talk to Inspector Hudberry. You busted his nose. Yup, stone crazy."

"I guess I am, but—

"I know. The direct approach." She chuckled. "Reckon I'm crazy too. Okay, Soldier. Let's do it."

THE STREET in front of the pub was clogged with ambulances and official vehicles. Police cars, their rooftop lights flashing, were positioned nose to nose to blockade either end of the block, and a police line had been established along the sidewalks at each intersection. Curious on-lookers along the street peered from everyway doorway and window.

Angel and I joined a cluster of the curious. Down the street, uniformed and plainclothes inspectors hurried about, in and out of the pub.

Angel said, "I don't see Hudberry. So I guess this was a bad idea and we should git gone."

"Tex, are you in or out?"

"Okay, okay. Wish me luck. I'm off to find the Inspector."

"I'll be waiting."

She grimaced. "And the fun begins."

She stooped under the police line before the Bobbies, stationed several paces away in either direction, could intercept her. She sashayed down the street toward the pub like she owned the world. The Bobbies scrambled after her.

I didn't wait around to see what happened next.

18

Fifteen minutes later, Angel and Hudberry walked past where I stood.

I had angled around to the backside of the block, made it over a wooden fence that I guess the cops figured was enough to block access. I waited where the fence bordered the sidewalk but was set back from it, beyond sight of both the cops and the onlookers. When they had passed me, I stepped out onto the sidewalk behind them.

"Inspector."

I could tell that he recognized my voice. He turned slowly. He sported a strip of white tape across the bridge of his nose. His eyes had that blackness that results from a broken nose.

He said to Angel, "I must be getting old, Miss McGuire. You told me that Jimi wanted to see me." His blackened eyes glared. "I knew from the descriptions that you were the ones who ran off after the killings. I'll see that you do time for this, young lady." He said to me, "As for you, you bloody bastard, put out your hands. I'm placing you under arrest. That business on the bus may win you leniency from the court but not from me." He produced a pair of handcuffs from a pocket and advanced in my direction.

I shifted my jacket aside so he could see the .45 tucked beneath my belt.

"You're welcome to try, Inspector, but I wouldn't advise it."

He lowered the handcuffs. "Good Lord. You'd shoot a police officer? It would be prison for both of you."

"Let's not find out what I'd do. We need to talk."

He drew himself ramrod straight. "You have that spot on. And we'll start by you dropping that weapon right now and allowing yourself to be taken into custody. There is no alternative."

"I can think of one. We talk. I leave."

He glanced coldly in Angel's direction.

"I must say, miss, that your involvement in this both surprises and saddens me. You associate with unsavory types. The whole idea of a crash pad positively reeks of social anarchy. But it is, after all, a free country. But something like this…I advise you to walk away, Miss McGuire, and instruct the first officer you see to come to my assistance." The blackened eyes returned to me. "Now hand over the gun, Soldier. You might kill me but you'd never escape alive."

"Don't underestimate me."

"No fear or reverence for authority, that's how you fancy yourself, is it? Mister, you overestimate yourself and you underestimate Scotland Yard. Drop your weapon. We know who you are." He rattled off my name, rank and serial number.

I said, `"So you found my duffel bag."

He said to Angel, "Do you know what this man did last night? Or are you a part of that too? A homicide? How far would you go for this man, and why?" He shook his head slowly. "Sad. Very sad. I advise you again to disengage."

Angel said, "I suckered you, Inspector, getting back here for this. You're not a man to forget something like that. I'd say my happy days in your city have just about reached a conclusion. I've thrown in with Soldier."

Hudberry turned to me. "Miss Blanchard's murder looks like what the tabloids will call rough sex that got out of hand. Drugs. No forced entry. It doesn't look good but a crime of passion, well," he shrugged expressively, "you might con yourself an insanity plea. Combat fatigue, that sort of thing. Play to public sentiments against the war. But killing a police officer? You'll be signing your own death warrant. Drop the gun, Soldier. You're out of the game."

"Inspector," said Angel, "he didn't kill Sydney Blanchard."

"And why would you say that, miss? We have evidence to the contrary. Yes, Yank, there's your duffel bag in the boot of Miss Blanchard's car and that's all we need to make an arrest at this point but beyond that, the officer you dodged when you fled the girl's flat has made a positive ID." His voice took on a paternal tone. "Give it up, Soldier. I call you that because that's what you are. You will gain nothing by shooting me. I have a wife and daughter."

"Yeah, I remember. A daughter who likes Jimi Hendrix records."

"Hand over the gun and come with me. You know it's

the right thing to do."

"Stop talking to me like I'm a traumatized vet."

"Then stop acting like one, laddie."

"Inspector, someone else killed that girl and tried to make it look like I did it. There was no rough sex. There were no drugs. As long as you're so damn sure that I did it, I'm going to have to clear my own name because no one else will. Now as long as I've got this gun, how's about I ask you some questions, then we'll be on our way? Why did you and that other cop show up last night at Sydney Blanchard's flat?"

One of the police tech vans passed the alley where the three of us stood. To anyone glimpsing us from inside the van in the seconds it took for the van to pass, we were just three members of the investigative swarm in conference.

Hudberry said, "An anonymous call reported that foul play had occurred at that address. I answered the call because I'm looking for Jimi Hendrix, and I brought backup because I didn't fancy another poke in the nose. My informants are talking about something big going down on the streets but nobody seems to know what it is except that it involves Gearson. Gearson has gone to ground. I thought Jimi, having dealt with Gearson recently, would know where he was. We have an informant imbedded at the club that you and friend Jimbo were at last night. I was reliably informed that he left with Miss Blanchard."

Angel said, "Inspector, we're looking for Jimi."

Hudberry pointed a finger in my direction. "Let's talk about you. I want you for this." He indicated his nose. "Now either try to use that gun, damn you, or hand it over and put out your hands for these cuffs."

I said, "No wonder you Brits ran the world for so long. You've got brass balls, mister. You put those handcuffs away and I'll forget I'm packing, how does that sound?" The pistol went back into my jacket pocket.

Hudberry considered this for a whole thirty seconds. Then he returned the bracelets to his pocket.

"You're a ballsy one yourself, laddie. You really should come with me, you know. I assure you, you will get fair treatment. I want whoever is responsible for what just happened here," he nodded toward the pub, "and for whoever committed that murder last night. The Blanchard girl was only a few years older than our daughter."

"If we're going to talk, let's first talk about Chet Daly. Would you like to know what he told us before someone killed him?"

"I would."

"He said there's a CIA hit team in London, most likely a spotter and the assassin. Or they could be freelance mercs, sub-contracted by the CIA. Their mission is to kill Jimi Hendrix."

Hudberry's short laugh was a snort of derision. "You mean to tell me that someone considers that mumbling, spaced-out guitar player to be a threat against the U.S. government? I say, that's rather ridiculous."

Angel said, "I thought the same thing until someone shot Daly dead right in front of my eyes. Now I'm a believer."

I said, "Inspector, what have you got so far on the shooter? You know it wasn't me because there's a pub full of witnesses who saw us standing next to him when the shooting started."

He said, "Heavy caliber rifle. A rooftop across the

street. That's what our tech chaps have concluded from the bullets' angle of entry. Officers are searching the rooftops but so far, nothing."

"This morning could have been the hit team's first opportunity to shut Daly down and right now they're hoping they got to him before he spilled any beans to us."

Hudberry said, "And what about the Blanchard girl? Are you going to blame that on the CIA?"

Angel said, "If they're fixing to kill a superstar like Jimi Hendrix, why would they hesitate over a little nobody like a Carnaby Street shop girl?"

"And what would be their motive for killing her?"

"Maybe Sydney spoke to this Chet Daly before he talked to me," said Angel. "He wanted to warn Jimi and if he knew about me, maybe he knew about Sydney. Maybe that's why she wanted to get Jimi out of that club and alone, to warn him that he was a target. They killed Sydney to silence her."

Hudberry managed to sneer in a very polite way. "It's far more likely that Miss Blanchard was engaging in the excesses of those sexual freedoms you women of today seem so terribly fond of, and things went tragically wrong for her."

I said, "Inspector, you need to trace the CIA connection."

"Are you giving me orders, mister?"

"Just passing along intel."

"Indeed. Well, Her Majesty's government and Scotland Yard in particular are most grateful. You're serious about a CIA hit team?"

"Serious as cancer. That could be what your informants are getting wind of."

"Any other intel you wish to pass along?"

"Well, there's a posse of German thugs running loose in your town. They're trying to get their hands on Jimi too. Sydney Blanchard was close to Jimi. There's your connection to the Germans. They could have pressured her to set Jimi up and that's when things went tragically wrong, as you put it."

Angel said, "And there's my ex-husband."

Hudberry frowned. "Bandy McGuire? What about him?"

I said, "He showed up at the Blanchard girl's flat last night. When they left together, Sydney was still alive."

"And how do you know this?"

"It's a long story."

"I'm sure it is. Just the same, I'd like to hear it."

"Inspector, it's a story I'd like to tell but it's going to have to wait until I can hand over the whole story."

"I doubt if I'll wait that long."

"It's not going to be a long wait," I told him. "It's happening fast. I could use some sleep. I've been sapped twice and one of those times some son of a bitch tried to frame me for murder. Maybe I have spent too much time in a war zone. I sure can't seem to readjust to what passes for civilization around these parts so I'm going to give up trying. I have a friend in trouble. I owe him my life. I'm going to rattle this city like a damn cage and I'm going to find him."

Hudberry cracked a tight grin. "Damn me for a fool, Soldier boy, but part of me admires you, I have to admit. You are something, sir."

"Don't call me sir. I'm an enlisted man."

"You're a wild card, is what you are. Three homicides

in a few hours. You can be quite sure that the powers that be will not be satisfied until those murders are solved. And here comes Soldier, like a storm whipping through London. You know, son, I do believe that I shall let you walk away this morning. You've provided me with intel and protestations of innocence and as a matter of fact, I'm half inclined to believe you. You're a barbarian on the loose in civilization. But I can use you."

It was my turn to grin. "I'll just bet you can."

"Go on. Rattle their cage. You're a suspect in the Blanchard murder and you're sought after as a material witness to these pub killings. But you two go on and outmaneuver the whole of Scotland Yard, if you think you can. Ultimately you will be apprehended and charged and when you are, I will have everything you know in trade for any prayer of plea bargain. Bandy McGuire, eh? Is Gearson tied up in this? I've been working to put that bugger behind bars."

I said, "I'll tell you when I find out. Where would you look for Bandy if you wanted to find him?"

"As a matter of fact I do want to find them. That's one of the things I wanted Jimi to tell me last night. I wish I knew where Bandy and Gearson are and that's God's truth, but I don't know."

I said, "Then we're done here. I'll be seeing you, Inspector."

Hudberry said, "Enjoy your freedom while it lasts. However this shakes out, son, this *is* civilization. This is not the jungle. London is *my* town. You're a worthy adversary, Soldier, but you will not succeed."

19

IT STARTED RAINING AGAIN. A STEADY DRIZZLE, MORE THAN a mist, that reminded me of the monsoon in Nam except this wasn't a nourishing soaker but a denseness that enveloped the city with the forewarning of another impending downpour. A dark, miserable day.

The cabbie who picked us up, a rosy-cheeked grandpa past retirement age with a gruff but chatty demeanor, tried at first to make conversation about the weather but after having his two attempts rebuffed with monosyllable replies from me, he gave up and just drove. The cab had a sliding glass panel between driver and passengers. I closed it. The only sound in the taxi was the steady back and forth of the windshield (I mean, windscreen) wipers.

Angel's fingers, icy cold, reached over to entwine themselves with mine. I'd caught a look from her when she heard me give the driver the address.

She said, "You think Monika knows where Bandy is?"

"No, but she might know where Jimi is. After I got

away from Sydney's flat last night, I went straight to Monika's to see if Jimi was there. No luck."

"And you think our luck's about to change?"

"Let's find out."

"Hudberry honestly believes that you killed Sydney."

We made eye contact. The moment held.

I said, "I haven't killed anyone in London."

She did not release my hand but her gaze shifted to watching the passing street scene beyond the rain-streaked windows.

MONIKA DANNEMANN ANSWERED her door wearing an ankle-length blue silk robe with embroidered Chinese dragons. Barefoot. Painted nails. Ankle bracelet. Nice ankles. The fact that she was ten years older than the crowd she ran with was apparent, in the gray light of a new day, in the first trace of crow's feet at the corners of insecure eyes and at the corners of a mouth that drew tight. She held a smoking cigarette in her right hand. She had brushed her hair but at nine-thirty on this bleak morning, Monika exuded a washed-out demeanor.

I said, "We're looking for Jimi."

"Is that so?" The German accent was slurred. "Last night at the club you were very cold to me, Soldier. Very impolite. I don't think I like you." She looked past me and said in a neutral voice, "Hello, Angel."

"Good morning." Angel tightened her collar against the cold mist. "Do you mind letting us in?"

I said, "I need to talk with Jimi."

"Jimi is always running and no one ever catches him.

You are the only person I ever saw who ran *with* Jimi so I especially don't like you."

"Will you let us in?"

The door drew inward. She gestured us in.

"Very well. Would you like tea?"

"No thank you," said Angel. "We're sorry to barge in like this, Monika, but it's important."

A well-kept flat, sparsely but tastefully furnished. Framed paintings and photographs adorned the walls. Fresh flowers in a cut glass vase. An acoustic guitar leaned against one corner near a cane rocking chair.

"I wish I knew where Jimi is." She sank into the rocking chair and studied the cigarette smoke she exhaled. "Why does he treat me so?"

We sat together on a divan that faced her.

Angel said, "I've known the man longer than you have, hon. I adore the man. But he is a man and that's the way men are."

Monika said, "The last I saw of him was last night at Ronnie Scott's. Jimi made a fool of me. He left me there to find my own way home. He left with that Blanchard bitch."

Angel said softly, "Monika, you shouldn't say that."

"Why not? The woman is a brazen slut. A dirty rotten little whore, while all of the time she acts so sweet and is just a little shop girl who wants to help my Jimi. Ha. I know what her game is. I know what goes on, the flirtation between them. I know everything because I am Jimi's fiancée."

Angel said, "Monika, there's something you need to know."

"Of course you will defend her," said Monika. "Jimi has

been with many women. I understand that he is desirable. But Jimi has vowed to me that he is now mine alone and so he is. Sydney should respect this. She is a temptress. A whore."

I said, "That's the last time you saw Jimi, when they left the club together?"

"I told you that, yes. The little whore."

"You didn't follow them to her flat?"

Her nostrils flared. The line of her mouth tightened around the cigarette. "Is that where they went? No, I did not follow anyone. I couldn't, they left so fast." Her eyes narrowed and grew sullen. "Why do you ask me these questions? Why is it important that you find Jimi?"

Angel said, "Sydney Blanchard is dead. Someone murdered her last night."

The cigarette dropped from her fingers and fell to the floor.

"Jimi…"

I picked up the cigarette, snubbed it out in an ashtray.

"That's part of it. Do you have any idea where we could try looking for him? Take a few wild guesses."

"*Mein Gott.* Don't tell me Jimi killed the little whore!"

"Don't even start thinking like that."

She gnawed on one of her knuckles. "I wonder what you are thinking and what you would do to protect your friend. Your question about me following them last night. Do you think I killed Sydney?"

"The only thing I think is that we're wasting time. What happened yesterday at Angel's crash pad? Why were you so angry and why was Jimi dodging you?"

A wistfulness warmed Monika's eyes. "Yesterday began as such a good day for us. At about two in the afternoon we had tea in the little garden outside here." She gestured to drawn drapes. "We went to the bank, a drug store and to an antique market. Jimi bought some shirts and trousers. We came back here. I took pictures of him playing his Stratocaster guitar."

Angel smiled. "The black beauty."

"That's the one. Jimi is relaxed when he is with me. I offer him sanctuary against the madness that always is closing in on him. I keep him grounded."

I said, "When you were out and about yesterday, did you notice anything that might indicate that you and Jimi were being followed?"

Monika embraced herself as if against a sudden chill. "No, nothing like that. Jimi was very high, you know. I was busy with the traffic and with guiding him about."

"What are your drugs of choice, Monika?"

She sat up a little straighter. "I don't think that is anybody's business."

"It might be if Jimi OD-ed on something that you keep around."

"There are only my sleeping pills. Vesperex."

Angel caught my eye. "A German brand. Real heavy duty. You've got to be damn careful with 'em." A wry grin. "That's the voice of experience talking."

Monika said, "I have warned Jimi about this. He's going through so much right now. I took twenty-nine photos of him yesterday at his request. He was mellow and he wanted me to capture who he truly is. Jimi is changing his image from the flamboyant stage performer. He can help to make the world into a better place but his wild image is blocking that. My pictures are softer, different from his image. I show his private side, Jimi is relaxed and happy."

I said, "Sounds great. So how did things go from being relaxed and happy to you trying to chase Jimi down at Angel's? You were screaming something about him running out in the middle of a fight."

Monika rocked herself in the rocking chair.

"He had me drive him to someone's flat near Marble Arch. He wouldn't say who. I was good enough to drive him there, but not good enough to be invited up to meet his friends. I had a right to be angry. Jimi said it was because they were not his friends. He said he wanted to show them he could cop. He was dropping off something for someone."

"And you have no idea who Jimi went to see?"

"I do not. I told you that. I do not like having to repeat myself. Jimi sometimes borrowed money. Perhaps he was paying off a loan. I often lend him money but as a gift, you understand? I never ask Jimi to pay me back. He said his manager kept him broke so as to better control him."

"Michael Jeffrey."

"That's the one."

"Do you know a man named Tobe Gearson?"

"No, I do not. I waited for Jimi yesterday for thirty minutes and then I rang him on the building intercom and told him to come down, that he was being rude and I was tired of waiting. He told me to come back later! I became very cross when he said that. Then he started yelling that I wouldn't leave him alone. I cursed him and told him he could damn well go to hell and I drove away. But of course I had a change of heart. And so I drove back but this time no one even answered the intercom. I can imagine Jimi and the others hearing me but laughing at me instead of answering. I became furious. When I heard he was at Angel's, I went there to confront him. That is when he ran off with you. Jimi does not like confrontation."

20

IT WAS STILL DRIZZLING RAIN WHEN WE LEFT MONIKA'S flat.

During our visit, a black limousine had drawn up in front of our taxi waiting at the curb. The limo occupied the full expanse of a No Parking zone directly in front of the hotel, as if daring someone to try and tell it to move.

We strode double-time past the limousine. I could see nothing in its smoked glass windows except our reflection.

A sibilant mechanized whisper and the rear window lowered. A man peered out at us. About forty. Clean cut. Prominent cleft chin. Receding blond hair combed straight back and a military moustache, severely clipped. Expensive steel rim glasses.

"Excuse me. May I have a word with you, *bitte?*"

A precise, clipped German accent.

I eased my fingertips closer to the concealed .45.

I said, "Last Kraut I had anything to do with knocked

me unconscious with a sap. Another was about to throw Jimi Hendrix off a roof."

"My name is Klaus Mueller. Those men you refer to were following my orders. Please join me in here out of the rain. Let us talk."

I released Angel's hand but I kept my right finger curled around the Colt's trigger.

"Okay, *Herr* Mueller, you've aroused my interest. Keep away from the door or any buttons while I have a look." I opened the car door. "You alone in there?"

"Very much, as you can see. The driver hears nothing."

The limo's interior was warm with plush bench seats, soft lighting, a TV now turned off and a state-of-the-art sound system that provided low, jazzy background music.

Mueller was a heavyset man in a Saville Road suit and expensive shoes. The driver sat at attention beyond a dividing panel of glass.

Angel gave me a small shove at the base of my spine.

"Come on, let's get in. It's pouring out here."

Mueller leaned forward to address her. "I beg your pardon, *fraulein*, but I wish to speak with the gentleman alone."

Angel gave me another stiff elbow, this time in the kidneys. "Come on. I'm getting wet and not in a good way."

I straightened from peering into the car's interior.

I said, "He's right."

"What?"

"Wait for me in the cab." I didn't phrase it as a sugges-tion. "You don't need to know things that could land you a life sentence in prison."

"Oh, but it's okay for you. I'm in this with you, Soldier."

"You are as long as I say you are. Wait for me in the cab."

Her chin lifted pugnaciously. "I'm not used to being spoken to like that."

"Please wait for me in the cab, Angel." I tried to smooth the edge off my voice. "It's for your own good. This won't take but a minute."

Long pause.

Finally, "It better not. Okay but if this big boat sets sail," she gestured to the limousine, "I'm having our cabbie stick to it like white on rice."

"Deal."

I drew the car door shut, sealing me in and shutting out the world as if no busy, rainy urban world surrounded us. The cozy interior, with its muted jazz, was a world unto itself.

Mueller said, "So kind of you to join me. May I call you Soldier?"

"I don't give a damn what you call me. You asked for my time, so here it is. What do I get in return?"

An amused smile reached steely eyes. "Ah, *sehr gut*. You are a man of directness. The TV news reports are broadcasting your military ID. The photo does not really do you justice. I can see how you can walk the streets without being recognized. You are on leave before reporting for duty in Germany. The authorities are seeking you in connection with the murder of a woman last night. You are as I imagined you from the report given me by my subordinates."

"How are your boys?"

"Otto has a severe concussion."

"Sorry to hear that. I don't like being sapped, myself."

He reached into an inside breast pocket and produced a thin box of cigarillos. He offered the opened box to me. I declined with a shake of my head. He fired on up for himself.

"This whole business has been mishandled from the beginning and I fear that I am to blame."

I said, "Let's see. Monika Dannemann is a German national. And you?"

Amused steely eyes held mine.

"The same."

"You've been covering her every move, haven't you?"

"Indeed, I have."

"That's how Otto and his boys found us at that hamburger joint. They were tailing Monika when she went to Angel's looking for Jimi. They followed us after Sydney Blanchard picked us up outside of Angel McGuire's."

He said, "Sydney Blanchard, yes. That is the name of the murdered woman, is it not?"

"I think you know damn well that it is. By the way, the man who was about to throw Jimi Hendrix off a roof. He was following your orders?"

"Perhaps I should explain."

"Perhaps you should."

"Mine, you see, is not a savory past. I may appear the epitome of taste and success but in reality I am no more than, if I may speak frankly, a well-groomed hoodlum off the street."

"I'm not blind. You haven't glossed it over that well."

"I came of age on the streets of Munich. Those are

mean streets, my friend. I made my bones, is that how you say it, when I was fourteen."

"When we say it, it means you've committed your first murder."

"By my twentieth birthday I had killed four men and one woman, and I knew none of them. They were only jobs to me. I worked my way up very high to the rank of chief enforcer when circumstances took a turn, shall we say. Life became unhealthy for me in Munich and before you know it, I am in Düsseldorf. I have the connections to get so high," he made a mid-level gesture with his right hand, "but no higher. It is a matter of having to prove oneself all over again, you see."

"What I don't see is where Monika fits into it?"

"Her family is prominent and powerful in Düsseldorf."

"Are you shadowing her on their behalf?"

A mild snicker. "I and my associates have absolutely nothing to do with the Dannemann family, nor with any of their business or social concerns."

"In other words, you're using the wayward daughter as a shortcut to make your name in a new town. There are those who don't like her dragging a good family name through the mud by assorting with a black rock & roll musician. An accident happens, like falling off a roof, Jimi goes missing, something like that and he's no longer in her life whether Monika likes it or not, and she has nothing to do with it. But you'll have creditability where it counts on those mean streets because you made a hit that no one can trace and it benefited the upper echelon even if they had nothing to do with it. That's where the connections and contacts are."

"You understand perfectly."

"Today you're keeping Monika under surveillance, hoping Jimi will show up again and this time you'll take care of him personally."

He smiled the way a snake smiles. "That was my intention but, as you say in English, I am about to call it quits. Do you know where Jimi is, *Herr* Soldier?"

"Not a clue."

"Pity. I was hoping you could share that information with me before you are indisposed. I have connections in London. Business associates, you might say. Rumors on the street are abuzz with the law coming down like a hammer on anyone caught aiding and abetting you."

"You're one connected wiseguy, Klaus. Was that sniper who just killed two people in a pub one of your boys? You don't think the cops wouldn't love to get his mitts on you?"

An idly dismissive gesture. "I have no idea what you're talking about. I am an outsider in London, much like yourself. To the authorities, I am an unknown. I keep a low profile, is that how you say it? My only objective is to eliminate Hendrix from *Fraulein* Dannemann's life, make it look like an accident or a suicide, and then return to Düsseldorf."

"Does Monika know you're hovering around, keeping an eye on her?"

"Certainly not. She is but a typical middle-aged spoiled woman born to privilege who cannot seem to hold onto a man. She attached herself to Hendrix. From what we have observed of them, she is an emotional parasite, artistic and possessing a striking beauty, it is true, but man to man, my friend, I will tell you that she is nothing but pure trouble. Given that he has not shown up here at her flat, Hendrix may have finally deduced that for himself." Cold eyes studied me. "May I ask what your interest is in all of this? You seem to be everywhere."

I said, "Let's talk about what you've been up to. Were you shadowing Miss Dannemann last night?"

"I was. We followed her and Hendrix to the club. I observed Hendrix leave the nightclub without her. He left with the young woman who was murdered. You hurried out of the club and followed them."

"And what did Monika do?"

Mueller shrugged. "What I have been doing since I came up with what I thought was a brilliant idea, although it's shown signs of becoming more trouble than it would be worth. She came home alone. I know because we followed her."

"We?"

"My driver and I."

"She came straight back here to her flat?"

"Correct, and this address has been under surveillance ever since either by myself or one of my men." He turned his attention to chain-lighting a fresh cigarillo. "Tell me, Soldier, did you kill the Blanchard woman as the police suspect?" His eyes rose to meet mine with an oily smile. "She was little more than a child, I am told."

"Someone's trying to set me up."

"Of course. Would you take the fall for your friend Jimi, if it was he who murdered the girl?"

"Don't be stupid. So if you followed Monika home last night, you conveniently alibi yourself and her. A paid employee, your chauffer, to back you up. But maybe you didn't tail Monika home. You could have tailed me tailing Jimi. A regular parade that ends at Sydney Blanchard's flat. You conked me where I was eavesdropping outside her flat, and then you killed the woman after Jimi left. Or did one of your boys do it for you? She was dead and I would go down for it. With my connection to Jimi, he'd be drawn into it and the tabloids would eat it up. Jimi would be discredited even if he wasn't accused of the girl's murder. That's your motive. Make him a social pariah so even Monika would shun him, leaving you to go back and be big noise in Düsseldorf because you engineered it."

Mueller drew his back straight, an attempt to look haughty that failed.

"I can assure you nothing of the sort happened. I swear to you, my friend, I had nothing to do with that woman's murder."

"Stop calling me your friend, you piece of shit in a suit."

He said, as if I hadn't spoken, "The authorities shall soon enough make a connection between the unpleasantness at the hamburger emporium and Jimi Hendrix's disappearance in the wake of *Fraulein* Blanchard's murder. I have decided that it would be prudent for me to depart the United Kingdom before that happens."

"You have no idea where Jimi is?"

"I have no idea and I couldn't care less. The incident on the roof, the altercation between you and my men, it is regrettable. I truly apologize for it. But if something has happened to Mr. Hendrix, well," again the shrug, "my work here is done. I will find another way to establish prominence in Düsseldorf."

"There's a murder team prowling around London with orders to eliminate Jimi. Know anything about that?"

"Eliminate him? You mean, kill him?"

"That's what I mean. You're not stupid enough to be a part of that, are you?"

"I have no knowledge whatsoever of this matter. Yes, I think it is time for me to return to Germany."

"The CIA could be involved. Is that air too rare for you, Klaus?"

"The Central Intelligence Agency." He smirked through the haze of cigarillo smoke. "I have had dealings with them. They generally use local talent when they stage a black op. I once killed a man for them in Munich. I was only a young man, of course."

"Don't tell me more than I need to know. I need to know whatever you can dig up for me about a hit team like that in London, looking for Jimi just like we have been. Can you do that?

Mueller said, "First you insult me, and then you request a favor."

"Favor hell. I'm giving you a chance get home to Düsseldorf with your ass intact. All I have to do is make an anonymous phone call about you to a certain inspector I know and he'll have every airport and dock under surveillance. You'll never get out of England, and I know you don't want that."

I watched a calculating mind behind those steel-rimmed glasses weighing options, possibilities and consequences.

He said slowly, "Perhaps we could work out an arrangement. *Ja*. We will establish a bond of trust, you and I, and after you are stationed in Germany, we could work together. There is much money to be made."

I glanced out the smoked window. Our taxi cab remained parked behind the limo. Angel hadn't lost her temper waiting and ordered our driver to take off and leave me here.

"One step at a time, Klaus. Talk about now."

Mueller said, "Very well. In exchange my tapping my resources for such information, if and when you are interrogated, I would ask that you refrain from mentioning me to the police. You don't know who was behind the attack on Hendrix yesterday at the hamburger restaurant. From what I understand, the fellow often mingled with unpleasant company like the loan shark, Gearson. But as for me, leave me out of it. If you can give me your word on this, in the time remaining before my departure from London, I will endeavor to learn what I can. But you ask for a lot. These are very dangerous people that you ask about. International killers."

I said, "I thought you wanted everyone to think you're a tough guy. If a Scotland Yard man named Hudberry gets his hands on you, you'll make one hell of an impression on the Düsseldorf boys from a U.K. prison cell."

I reached into my back pocket. His eyes widened, and then relaxed when he saw that I wasn't reaching for a weapon. I opened my wallet and glanced at a piece of paper that had the address and phone number of Angel's crash pad. I recited the phone number.

"I can be reached there. Call me when you come up with something."

He opened a panel in the door, withdrew a notebook and wrote in it. He extinguished his cigarillo without lighting another.

"You know," he said, "there is another way for me to insure that you will not cause me difficulty with the police."

I paused with my hand on the door handle.

"You mean, have your chauffer pump a bullet through my head?"

"All I have to do is nod."

I glanced over my shoulder.

The divider had been slid aside partway by the chauffer, a wiry-eyed little guy with a serious mole at his left temple. He held a silenced revolver, aimed at me.

I said, "You won't give him the nod. You want to get away clean from this mess. Things would only get messier if you killed me."

"*Auf Wiedersehen,* my friend. Meeting you has been an interesting experience."

"Buddy," I told him, "I'm the furthest thing from a friend that you'll ever have."

21

TIED TO A KITCHEN CHAIR. HE HEARS A TELEVISION. A cheesy British game show.

Bandy sees Jimi stir.

"Well then, look who's decided to come back and visit the world of the living. Top of the morning to you, Jimi."

"Bandy, what the hell is going on, man? What are you doing?"

"Me, I'm following orders," says Bandy. "You, you're being held here under house arrest. That's all I know about it and that's all I'm saying about it. Sorry, mate. That's just how it is."

Bandy finishes off the beer, gets up and saunters out of the room. Sounds of a bottle being tossed into a receptacle, a refrigerator door opening and closing and of another bottle cap being popped.

The wooden chair Jimi has been tied to does not belong in the room he's in. Sunlight shines through a row of tall windows that line one side of an oak-floored room. The windows are half-raised and through them drift the sounds of the country, crickets and birdsong, an absence of vehicle or machinery noise. The opposite wall of the room holds sturdy shelves lined with books from floor to ceiling. There is a cold fireplace, assorted divans and stuffed chairs and this couch and the TV. Straight ahead is what looks like a door to the outside, maybe twenty-five feet away. An expensive-looking, classy home.

Bandy returns to the couch.

"Wish I could offer you a beer, Jimi. Matter of fact I'm glad to see you coming around. Man, you were out. I was getting bloody tired of watching you snooze. What the hell were dreaming about, laddie? It sure was like you didn't want to wake up."

Jimi says, "I was dreaming about spaceships and dragons and butterfly women who would take me away. I wasn't dreaming about nothing. Bandy, I thought we were supposed to be friends."

"We know each other," Bandy concedes. "Sad to say, bro, but there's a difference." Bandy takes a swig of beer. "But it ain't personal, Jimi. I've got nothing against you, mate. I'm being paid to do this, I am, and it's good money that can be put to good use."

"My people can pay you to let me go."

Bandy snorted. "That's funnier than you know, mate."

"Are you working for Mike Jeffrey?"

"Now let's be realistic. Would I be likely to tell you if I was?"

"Where am I?'

"That's a bloody cliché, is what that is. And it gets the same answer."

"If it's not that prick Jeffrey then it's Gearson, isn't it?"

Jimi again studies his surroundings. "But Gearson's a street hustler. A loan shark. This ain't his place."

"You've got that right. You're being made an example of and that's a fact, it saddens me to say."

"Bandy, for crying out loud. You're not going to keep me tied to a chair after all the times we sat around your ex-old lady's pad blowing hash and snorting line."

Bandy's features darken. "I wouldn't bring that bitch Angel into it if I was you." He raises a clenched fist that is only slightly smaller than a country ham. He waves it before Jimi's face for emphasis and says through gritted teeth, "I still think about busting bones in her face just to see if she could ever draw another man to her after I got done."

"Look Bandy, let's talk about that later. Right now how's about untying me, bro? What kind of joke is this, tying me up to a damn chair?"

"I told you."

"Yeah, okay, you're getting paid. But see, I know something about you, Bandy. You're still in love with Angel."

"You shut your mouth."

"She told me something about you the last time we talked. Something you ought to know."

Bandy's massive head tilts with curiosity. "About me?"

"I promised her I wouldn't tell. I shouldn't be talking to you about her private feelings."

"You should if they're about me. Look here, Jimi, how's about I get you a beer and hold the bottle for you while you drink it."

"Screw that. Bandy, if you want to hear what Angel told me she really wants to happen between you two, you're going to get me a beer after you untie me from this chair."

Bandy considers this.

"It will be my arse if you pull anything funny. Jimi, you've got to promise me that you won't try and get away if I do untie you. That you'll just hang out with me here and, how do you Yanks say it, shoot the breeze. I reckon you're right. I do think about Angel now and then. She was a swell gal while it lasted between us. I kind of wish it never ended. Between you and me, I guess I sort of wish I was still in her heart."

"So untie me and I'll tell you what she told me."

Bandy continues to consider this. "And you promise to tell me what she said?" There is wavering doubt in his eyes and a trace of hope in his voice.

Jimi says, "I promise."

"And you promise not to try and bust out of here?"

Jimi looks around again. "Man, this is some hip place. Come on, Bandy, where we at? Who's paying you?"

"Forget that. Just promise me, Jimi."

"All right, all right. I promise. Jesus, untie me, man. This is ridiculous."

Bandy sighs. "Yeah well, I reckon it is."

He sets his beer aside and rises to his feet, reaching into a pocket to bring something out. He flicks his wrist. A six-inch steel blade gleams in the sunlight.

Jimi said, "Damn. You're King Kong with a shiv."

Bandy makes quick work of prying the blade under vital lengths of clothesline. and with several quick flicks of the switchblade, the clothesline loosened.

"Just bloody well remember, mate, there's plenty more

where this clothesline came from all over again if you try anything funny."

Jimi shrugs and his restraints fall away.

"Jeez man, trust me why don't you? And how's about that beer?"

"Righto," says Bandy. He folds the blade and returns the knife to his pocket. "One beer coming up. And uh, thanks for not blaming me for what's happening here, mate. We'll sit down and talk gentlemanly like the friends we are, eh? And you'll tell me about Angel and maybe even what you think I should be doing about it."

He walks to the kitchen. The refrigerator door opens.

Jimi bolts out of the chair. He storms down the short hallway, passing the kitchen where he catches the briefest glimpse of Bandy elbowing the refrigerator door shut.

Jimi knows that Bandy has seen him but he doesn't stop. He reaches the front door.

Bandy shouts, "Goddamn you, Jimi!"

The beer bottle hits the door with a *thunk!* Glass shatters. Beer splashes in Jimi's face.

Jimi grabs the door handle, tugs it open feverishly and the door swings inward.

He's free!

Before him the lawn of an expansive estate is a carpet of jade green, dotted with well-tended shrubbery and small trees. The day is bleak and overcast. Dark clouds smother the sky. A ten-foot-high stone wall that encircles the property. A long driveway, a graceful sweep of gravel, leads to what looks like a blacktop country road. A gate of ornamental wrought-iron bars the entrance but Jimi is tall and if he takes a running leap at that gate, catches hold of its ornamental topping, he could swing himself over and—

A huge black dog comes tearing around the side of the house, barking angrily, but before it has made it halfway across the lawn, Bandy's voice is so close it sounds like it comes from inside Jimi's head.

"Got you, you lying bastard!"

Bandy launches himself in a running tackle. Takes Jimi down.

They tumble across the grassy slope. The sky and the emerald green sea of grass cartwheel around Jimi. When he stops rolling, he tries to stand. A sudden wave of nausea and dizziness overcome him and propping himself on one knee, he tries to regain his balance.

Bandy has already regained his footing and is advancing on him with rage flushing his features. This time Bandy is King Kong with a gun that resembles a toy clutched in his meaty fist. He easily takes Jimi down again with a short, swift kick. Then Bandy is on him, pinning Jimi to the lawn with a knee to the base of Jimi's spine. Bandy's left forearm encircles Jimi's throat in a choke hold. The muzzle of his pistol grinds hard into Jimi's right ear.

"I guess you don't hear so good, you son of a bitch." Bandy is short of breath. "I said no funny business. Now when I let you up, I want you to march your black arse back into that house. I'm tying you up again, Jimi." He exerted pressure on the gun muzzle for emphasis. "You give me any more trouble, I've got permission to start breaking your fingers."

22

IN OUR TAXI, ANGEL SAT WAITING WITH HANDS FOLDED primly in her lap, lady-like as hell. The driver slipped the cab into gear even before I'd latched the door after me and steered us sharply around the limo. With a forward thrust that pitched me into my seat, we rejoined the traffic flow.

I nodded at the driver beyond the closed partition. "So you've got the old boy cross with me too, eh? I hope you're not one of those women who sulk."

"I'm not sulking. I'm trying to exercise self-restraint. One time when I was visiting my sister and her husband outside Waco, me and their little boy were sitting there on the porch when a mean old rooster crossed the yard and came right up and pecked that little boy on the arm for no reason at all. Tyler screamed. The rooster had broke the skin and it must have hurt like the dickens. That got me mad. I took that little boy in to his mama for patching up. The poor little guy was raising holy hell when my sister went to work on him. Me, I was so pissed off I went and got Tom's shotgun. Then I went out and blew that dumbass rooster's head clean off. That's how mad I am right now, mister."

"Okay, you're not sulking. I'm glad there aren't any shotguns handy."

"I am not a woman to be left on the sidelines."

We traveled for awhile in silence.

I said, "Just out of curiosity, where are we going?"

"His name is Dave Henry. He was a friend of Bandy's."

"Was?"

"Bandy's a strongarm thug and so was Dave. That's the long and short of it. The roadie gig where I met Bandy on that tour, Tobe Gearson knew people who knew people who got Bandy that gig when it became convenient to get Bandy out of the country for awhile until something, I don't know what, blew over. I didn't learn about any of that until much later, of course, like after we were married." She rolled her eyes. "Jeez, I was so stupid."

"Sounds more like naïve. So why are Bandy and Dave no longer friends?"

"Me."

"Ah ha."

"Bandy and I were going through a rough spell. We went through a lot of rough spells, considering the short time we were married. I needed a place to crash one night when Bandy was being a real jerk and somehow I ended up on Dave Henry's couch for a night. It was just the two of us, alone. Of course, being a dude, Davey came on to me and I had to gently rebuff him and I swear to this day he respected that. He spent the night alone in his bedroom and I slept on the couch. Of course Bandy didn't believe a word of that and I guess no one else did either, so naturally it came to a blowup between them. They'd worked as a team for Gearson, and for Mike Jeffrey. But guess what."

"What?"

"Turns out that dumb Davey had a crush on me all along. Turns out the poor boy was head over heels in love with *moi*. He told everyone but me. He just flat lost it after that, the way some people do. Started to mainline and hitting the bottle. Anyway, Bandy stopped working with Dave."

"You have quite an effect on men."

"Yeah, I seem to."

"What's your secret?"

"Stop playing with me. It's like being a woman. Sometimes it's a blessing, sometimes it's a curse."

"Fair enough," I conceded. "Okay. Why are we rousting a drunken doper has-been when we could just go straight to this guy Gearson? If Bandy works for Gearson, Gearson could be our handle."

"He could be. Problem is I never met Gearson. He's just a name to me. I wouldn't know where in London to start looking for him. It's not like he operates out of an office."

Our cab drew to the curb on a street of tenements, in front of what looked like a derelict building until the front door opened and a shabbily dressed, middle-aged man wearing a beret emerged, wearing a backpack. He moved sprightly down the front steps to the sidewalk and headed off down the street.

I eased open the sliding panel and passed the driver enough folding money to raise both of his eyebrows.

"Wait for us."

"Right you are, guvnor."

The low black sky chose that precise moment to release its fury with one mighty crack of thunder that probably rattled every window in the city. Rain clawed at us, the wind a whipping spray, as we hurried from the taxi to the front doorway. I held the door open for Angel and we stepped inside.

The old structure had the smells of every old rooming house in the world. The stale smell of mold and old cooking and too many souls existing under the same roof over too many years. We climbed creaking stairs to a narrow third-floor corridor, dimly lit by only one low-watt bulb at the far end. Bare wood floor. Plain walls.

Angel indicated the door we wanted. Instinct inched me one step aside from the door. I indicated with a nod that Angel should do the same. She picked up on the play with no reaction other than to ease away from her side of the door. Bullets can pierce doors with no problem.

I knocked on the door the way an impatient cop would. "Dave Henry, open up." I knuckled the door a few more times.

Vague movement from inside. A man mumbled.

I gave the door a thump with my boot. "Open up in there."

Someone inside leaned against the door.

"Don't wanna talk," croaked a raspy male voice. "Dave don't live here no more. Go way. Don't wanna talk. Don't wanna, damn your eyes." He lapsed into unintelligible gibberish.

Angel said, "Dave, it's me. Angel."

"Angel?" Stunned by the inconceivable. "Angel, is that you?"

"Yes, it's me. Davey, open the door. We want to talk to you."

"Who's with you? Angel, have you really come to see me? Really?"

The tightness around Angel's eyes and the pinched corners of her mouth told me she wasn't enjoying herself, but she spoke in a stage whisper, her words honeyed with the caress of Eve offering Adam his first apple.

"A friend is with me. Open up, Davey. Let us in, luv. Please."

Angel McGuire could have gotten a preacher to jump through a stained glass window.

A series of clicks. Locks unbolted and unchained. The door opened.

Dave Henry was like the building he lived in. Derelict but somehow managing to hold on. A pock-marked face, book-ended by a pair of cauliflower ears. Glassy-eyed and pasty with dissipation. Three days worth of stubbly beard. He looked like a man shrinking inside his own body. The worn slacks sagged. The black t-shirt was soiled and seemed to be hanging on a scarecrow.

When Angel stepped past him, his eyes lowered as if she was a queen. The eyes came back up when I paused on the threshold.

"Inside," I said.

He might have taken me a couple of years ago, or tried to. The ghost of that man flared briefly in his eyes, replaced by caution and fear. He backed into his room.

A squalid little room. Close. Musty. Tattered armchair against one wall. Low table with a double heating plate. Metal-frame bed, unmade, and a door that led to the bathroom. Overflowing ash trays. Beer and whiskey bottles littered the floor and furniture.

Without taking his glassy eyes from me, he croaked, "Angel, what's going on? Who's this bloke?"

Angel said, "Be nice, Davey," in the same voice she'd used to get us in. "This is my friend Soldier."

Dave squinted, taking me in from head to foot and back again. "Looks like a soldier. Big, ugly, tough son of a bitch." He weaved back and forth, maintaining his balance with effort. "I was that way once, I was. Do you believe that, mister?"

I stepped inside and tapped the door shut with my heel.

I said, "We're not here to trip down memory lane."

He said, "Angel, I've always been sorry about what that happened between you and me. Bandy came on so tough. He beat the bloody crap out of me, did you know that?"

Angel said in a softer voice, "I know, Davey. I heard. Dave, we've come to see you because we need some information and we need it quick."

"I was no match for him. Bandy beat me down in public not once but twice, he did. And then you stayed with him." He sat on the edge of the bed. He peered down into his clasped hands and said in a hollow, empty voice. "I should have been more brave. I should have fought for you, Angel. But that goddamn Bandy. We killed a guy once together, y'know."

Angel said, "Dave, stop. I don't want to hear about that."

"Okay. Yeah, you're right. You're a smart one, you are, Angel. A good woman. If you just gave me another chance, it could be different."

I said, "Stop it. She just told you we need your help. Angel says you know where we can find Gearson. We're looking for him and Bandy, and we're in a hurry."

He ignored me and said to Angel, "Get rid of this guy. Got me some smack. I'll share it with you, Angel baby. If God made a better high, He kept it for Himself."

Angel grimaced. "I don't do that and neither should you. Do you know where Bandy is, or Gearson?"

He made a dismissive gesture and almost fell off the bed. "Still hung up on Bandy, eh? Come on, Angel. He'll never find out. We ain't mates, me and him, like we was before. I'll be good to you, I promise I will." He seemed to remember that I stood next to him. He turned with those glassy, droopy eyes peering up at me. "Go on, cop a walk. Already told you. Don't wanna talk. Go on now. Go away."

I said to Angel, "This ain't working. We're wasting our time. Open the window."

Wind and rain pelted the window glass.

Dave Henry gaped from one of us to the other. "Open the window? Are you crazy? It's bloody raining cats and dogs outside. What's he talking about, Angel?"

Angel said, "Yeah, Soldier. What are you talking about?"

"You heard me. Open the damn window."

She started at that as if jolted with a small electrical shock. Then she went to the window, glaring at me every step of the way.

Dave Henry said, "That's no way to talk to a lady." He mumbled something that sounded like he was calling me a dirty name.

I said, "We need answers and we need them now."

I grasped him with one hand by the scruff of his scrawny neck and yanked him to his feet. He tried protesting but the words came out as startled jabber.

Angel struggled to raise the window. She must have sensed my intention because her expression said she was approving of this less by the second. She managed to raise the stubborn window. Cold rain was wind-driven into the room as if through a funnel.

I dragged Dave Henry across to the window. He emitted a shrill yelp when he too realized what was happening. I think Angel cried out "Soldier, no!" but I couldn't be sure over the noise Dave was making. I gripped the back of his wide leather belt and hoisted him bodily out the window.

Dangling over the street below from three fights up, with gusts of wind pelting him with driving rain, he suddenly became quite lucid.

"Are you insane? *Stop!*" He had to scream to be heard above the raging elements. "Pull me in! You'll drop me!"

"That's the idea," I called. "It's an interrogation technique that's damn effective. Three weeks ago my squad was being evaced with two VC prisoners and we needed intel fast, just like I do now. It was a matter of life or death for a platoon of American soldiers. Know what I did onboard that evac chopper?"

Angel reached out but stopped short of touching me, unsure of herself. "Soldier, stop. Haul him back in. You're not in Vietnam."

"No," I told her, "but the situation is the same." I resumed calling down to the soaked creature below. "We needed that intel fast, Davey. I held one prisoner outside the chopper in flight, just like I'm holding you now. When that VC idiot thought we were bluffing and wouldn't tell us what we wanted to know, I let him drop. His partner got real cooperative, real quick."

He screeched like a big-ass bird. "No!" He was reaching desperately for something to hold onto but the outside brick wall was smooth and slick with rain. "Pull me up! Don't let me die like this. Angel, *save me!*"

Angel stood next to me and shouted down at him, "Do what he says, Davey. Tell us what we want to know. He won't hurt you." Then she lowered her voice and the fingers of her hand tightened on my arm. "You hear that, Soldier? You won't hurt him."

I shifted my weight, causing Dave's head to bump against the brick wall but not too hard.

Another screech. Then, "Okay, I believe you. Krikey, don't kill me! I'll tell you anything you want to know, just pull me in!"

I hoisted his bantam weight back into the room. I released him with a throw that sailed him across the room. He smashed, upside down, into the opposite wall.

Angel closed the window.

Dave Henry's ragged breathing filled the room. He cowered in a corner, peering at me with desperation.

Angel said, "We've got to get out of here. People heard him screaming. They'll call the police."

I said, "I doubt that. Not in this neighborhood." I moved in, boxing Dave into a corner. "But in case she's right, Davey, cooperate fast, why don't you?" I squatted down in front of him. More field interrogation technique. He had to be reminded that he wasn't out of the woods yet. I delivered an open backhand slap across his pasty face. "Talk."

He was out of breath. "I swear to God I don't know where Bandy is." The words poured from him in between gulps for air. "Oh sweet Jesus, I don't want to die."

Angel said, "Davey, what about Gearson?"

I said, "Bandy works for Gearson, right?"

"Aye, he does. And for Mike Jeffrey. Him and Bandy do off jobs for Mr. Jeffrey, you might say."

"So where is he, Dave? This is where you buy your life. Where do I find Gearson?"

He must have seen something in my eyes. He started trembling.

"I'm trying to help, mate, swear to God I am. Ask me something I know for krikey sake but please don't throw me out that window!"

Angel said, "Who's he sleeping with these days?"

Dave said, "Bandy? Any damn thing with three holes and hair."

I said, "Tobe Gearson. Who's keeping his bed warm?"

Angel said in a small voice, "Actually I was talking about Bandy, the no-good bum."

I spoke sharply to Dave. "Who does Gearson see?"

Dave gulped audibly. "Please don't make me rat on him. Gearson will kill me!"

I said, "I thought you didn't want to fly anymore." I leaned forward, reached around behind him for his belt. "You've worn out my patience. Angel, the window."

He screeched like he had when he was dangling.

"*Wait!* I just thought of something!"

"I kind of thought you would."

"Gearson is dating some dancer at a club down in Wardour Street."

"Names, Dave. I want a name."

"Raven, they call her. Corner her, why don't you? She'll know where to find sugar daddy."

"Girls like that work at night. Where do I find Raven during the day?"

"At the club. The Tit Tat. She does a noon show for the lunch crowd."

I glanced at Angel. "You know the place he's talking about?"

"I can't say I've ever been there but yeah, I know where it is. It's one of Mike Jeffrey's clubs." When I rose to stand beside her, she said to the miserable, rain-soaked man cowering in the corner, "Thank you, Dave. I'm sorry this had to happen. You've been very helpful. But just one more thing before we go. What do you know about Jimi Hendrix?"

"Uh, I like his music. Now leave me alone, Angel, you and your bloody mad Yank. It was because of you that everything went wrong for me and they call you Angel! Me and Bandy having our falling out, Gearson throwing me down and me coming to this. I love you, Angel. You drove me to this."

Angel said, "No, it all happened because you've been stupid. You can turn your life around and start getting smart again anytime you want to. But I'm not the girl for you. You're just like Bandy only not as mean and that's not saying much, is it? How would I have been any happier with you than I was with him? You never had a chance."

The cowering guy, in his puddle of rainwater, said, "Angel, I'd do it again, hand to God."

"Dave, I'm sorry."

I said, "Aw for pete sake," and drew the .45 from under

my jacket.

Angel gasped. "No, Soldier, *don't!*"

Dave Henry scrunched down, trying to make himself smaller in the corner. I bent over and clipped him a quick tap with the gun barrel that caught him along his left temple. His body relaxed and he slumped over onto his side. I put away the .45.

Angel watched with troubled eyes.

"You're a mean bastard."

"When I have to be. This way your friend Davey doesn't get the chance to put himself back in solid with Gearson by warning Gearson that we're after him."

We let ourselves out.

Angel spared a parting glance at the unconscious man.

She said, "The poor fella," as if she really meant it.

23

Our rosy-cheeked grandpa of a taxi driver sat sideways, reading a racing form when we hurriedly clambered into his taxi to escape the rain. He set the folded form aside with a cheery smile.

"Next stop then?"

I said, "Do you know Tit Tat Club in Wardour Street?"

His crinkled eyes danced from me to Angel and back again, as if seeking confirmation that he'd heard right.

Angel made a wry face. She said to me, "The good driver is not used to answering that question with a lady in his cab."

The driver actually blushed. "Right you are, ma'am. They do call it swinging London, eh? Yes, sir. I know where that club is and I know the fastest way to get there."

"We've got a lunch show to catch."

"Be there before you know it, guvnor."

And away we went.

I shook a smoke loose from its deck, offered Angel one and fired us both up. It was a gray, dark world passing by outside. Vehicles sloshed through the streets with their headlights on.

Angel closed the divider between us and the driver. "I wish I hadn't seen you do those things you to Dave."

"That's nothing. You should have seen what someone did to Sydney Blanchard."

"I was starting to like you, Soldier, and maybe I still am. I mean as a person. You're an intense guy." She studied me through a twin stream of smoke exhaled through her nostrils. "So sure of yourself. Not cocky but, I don't know, so different from the men I've known. I left Texas because I was running away from men like you. So macho. So confident in yourself and in what you're doing that you're almost arrogant. But you're not arrogant. You're...what? Principled and impatient. That's what you are."

"Hudberry called me a barbarian."

"You act like a barbarian if anyone or anything stands in your way, while I'm trying to act like a Buddhist and not judge. You are the way you are and, frankly, that's kind of scary. That story about dropping the Viet Cong from the helicopter. Was that true?

"Up to a point. I wanted to impress Dave."

"What really happened?"

"The VC talked. Who wouldn't? I pulled him back in."

"Sydney was murdered last night and since I met you this morning for breakfast, I've seen two people gunned down in cold blood. Violence follows you. You breathe violence. I watched you nearly kill Davey and then club him unconscious with a gun. My God."

I said, "You're talking about a punk who beat up and maybe killed people for money until he flipped his lid into la-la land. Have sympathy for the victims he was paid to terrorize."

She laughed. "Y'know, you being so damn logical could get on a girl's nerves. All right, all right. I guess it's just that as someone who's trying to live an ethical and peaceful life, I feel a little guilty about what we did back there." She snubbed out her cigarette in the door tray. "And it all started because Dave was a nice guy who offered me a couch to sleep on one night when my old man wanted to beat my head in. Dave was a gentleman about it and look what it got him."

I said, "You don't have to convince me that life isn't fair. Try writing letters to mothers and fathers informing them the sons they raised have been cut down by enemy fire in a jungle halfway around the world."

"You're right, Soldier. You're risking your life to help a friend. I'm sorry for judging you."

"We've got our lead on Gearson."

"Ah yes, Mr. Gearson's girlfriend, if that's the word. I've never been to a strip club. What a day. What a day. And what are we going to do about Raven when we find her? Dangle her out another window?"

"Not unless we have to. We're going to start by keeping our distance. We ID her and keep an eye on her after she gets off work."

"I see. She leads us to Gearson and Gearson leads us to Bandy and Jimi."

"And maybe to whoever killed Sydney Blanchard."

"What if it's a dead end?"

I lit us another pair of cigarettes.

"Then we start over. Damn, it really pisses me off that

a sensitive, artistic guy like Jimi got caught up in something like that."

"I hate to say it but our friend deserves some of the blame. He's a lost soul and he's made some wrong choices. But then, haven't we all?"

"When I read the letters he wrote me over in Nam, he sounded like the guy I knew. In those letters his head was screwed on right."

She nodded. "And then there's you."

"What about me?"

"Well, since we met this morning, you've been a bull charging through every china shop he can find."

I gave her a tight grin. "Yeah, but with purity of purpose."

"I know. I sensed that yesterday when you showed up at the crash pad, the first time I saw you. That pureness of purpose redeems you."

"Forget redemption. I'm a lost cause."

"Soldier, no one's a lost cause. You were wounded in that war, not in your body but in your psyche. Vietnam. You're still there."

"I should be on patrol with my squad. You wouldn't understand."

"You're right. Vietnam. I hate the sound of the place and I've never even been there. And here you are, suffering the hurt deep inside where no one can see."

I said, "I want to find Jimi, that's all. I want to get out from under."

"I know that. But Soldier, you're not in Vietnam anymore. You need to let your mind and your spirit catch up with your body. You haven't done that yet."

I didn't know what to say, so I kept my mouth shut.

Before long our taxi drew to the curb near The Tit Tat Club, a two-story structure marked by a flashing red and yellow neon sign, sandwiched between a sex toy novelty shop and a nondescript structure that, in this neighborhood, could well have been a cathouse.

I handed the driver some more money. "Wait for us?"

"Right you are, guvnor. You lovebirds have fun."

A barker stood on the sidewalk in front of the club.

"In here, folks! Right this way! The prettiest girls in London! Passable food! Cheap drinks!" When we stepped by him on our way in, he prattled, "Excellent choice, dear hearts, and have a good—"

The rest was lost beneath the din of recorded rock music that vibrated the floors and walls of the smoky club. On small, strategically placed round stages, curvaceous young women danced provocatively beneath soft stage lights.

The joint was jam-packed, four deep at the American bar that ran the length of the place. A large mirror behind the bar gave the illusion that the place was twice its size. The parties squeezed into the row of tables along the opposite wall hardly had elbow room to raise their glasses. The rock music boomed from speakers to either side of a curtained stage at the far end of the place.

I tipped a hostess to get us past a velvet rope and into a warmly paneled and carpeted, dimly lit dining area with discreetly distanced booths and tables. Our table provided a good view of the stage but was well removed from the cacophonous hubbub of the bar. The tables here were occupied by lunching businessmen and a smattering of couples. A pretty waitress came over promptly and was only mildly surprised at our order of two Coca-Colas.

I became aware of Angel's concentrated attention on three guys who were in the process of shouldering their way through the crowd, having just come in while I ordered.

She said, "The one in the middle. That's Michael Jeffrey. I told you he owned this place."

He was in his late thirties. Camel hair coat worn over his shoulders. Aviator sunglasses. Slicked-back hair curled over his collar. Average build but the way he carried himself with a lumbering swagger gave the impression of bulk and menace. The point bodyguard cleared a path and people looked glad to step aside. The second bodyguard stayed close behind him.

They passed through a curtained doorway beyond the bar.

I said to Angel, "Excuse me. I'll be right back."

She touched my wrist. "You're going to confront him?"

"Do you have a better way to find out if he knows where Jimi is?"

"Uh no, I guess not. Uh, what should I do?"

A fanfare sounded from the main stage beyond the sea of heads. The dancers on the smaller stages stepped down.

A voice announced over the sound system, "And now, ladies and gentlemen, the moment you've been waiting for. Without further ado, I give you...Raven's Fantasy!"

A pumping bass line backbeat. The curtain rose on a stage, empty except for a dais. Fog swirled in from a smoke machine, creating a dream-like quality. In syncopation to the beat, two dancers—one male, one female—swayed sensually, approaching the dais from opposite sides of the stage.

I said, "You keep an eye on Raven. I'll try to be right back."

"That's reassuring."

She released my wrist and turned her attention to the stage.

The woman was slim, with a muscular litheness. Black hair, stylishly short, framed her high cheek bones, lush lips and sensual eyes. Her hips were encased in a bikini bottom. She wore a smile and a shawl of Oriental pattern, bright and shimmering in the softened stage lighting. She wore white nylons and high heels. The male dancer, clad only in a loincloth, was muscular and tall, with a well-developed physique.

I brought an elbow into play and nudged my way through to the curtained doorway beyond the bar, through which Jeffrey and his bodyguards had passed.

24

I FOUND MYSELF AT THE FOOT OF A DOZEN STEPS THAT took me up into a gloomy hallway with doors along one wall.

The bodyguards stood in front of the first door.

The bodyguard on the right said to me, "What do you want?"

The second one sneered, as if dealing with errant, horny guys was nothing new. "No girls back here, bloke. Try the house next door. The loo's out front."

I could only guess that the loo was the men's room.

I said, "I don't want a girl. I want to see Mike Jeffrey."

"Let's take him," the first one said out of the side of his mouth.

They came at me fast. The one on the right drew back a fist adorned with old-fashioned brass knuckles. His partner brought up a leather sap from his back pocket.

I dodged the swing from the brass knuckles while I caught the wrist of the other arm that was swinging the blackjack. I thrust back on the wrist, causing him to clobber himself between the eyes hard enough to knock him off his feet. Then I caught the other's arm at the wrist and shoulder and brought it down sharply across my knee. The *crack!* of snapping bone was loud enough to hear over the thumping music from out front. This one dropped too, moaning next to his semi-conscious partner.

I sensed someone behind me.

Jeffrey stood in the open doorway. Up close, his features were fleshy, pasty.

"Looks like I need to hire some competent help."

I said, "Let's talk."

"What about?"

"Jimi Hendrix. He's missing."

A pair of bouncers rushed into the hallway to join us. Muscles bulged beneath matching black t-shirts. They took in the situation and started toward me.

Jeffrey raised his hand.

"Let him be." He indicated the fallen bodyguards. "Get these rummies out of my sight. They're fired. See that they bounce when you toss them out."

"Yes sir, Mr. Jeffrey," they chimed in unison.

They each tossed one of the bodyguards over a shoulder and trundled them away.

Jeffrey said to me, "Step inside."

"You first."

His eyes drifted to my right hand, hovering near the concealed .45. He knew I was packing. When he stepped back in through the doorway, his hands remained in clear view. He made no sudden movements.

It was a nondescript office except for the huge glass window that provided an ideal vantage point, a bird's-eye-view, of the crowded club interior. I remembered the mirror behind the bar. I couldn't make out Angel because of the angle but the view of the action onstage was clear enough.

The show was heating up. Raven's shoulders were shimmying, their roundness accentuated by the artfully draped shawl. The dancers undulated, eyes closed, in a steamy embrace, his lips traveling from an extended kiss to her throat. One of his hands slid beneath the shawl. Raven leaned her head back and mouthed a silent moan.

The office was soundproofed, creating the strange effect of viewing the club as if seen in a silent movie accompanied by the classical music that came from unseen speakers.

A man in a wheelchair sat behind a desk, waiting for us; a large-boned, gray-bearded man around forty, peering at me through thick-lensed glasses.

He said, "What the bloody hell?"

Jeffrey cleared his throat. "Owl, I've got to ask you to excuse us for a little while."

"Excuse you? What the hell, Mike? This is my bloody club!"

"No, it's my club," Jeffrey said in what was almost a whisper. "You run it for me. You get yourself diddled by the girls working here with a snap of your fingers. All that and more. You've got yourself a sweet berth, you have. So when I request a little privacy around here, I fucking damn well get it. Now isn't that so?"

Owl glared at me. He said to me, "Fuck you, mate," spun his wheelchair around and wheeled himself through a hinged door in the wall behind the desk.

Jeffrey waited until the sound came of another door being opened and closed.

He said, "Owl stopped a bullet for me in Damascus. Now who the hell are you? What's this about Jimi?"

"I'm looking for him."

He leaned back against the desk, his arms folded. "Everyone's looking for brother Jimi. My solicitors. His solicitors."

"And you? Are you looking for Jimi?"

"Me? That's why I pay the bloody solicitors and so far it's been money down the drain."

"So you're Jimi's career."

He lit a cigarette and said between puffs, "I was his manager. Don't blame that train wreck on me. And don't waste my time with idle chit-chat. I'm talking to you because you kicked the asses of two former SAS officers on whom I was also obviously wasting good money. Who are you? What's this about?"

I said, "Owl isn't used to being excluded from the conversation, is he?"

"What of it?"

"I notice things. It's my nature. So you don't know where Jimi is?"

"I don't know where Jimi is." He stood up straight. "Is that it?" He patted a pocket of the camel hair coat. "I stopped in here to pick up the receipts, not to make friends. We're done. I'm a busy man."

"How about Bandy McGuire?"

That got me a curious frown. "What about him?"

"I'm looking for him too."

"I don't know where Bandy is."

"Tobe Gearson?"

"Not a clue."

"I thought those boys work for you."

"They do, when I've got work for them. I haven't seen either one of them in weeks. Wouldn't know where to look."

"Kind of early in the day to be picking up receipts, like you need some fast cash. Taking a trip, Mike? Got a reason to leave town for awhile?"

He slipped off his shades so I could see his eyes. Narrowed eyes. "You're a cheeky bastard. What the hell are you talking about?"

I said, "There's more than solicitors looking for Jimi, but I think you already know that. You're jumpy, Mike. Sending Owl off like that. Making the rounds early." I decided to go from observation to conjecture, and said, "You got a visit from the man in the Brooks Brothers suit and raincoat. I heard he was CIA."

There was a knock at the door.

Jeffrey called, "Get the fuck in here," and said to me in his near whisper, "I've got enough men under this roof to take you apart no matter how bad you are."

The bouncers who had carried out the bodyguards returned, accompanied by another pair of muscle-bound guys in black T-shirts. The four of them took up position just inside the office door, a pair to either side of me.

I said, "Brooks Brothers paid you a visit. How about a German slick named Klaus Mueller?"

He put his aviator sunglasses back on. He waved a hand at me, a nuisance he had lost interest in. "Walk. And watch your back if you're so damn observant. It's not me you have to worry about."

You can only stare down five guys for so long. It seemed like a good time to return to my date. I rejoined Angel.

She sat alone at our table, engrossed in the goings-on onstage.

The pulse of the music had intensified, much like Ravel's *Bolero*. The dancers writhed in a sensual embrace, their hands gliding across each other. Raven shrugged and the shawl dropped to form a luminous pool at her feet. The man lowered his lips and began to kiss and fondle her pale white breasts that were topped with taut brown nipples. Curls of artificial smoke partially obscured the entwined couple on the dais. The man slid around behind the woman, embracing her possessively.

Angel said, close to my ear, "Now that, darlin', is stimulatin', wouldn't you say?"

"See anyone else you recognize?"

"You think I wouldn't mention that? No, Bandy's not here and I've been looking." She nodded toward the stage. "At least most of the time."

I finished my drink.

"Let's get out of here."

Her eyebrows drew together. "You're not going to turn prude on me? Aw, Soldier. Let's stay and watch. They can't show much more. There are decency laws, you know."

"We got what we came for. We've seen Raven."

She finished her drink and accompanied me, muttering, "Let's hope we recognize her with her clothes on."

She took my hand when I reached for it. I steered us through the attentive crowd that erupted with a gasp and enthusiastic applause at something that happened onstage behind us just as we reached the entrance. Angel dug in her heels. Since we were holding hands like a couple of teenagers, I drew up short. We were too late. The curtain had fallen on whatever erotic tableau the dancers had assumed. Angel sighed her disappointment, and then stepped with me out under the canopied entrance of The Tit Tat Club.

The rain came in a steady downpour. Scurrying pedestrians were dark shadows with umbrellas, darting through the gloom, dodging the waves of water splashed across the sidewalk by passing vehicles.

Our cabbie was parked up the block. He switched on his headlights and drove forward to stop at the end of the canopy. We made it into his taxi with only a minimal dousing.

I said to Angel, "You get easily sidetracked."

"I have a healthy interest in sex. Is that a bad thing?"

"No, that's a good thing as long as we stay on mission."

"I know. It's about Jimi. But we wanted to get a good look at Raven, didn't we? How did it go with Mike Jeffrey?"

"He's a cool customer," I said. "Too cool for his own good. I got more questions than I did answers. We're still looking for Jimi."

The cheery driver turned to regard us through the open divider. We'd become old friends.

"Are me lovebirds having a quarrel, then?"

I said without conviction, "Mind your own business." I nodded at the Tit Tat. "How well do you know this place?"

"Try me."

"We want to tail one of the dancers when she leaves. Her name is Raven. Is there a back way out?"

"There is but she won't use it. The girls here are encouraged by the establishment to mingle with the customers after the show, before they leave. That's one of the draws. Skirts a couple of laws but who's to squawk?"

"Take us around the block and park where you were just now when we came out. We'll pick her up when she leaves."

He slipped the taxi into gear.

"Sounds good to me, guvnor. I'm aces on a tail job, I am. That is as long as she doesn't step out of the club and hail my cab."

"If she does, we'll get out as if you're just dropping us off. Earn yourself a big tip when you tell me where you took her."

He chuckled. "That's what I like about you, Yank." He merged with the slow traffic crawl along Wardour Street. "You know what you're doing."

"Let's hope so," said Angel. "What if Raven decides to leave the club while we're circling the block?"

I said, "She's not going out in the rain in that stage getup," and added to the driver, "but step on it just in case."

25

────────

We almost missed Raven.

Our driver glided his taxi into a parking space, up the block from the club. A sporty little Triumph tooled past us from behind and braked to a splashy stop before the canopied entrance of the Tit Tat Club. The Triumph's red racing stripe and the smooth lines of its white chassis stood out against the drab gray day.

Raven darted out wearing a trendy knee-length red slicker. The slicker wasn't buttoned but she clutched at its front as she hurried to the sports car.

Angel cracked a small grin. "Imagine that, running out into the rain in nothing but a raincoat and, well, nothing but a raincoat. Who'd have thunk it?"

I said, "Okay, okay, I never said I could think like a woman. Figures that a guy driving a sports car with a racing stripe wouldn't want to be the type to be kept waiting."

Raven slid into the low-slung Triumph, which rocketed away from the curb before she had closed her door. Centrifugal force took care of that.

I said to our driver, "After them."

"Righto," said our cabbie, and he slipped the taxi into gear. "Here's where I earns me pay."

He proceeded to exhibit an expertise at the playing of traffic patterns worthy of a professional undercover spy on a tail job, positioning us at least two car lengths behind the Triumph at all times, playing the lanes once we left Soho, staying camouflaged amid scores of identical London black taxis that dominated the traffic.

After ten minutes of this, the Triumph dutifully indicated a right turn before disappearing into the underground parking garage of a ten-story tower of steel and plate-glass.

Our man slowed his taxi to a crawl. We glided past the ramp leading down into the garage. "Curse the luck, guvnor. What now?"

"He could just be dropping her off. Let's give him half an hour."

He found a place to park and serve as our vantage point, then returned to his racing form. Angel and I smoked cigarettes and didn't say much.

At the thirty minute mark exactly, Angel said, "Is time for Plan B."

I said, "Okay. I'll stay here. You find a car rental place."

The driver said, "There's one of those about three blocks from here. She could be back with a car in a jiff."

Angel said, "But we're not sure it's Gearson driving that sports car. What if Raven plays the field? This is an awfully thin thread, hoping that Raven will take us to

Gearson and he'll take us to Bandy. Uh, we do know what we're doing, right, Soldier?"

A tight grin stretched my face. "We'll find out soon enough. Now go fetch us that rental and get back here fast as you can. I'll reconnoiter."

"Reconnoiter. Still a soldier."

I nodded. "Always a soldier."

I got out of the cab and handed the driver a wad of pound notes.

His eyes brightened as he made a quick count. "Right you are then, guvnor. It's been a pleasure being of service to a gentleman of your caliber."

"Likewise, you old salt."

Angel said, "One more question. What if it is Gearson and he decides to drive off before I get back?"

"Adapt and improvise," I said.

Her smile would have shamed Mona Lisa.

"Stay safe, Soldier. I'll be right back."

And they were gone. The rainy thoroughfare hissed with four busy lanes of traffic.

The lobby of the building looked inviting. Comfortable, warm and most of all dry with its wide marble floor, potted plants and wood-paneled walls. A conservatively dressed elderly couple were emerging from the elevator and strolling, arm in arm, across the lobby.

The rain worked for me. I angled in, timing my approach to intersect with them in the vestibule that separated the lobby from the street. The natural impulse of the civilized person compelled the man to hold the door open for me. We traded nods and I thanked him in passing. Their taxi waited at the curb and so they were off. I was alone in the vestibule. A security lock in the street door made an audible click when it closed after them.

I tried the lobby door but it had automatically locked after the couple. The vestibule, with its row of mailboxes set in one row, was as far as I was going to get. That was okay. I read the names over the mailboxes.

T. Gearson was in Apartment 8b.

Back into the rain, along a sidewalk to the garage entrance. I walked like a man who belonged; who knew where he was going and wanted to get out of the rain. No gate or manned booth barred entrance to the underground garage. I entered the dark world of chilled shadow and echoes. No one was in sight. There was an abundance of empty parking slots. People were still at work.

I found the Triumph with no trouble, parked near a locked door of solid steel with only a small glass window, through which I could see a small, plain lobby and an elevator.

A few minutes later when a late model Toyota approached the ramp from the street, Angel turned in out of the rain and braked to a stop next to where I stood.

My inclination under ordinary circumstances would have been to amiably slide her across the car seat so I could take the wheel. I prefer being the driver regardless of the vehicle I'm riding in. Always been that way. I'm a nervous passenger. But I was battling cumulative fatigue, with enough on my mind to have no inclination to learn the rules of the road by driving on the opposite (I couldn't help thinking of it as the wrong) side of the road, so I settled into the front passenger seat.

Angel's small smile said she understood, and she drove us deeper into the garage, rounding a bend before we reached the Triumph. She backed our rental car into a slot on the opposite side with three occupied parking slots separating us from the Triumph. She switched off the ignition.

We sat in the silent subterranean gloom.

Angel said, "Now what?"

"Now we wait. When Gearson leaves, alone or with the woman, we follow."

"And what if they don't go anywhere on this rainy afternoon? What if they decide to spend the night in?"

"Don't you ever get tired of being a pessimist?"

"I'm a realist."

"Okay, realist. I've been led to understand that Gearson is a man of the night. A street dog. He'll be hitting the streets by dark if not before." Her stare of unrelenting skepticism prompted me to add, "Okay, we'll give him an hour. If he's not down here and gone by then we'll try something else."

"Like hanging him out a window?"

"We'll see."

"And if it isn't Gearson?"

I said, "Stop it."

"You like me, don't you, Soldier?"

"You're okay."

"You do like me. And I like you. You're not the first dude fresh out of Vietnam that I've encountered, y'know."

I massaged the back of my neck, which ached like hell. I said, "I don't know if fresh is the word."

My eyes felt like they'd been rubbed with sandpaper. I leaned back against the headrest. I closed my eyes. The sigh of exhaustion that came unbidden sounded foreign to me. I tried to remember the last time I'd gotten a decent stretch of sleep. On the flight? We'd landed almost twenty-four hours ago.

Angel said, "Back in Texas I dated a guy who served over there. A real nice guy who knew how to take care of himself. He loved his mom, he believed in God, he even liked apple pie. He opened a hardware store on a VA loan and wanted a wife to raise his kids and live the American Dream. He married my best friend. He always said that war made a man out of him."

"You can believe that."

"I do. And last month another guy crashed at the pad for about a week. Said he'd fought over there and had his regimental tattoo to prove it. He'd been discharged and he was bumming around Europe and the U.K. and I do mean bumming. One day I walked in when he thought no one was around. He was shooting up right there on the damn living room couch. He was a ruined man."

"Yeah, it can happen that way, too. Depends on the man and on what he's had to face and deal with. There are too many variables for it to be easy to understand."

"I can see which kind of man you are, Soldier. Maybe someday you'll be running a hardware store in a little town."

"Angel, if it were to happen that day's a long way off."

"I see that too. You're a walking razor. I'll never know what you know. I know that. I've never walked a bloody mile in your shoes and I hope that I never do. But I think I understand."

"I believe you do."

She said, "I get why a man like you has to keep the

walls up. Where you've been, you make a friend, you trade stories about back home and the people and places you miss, you tell jokes, you get to know the guy, you go out on patrol and you watch his body get blown apart. You watch him die."

"He doesn't just die, Angel. He's blown to shit. I finally lost count," I told her. "It got to the point where every time I got to know a guy, that guy would buy it, seemed like. Like I'm cursed. People die when I let them get close to me."

"That's crazy talk and you know it."

"It's like yesterday when Sydney intercepted me at the airport. Did you know about that?"

A sad smile. "It doesn't surprise me."

"She was dead a few hours later."

"Well I'm around you and I don't plan to die anytime soon. As a matter of fact, Soldier, you make me feel alive."

Somehow our bodies melded and I gave in to whatever crazy emotion was stirred up in me by this woman seated beside me in a new-smelling rental car in a remote corner of an underground parking garage. I opened my mouth to speak and received a steamy tongue kiss that I returned in kind.

"Oh, I want you, Solider."

"You want me, lady, you've *got* me."

Our mouths locked again. Her tongue darted and slithered sensuously, penetrating, caressing my tongue. Her teeth nibbled at my lower lip. I grew rock hard. I maintained the clinch and eased across her, pressing her against the car seat. I half-mounted her as best I could considering that we were clothed and restricted by the close confines, like kids making out who were letting it go too far. She slumped down to facilitate the maneuver.

My left hand stayed around her waist while my right found its way under her blouse to cup her left breast. With no brassiere to impede roaming fingers, I cupped warm vibrant woman for the first time in a long, long while. I positioned one of my knees where it would do the most good. She gasped. Through layers of material, hers and mine, I felt the heat of her against my knee. Beneath me, she writhed in coital passion while I pinched her left nipple and we shared a searing soul kiss. She quivered and trembled, ending our kiss and gasping the word "Oh" as if it had seven syllables. I held her then while she quaked in my arms.

Then she eased out of my arms. She somehow managed to find a comfortable position kneeling on the floor. For some stupid reason I started to say no, this wasn't necessary. But those words died with the thought as she undid me and began returning the favor. I hadn't gotten a blow job since before I enlisted. It was over before it began, like the Fourth of July and a mortar attack with maybe some napalm and then it was me doing the quaking and the gasping.

When the moment had passed, she looked up at me and smiled.

"Welcome home, Soldier."

All I could say was, "Whew," as if it had seven syllables.

She seated herself beside me again, smiling a contented little smile, tidying us up with tissues.

Down the way along the opposite wall, the steel door opened.

Raven appeared, wearing a slinky thigh-length black

dress and high heels, accompanied by a lean, sharply dressed man in his mid-twenties who walked with the swagger of a hustler.

"Gearson," I said.

They walked to the Triumph without looking in our direction.

26

THE RAIN HAD LET UP WHILE WE WERE UNDERGROUND BUT the smell of it clung to the air, a humid presence threatening more of the same. Umbrellas along the thoroughfare had not been closed but there were more of them. Pedestrians who just had to be somewhere, taking advantage of the hiatus.

On two occasions the Triumph made sudden turns and the density of city traffic momentarily caused us to lose sight of it. I doubted Gearson was aware of us tailing him or was trying to lose us. Both times Angel managed to regain visual sighting and stay with them.

There was a renewed edge to me now. The primal jolt of sex had rejuvenated me. I was a little jangled, I'll admit it; uncertain about Angel and my feelings for her after what happened in the garage. She drove with a smile. We smoked cigarettes and neither of us spoke for some time.

Then she said out of the blue, "Do you believe in God?"

I hadn't thought about that one in awhile.

I said, "I believe in what most people mean when they say the word."

She eased us around a slow-moving van.

"Good answer. Me, I was raised Southern Baptist. I'm going to hell when I die. But I sure enough believe in the good Lord Almighty. Would you like proof that He has a sense of humor?"

"Uh, Angel, I'm not sure where you're going with this."

"I know. Do you want to hear the punch line of God's latest joke?"

"If it's funny."

"Oh, I'll let you decide that." Pause. Deep breath, making those firm, lovely breasts rise and fall. She plunged on. "Honey, the fact of the matter is I've sort of been exploring and enjoying the lesbian lifestyle now and then since that rat bastard Bandy McGuire soured me on dudes, I thought once and for all."

I said, "I don't think that's funny at all."

The traffic slowed to a stop. The Triumph idled three cars ahead of us at a busy cross-town intersection.

She said, "That damn Bandy. I'd like to see him dead for the way he killed my trust in men, for him teaching me the way you men really are." Her voice didn't convey anger, only regret and conviction. "Men are so selfish and rough. A woman knows how to treat another woman in just about every way there is."

She hesitated, no doubt expecting me to voice a reaction of some sort to indicate how I was receiving this information.

I coughed to clear my throat and managed, "Well uh, so what happened between us?"

The stoplight changed. Traffic inched forward.

Angel said, "Well, the fact of the matter is I do love guys. I guess that's why they keep falling in love with me. Dang it, I'm just a doggone flirt is what I am. I'm what they call AC-DC back in Texas. Maybe they call me that in London too, for all I know. Guess I sort of like playing on both teams."

I said, "I read a lot of science fiction when I was a kid. My favorites were the stories where someone would find themselves stepping into another dimension. That's me in London. That's me and you."

"There's something else you've got to know. I should have mentioned it before this. I don't think it has any bearing on this but, well, you need to know if you want to know me. If you want to understand."

"Understand what?"

"Sydney. Sydney and I were lovers. It only happened a couple of times between us. Three times, actually. I hope that doesn't make you feel uncomfortable."

"Were there others?"

"A few. Most of the time since Bandy I've sort of enjoyed the freedom of being celibate but every once in a while I sort of get that itch you can't scratch. But Sydney was the last one. With Sydney it was lovely and sweet and very hot. But it's a busy world full of complications and other people's energy. We stayed friends but the sex part of it went away. I think that's really how we both wanted it, to be just friends. She was a beautiful young woman. She deserved a long and bountiful life. So there it is."

"How long has it been?"

"It ended after the first of the year. January is a dreary time in England and I've always wondered if maybe that didn't have something to do with it. Not that it matters now. So I guess it's been about eight months. We see each other at the clubs, I've been to the shop where she works…where she worked." She swallowed audibly. "Poor thing," she said with quiet reverence.

I said, "Did you kill Sydney?"

Her eyes tightened and grew hard. "Are you joking?"

"I'll take that as a no."

The hard eyes softened. "I guess you had to ask me that, or you wouldn't have. No, I did not kill poor Sydney."

"Have I turned you off yet? That's the term, right?"

"Yes, that's it. Mister, you just flat turn me on. Your strength. Your devotion to a friend. Your directness. You'd stoke any woman's furnace if you didn't scare her off first."

"Well, uh, thanks for taking the initiative."

"You've been out of circulation for too long. You don't seem to know what you've got, bub, so I figured you needed a lift, so to speak. Sometimes I do charity work."

"Ouch."

"Well it's true. "

She was getting under my skin but in a nice way. This bantering between us was energizing me too.

I said, "Guess I can't blame you for liking girls."

"How's that?"

"Well, considering all the gorgeous women out there after this sexual revolution I read about, who wouldn't want them, man or woman?"

She sighed and shook her head. "That's so the way a man would see it. "It's not just about sex. When my time comes, I want to die knowing that I've *lived* my life. That I haven't short-changed myself."

"You could never short-change anyone, Angel. It's not your nature."

"That's sweet. Do you want me to fall in love with you, Soldier?"

"Don't be silly. What could I offer a woman? I'm nothing except the things I've done. I destroyed. I've killed people, many people. I've done terrible things."

"Stop it. That was war. You never killed out of greed or because there was cruelty in you."

"It's the life I've chosen. My future is duty, not love."

The traffic jam loosened up and resumed flowing. Angel shifted lanes to maintain our tracking position. The Triumph started easing ahead of the pack.

Angel said, "You fascinate me, Soldier. Guys like you who are honestly tough. You're a rare breed, my friend, and I speak from unfortunate experience. There are a lot of scared little boys walking around in men's bodies. But you guys, I mean the ones who put your life on the line for something you believe in, something that matters, you're the real men. Your passion run hotter and deeper than the rest because you're not like the rest. Ancient societies had a warrior class, and that's what you are today. You don't run with the herd because you can't. You don't even know how."

I rubbed my eyes. It felt like grinding sand into them. Now instead of seeing Pulaski stepping into that booby trap every time I closed my eyes, I kept seeing the corpse of a pretty young woman with the back of her head turned to strawberry jam.

I said, "I'm just trying to keep my head above water, help Jimi and I want to nail the bastard that killed Sydney. I've got the sense of separate threads intertwining.

Someone for some reason has Jimi. That's the only way it plays unless Jimi is dead, and I'm not willing to accept that. Sydney is dead after getting Jimi off to herself. Your ex-husband is tied into it. Chet Daly is dead after telling us about a hit team. Those are the threads that I've got to untangle if we want to put the finger on Sydney's killer."

"Jimi's at the center of everything, isn't he?"

"He's why I'm here."

The Triumph turned onto a secondary through street. Angel tapped the rental car's brakes. We fell back a few more car lengths as traffic started to thin out and our surroundings morphed into a world of sedate greenery, sparse traffic and walled estates.

Angel held way back but we kept the Triumph in sight.

Up ahead, the Triumph braked. Properly signaled. Wheeled into a gravel driveway, stopping before a wrought iron gate set in a ten-foot-high brick wall.

Angel lightly tapped our brakes. "Shit. Now what?"

"Keep going. We're just traffic driving past. They don't know they've been followed or Gearson would have initiated some sort of evasive maneuver before coming here."

We sailed past. The gate was opening automatically, revealing the vast green acreage surrounding a sprawling house on a hill, and then we were past the driveway.

Angel said, "Do you think Jimi's in there?"

"The hell if I know. Whoever and whatever is in there has money to back them up and plenty of it."

"That's what it's all about, isn't it? All they want is their fucking money and to get it they don't mind destroying human being. God, I hope he's all right."

"Me too. Pull over there behind those bushes. Kill the engine."

Angel steered us in behind the brush, braking to a stop beside the wall, nosing the Toyota's front end in far enough so as to effectively conceal the vehicle from passing motorists.

"And now?"

I eased open my door. "I didn't see a gate guard. Their security is nonexistent. Amateurs. You wait here."

"Like hell." She eased her door open. "I'm staying with you, fella."

"No, you're not. I've got enough to keep me occupied. I don't need to be covering your sweet ass, too."

"Thanks for the compliment but I can take care of myself. You think they grow us gals quiet and meek back in Lubbock?"

"I don't want to find out. Don't debate me on this, Angel. I'm going in, you're staying here."

"I'm not debating you. I'm stating a fact." She lifted a foot to indicate her Converse sneakers. "I even came dressed to go sneaking. You've taken on a partner for this run and I say we stop talking about it."

I said, "Okay, let's do it."

27

———

TIME CRAWLS.

Bandy has tightened the knots of the clothesline binding Jimi to the chair. After the escape attempt, Bandy seethed with anger.

He called someone on the telephone. "The fucker tried to make a break for it, G. That's right. No, he won't be going anywhere for awhile. He's tied up like a Christmas turkey, ready for slicing if he wants to try any more funny business. You call money man and tell him what happened but that old Bandy's got everything under control. All right then. You're still coming out? Ah, you and your women. That stuff will cost you your life, G. All right, all right. Just be here."

Bandy hung up the phone and had flung himself upon the couch, pretending Jimi wasn't there.

Jimi said, "Bandy, who's the money man? That's Gearson you were talking to. Who's paying you guys to do this?"

"Shut up, Jimi."

"Is it my own manager? Did Mike Jeffrey set this up? Squeeze me dry until there isn't anything left and throw me to the wolves after cheating me blind?"

Now, thinking about it, Bandy slouches lower on the couch. "Forget it, Jimi. Just bloody forget it and let's get through this, what say?

He doesn't expect a reply, and he doesn't get one.

He slips in and out of consciousness, partly from being slapped upside the head and partly because, being tied to a kitchen chair, there isn't a whole lot a man could do except sleep or listen to the monotonous drone of the television. At one point he managed to persuade Bandy to let him have a couple of tokes on the hash pipe Bandy kept smoking. Bandy did not untie Jimi's arms this time but held the pipe to Jimi's lips with one hand and a lighter flame to its bowl with the other. Bandy similarly fed him a couple sips of beer.

With the TV set droning on interminably, his thoughts turn inward. He reflects not too much on what will happen. No one is going to kill him. He's the goose that lays all their golden eggs. He'll be okay. He'll survive this. It's the people and circumstances that have brought him to this, tied to a chair while he smokes dope with a dude who's threatened to break his fingers. How did he ever wind up in such a point in time and space?

He considers Monika. He likes having a foxy blonde on his arm when he goes clubbing. Monika has a tender heart beneath the sophisticated veneer she sometimes works too hard at maintaining. Too often her insecurities make her a real drag to be around. She likes to cause a scene.

Only a few days before they had been walking down

King's Road when a man in a chauffeured Bentley, with two women companions, rolled down his window and, recognizing Jimi and full of good spirit, had invited them to tea. Jimi said why not, despite Monika's reproachful glance, and they had followed the Bentley with Monika yapping in his ear the whole time about how she didn't like strangers and how she wanted to go back to her flat. But this was exactly the sort of spontaneous adrenaline rush he had lived his entire life by.

Turned out the young man was the son of an English lord. His opulent home was lavishly decorated in a Middle Eastern style. Jimi felt immediately comfortable seated on pillows, surrounded by grandeur, drinking first a spot of tea, then smoking hash and then drinking wine. But it wasn't long before Monika started making her mood known, becoming agitated because too little of the conversation involved her. This led to an ugly scene. She stormed out of the house. Jimi went after her. Yelling in the street. She called him a fucking pig. It was embarrassing as hell. She passed out in the passenger seat as he drove them back to her place. She had mumbled drunken apologies and pleas for forgiveness. She fell into bed, and awakened all apologetic and tearful. He heard of the troubled child that lived within her. Then she drew him in with her warm embrace and those gentle ways that he did like about her.

That was Monika.

He returns his attention to his surroundings because Bandy suddenly sits bolt upright and is reaching to turn up the volume of the TV, which is broadcasting a news report. The announcer is saying something about Scotland Yard investigating a homicide. Jimi concentrates on the screen.

They're showing a photograph of Sydney Blanchard. The camera draws back to show a well-coifed woman reporter who goes on to say that a suspect is being sought by the police in the woman's murder, an American serviceman on leave who has also been linked to the murders earlier this morning in a pub near Trafalgar Square. The anchor man moves on to another story.

It's like cold water being splashed in Jimi's face. His mind is instantly clear.

"Bandy, what do you know about that? Did you know Sydney was dead?"

Bandy continues to stare at the screen. "I did not. It seems that people have been keeping things from me."

"Damn man, did you kill Sydney?"

Bandy gets up. Crosses to the television. The TV goes black and silent.

"Don't talk crazy, mate. The girl was alive when you and I left her last night so you know it wasn't me what done it. Bloody hell. I've got things to find out."

Bandy clunks his beer bottle down and picks up the telephone. He dials from memory.

Jimi says, "That's right, call Gearson. See what he's got to say."

There's the sound of a car horn beeping.

Bandy laughs. He sets the phone aside.

"Don't have to call him. He's here, ready to relieve me right on schedule."

Jimi says, "So that's your story? You had nothing to do with Sydney's murder? The last time I saw her, she just wanted to be alone with me. She offered me a port in the storm. I can't believe she's dead."

Bandy said, "Best to mind our own business is the creed I live my life by. It's healthier that way. As for Sydney, well, Bandy McGuire has done some evil, despicable things in his life and I'll pay for them when my time comes but I ain't yet murdered no young girl child like her and I never could. Now shut up, Jimi. Gearson might not go so easy on you."

Jimi focuses on the turmoil within. A beautiful life, smothered. Snuffed out. Questions that burn for answers. Where is Soldier?

He wishes he could be more like Soldier. Jimi's war rages within himself, not the warfare that had hardened and toughened Soldier. Soldier is a human fighting machine, turned loose in London. Yeah, it would be nice to be more like Soldier instead of being a drug-addled, so-called musical genius who spends more time squandering his talent on dope and meaningless sex with strangers than reaching his artistic potential.

The brittle laughter of an inebriated woman reaches his ears and then Bandy steps aside to make way for Gearson and the chick with him. Gearson is his usual slick, swaggering self. Greased back hair and Elvis-style tinted aviator glasses. The woman with him is hot, tall and curvy with shoulder-length black hair. Impossibly high stiletto heels accentuate her figure.

Gearson says, "Well well, looks like you've got him done up right, Bandy." The rhythm of his speech matches his looks. Short and snappy. "Any more trouble?"

"Naw. No more trouble."

The woman giggles. "Hey, it's Jimi Hendrix."

Jimi says, "Well hello there, sugar. Welcome to the party. Do me a favor, will you? Call the police."

She giggles again and says, "Oooh this is cool, G. You didn't tell me—"

Gearson says, "Shut up, Raven. Sit until I tell you otherwise."

"Yes, daddy." Raven positions herself on the edge of an armchair.

Jimi says, "It makes perfect sense, G. You were the guy driving the car when Bandy snatched me, weren't you?"

"You catch on real quick, Jimi."

"This is jive, man. What's kidnapping me and holding me hostage supposed to prove?

Bandy says, "Gear, what's this about murder? The telly just said that Sydney Blanchard was murdered. You know anything about that?"

"Relax. We're totally in the clear on that." Gearson laughs in Jimi's direction. "You're the one who needs to fix an alibi. Everyone at Ronnie Scott's saw you leave with her last night. Ducked out on your own girlfriend."

Jimi says, "You're not going to kill me, so what the hell are you guys doing this for?"

Bandy quickly says, "I didn't tell him nothing, G."

Gearson says, "I'll tell you this much, Jimi. We're being paid to do a job—pick you up and bring you here and keep you here until we're told otherwise. We're being paid good bread to do it and if you ever go to the authorities about it, it will be your word against ours."

Gearson says, "It's business, Jimi, plain and simple. You knew we were a tough crowd when you came to us for help."

"You were a friend of Bandy's," says Jimi. "He's Angel

McGuire's ex. I needed get-by money while I dodged my lawyers, so you fronted for me. I told you I'd get you the money! I thought we buried the hatchet when I came by your place with that bag of reefer."

"Stop it," says Gearson. "This ain't about that anyway."

"Jeffrey's behind it," says Jimi. "Don't tell me he ain't. That dude thinks he's so mysterioso, flits about behind the scenes like a shadow, but he ain't nothing but a thief in the night and if you're his boys, you'll get the shaft too."

Bandy yawns and scratches his belly. "This here talk is way over my pay grade. He's all yours, G. I'm off duty. Anyone want a beer?"

Jimi says, "It's a power play. Before long some of Jeffrey's guys are going to show up and you bozos will hand me over but I'm supposed to tell the tabloids it was a heroic rescue by Mike but it's stupid. I see through that and so will anyone else."

Gearson brightens and claps his hands together twice. "Enough. Bandy, go get us those beers, and put on some music. It's like a morgue in here. What have we got?"

Bandy crosses to the rows of record albums lining shelves near the stereo.

"Got everything, G. Great collection." He studies titles. "Stones. Jefferson Airplane. Soul music. New one by the Beatles."

"Anything by Jimi Hendrix?"

Jimi says, "Aw shit, you guys. Come on..."

Bandy extracts an LP from the shelf. "Jimi Hendrix. *Are You Experienced?*"

"Well, put it on the turntable. Play it loud." Gearson leers at Raven. "This album's about you, honey."

She says in a hesitant voice, "G., don't be kidding me. Be nice."

"I am nice. And you're experienced, showing off everything you've got down at the Tit Tat. Get up on that table there. When the music starts, you give me and Bandy a private show, hear? Jimi, you can watch too."

Bandy looks and licks his lips. "Now you're talking."

Raven shrinks away from them. "But that's my job, at the club. I'm not working now."

Bandy snickers. "Bitch says she's off duty, G. You let her get away with talking back like that?"

Raven is wringing her hands. "Please, G., don't make me dance like that here, in front of them. I don't want to do that. It would be humiliating."

Gearson says, "Yeah, I know. Bandy, start the fucking music and get me a bloody beer."

"Right you are, G."

Heavily amplified opening guitar riff to *Foxy Lady*.

Bandy disappears into the kitchen.

Gearson says to Jimi, "You're going to love this. You love these Brit birds, don't you, boy?" He delivers Raven an open palm slap across the face that is loud enough to be heard above the music. "No one's asking you, bright eyes. Now get up on that damn table. I want to see you move. And put something extra into it for Jimi."

28

THE FIRST TIME I COMMITTED AN ACT OF VIOLENCE AGAINST another human being was in the wilderness, eight miles from the small country town where I was raised with what they call good Christian values.

I spent a lot of time on my own, by choice more than circumstance. I could have spent more time with my dad and uncles when they went on fishing trips or shot the bull getting pleasantly drunk around the barbecue grill while the women toiled in the kitchen, but I preferred finding a quiet corner somewhere and reading, freeing my mind to travel beyond my sphere of experience rather than interacting with the life I was living. I was a loner, but never lonely.

I delved into the lore of what are now called Native Americans but who in those days we just called Indians, the thankless legacy of a clueless explorer in Spanish service who sailed the ocean blue in 1492 and got lost, "discovered" America but thought he was in India. So to us they were Indians, and their legends and ways inspired me to spend time tracking game in the woods near where I grew up. I made no secret of this pastime but had trouble finding anyone who wanted to join me when I began hunting with a bow and arrow.

My parents weren't exactly supportive of these forays into the wilderness of low hills that surrounded our town, but with me reading science fiction novels by the ton around the house day and night—everything from Asimov to Zelazny—they came to regard my outdoor activities as some indication that maybe I did have an interest in the world around me after all. Mom and Dad became even more accepting the day, when I was a teenager, that I drove into the yard in my pickup truck with a deer I'd killed in season with my bow and arrow. We ate mighty fine that winter.

It was a different world for a teenager back in those days. Only three stations on the TV. No sex, at least not with someone else. No drugs. Listening to rock and roll records turned up so loud that your parents threatened to ground you and going to the Friday night sock hop in the gym was about as crazy as it got. I was virtually invisible to the sports jock strata of high school society, though I was popular enough with most of the kids in my class and with my teachers. I was a "good kid" who preferred spending his time alone, either reading a book or stalking through the woods...

The deer was a twelve-point, white-tailed buck that reached seven feet at the tip of his antlers. I can still see those antlers brushing the grass of a meadow as he grazed idly, occasionally pausing to survey the area, to make sure that he was alone.

He hadn't spotted me. I'd spent the better part of the

day tracking him with my bow and arrow. I wore buck-skin shirt, pants and moccasins. My hair was tied back with a leather headband, and slung across my shoulder was a quiver full of arrows.

The chill of Fall whispered on a pine-scented breeze. The buck looked up instinctively, senses on full alert at the whisper of the breeze.

I fired my first arrow.

It took the animal in the side. The buck reeled on its hind legs and then, with a desperate last gasp for life, fell over dead. I remember approaching that buck and standing over him in admiration. Squatting down, I stroked the animal respectfully. Then I drew my Bowie knife from its sheath on my hip and started to field dress the animal. After the first cut, I put my finger into the belly of that deer and tasted its blood, and then I ceremoniously streaked the blood on my face as if it were war paint.

This would have taken some tall explaining to Mom and Dad, but at the moment that wasn't important.

Approaching footsteps. Two hunters in camouflage fatigues emerged from the tree line. Overweight, middle-aged city dwellers gone hunting, but hardly at home here in my world. One of them tripped over a rock. With a curse he fell flat on his face, his rifle slipping from his hands. He picked himself up, still cursing, and retrieved the rifle, then leaned against a tree, doing his best to catch his breath. His partner was doubled over, laughing at him. Then they saw me.

I continued to field dress the deer.

They approached. Meaty faces, flushed from drink,

exertion and sunburn. They reeked of whiskey fumes. Their glazed eyes fell on the deer.

"Nice work, kid. We've been tracking him all day, so we're claiming this kill."

I didn't know what to do. I'd never even considered a run-in like this. I continued gutting the animal as if I hadn't heard a thing.

The second hunter snarled a curse. "Get back to your reservation, boy."

He tried to deliver a kick to my head with one of his size twelve boots. I got an arm up in time to block the blow to my head but he caught me hard enough to knock me over, separating me from my knife. They then proceeded like I wasn't there. Like I was trash, cast aside and forgotten. They drew their knives and stooped over the halfway eviscerated animal to continue what I had begun.

I said, "This is *my* kill."

A war cry sprang from me. Their eyes became wide saucers at happened came next and to tell you the truth, I don't know where it came from. It was like nothing I'd ever felt before, growing up as a geek loner in a normal rural household. But somehow in that moment a warrior burst to life inside of me with the roar of a tiger, summoned forth I guess by this confluence of aggression, the smell of blood, the blood of my kill smeared across my face, and these pathetic excuses for men who thought they could push people around and simply take with impunity.

My first arrow whistled through the air and struck the first hunter in the thigh. The drunken fool seemed to take a moment to believe this was happening, then he lurched over, gasping for air like a beached whale. The other one panicked and nearly fell over, reaching for his rifle. Another whizzing sound pierced the air and my razor-sharp arrow slammed into his thigh, toppling him. He grabbed at the arrow protruding from him. Both men were crying out in shock and pain.

I withdrew from the desecrated kill.

I went home and acted as if nothing had happened.

29

I COULD REACH THE TOP OF THE STONE WALL FROM THE roof of the Toyota. I drew myself up and, crouched there and bracing myself, I extended a hand down to where Angel stood on the car roof, reaching up to me with both hands. We made contact and she made it easy with a little leap and then she was there on the wall with me. She stretched out beside me.

From the direction of the main building, the vague sound of recorded rock & roll, being played at a very loud volume, carried to us on the quiet suburban afternoon.

Angel and I and dropped to the ground inside the wall. We landed on bushes damp from the earlier rain. The bushes didn't crackle under our impact but crumpled wetly.

She was no Special Forces op but the woman was game, shadowing me as best she could. As long as things didn't get hairy, as in people brandishing guns, she should be all right. And if the deal did go bad? Well, that was the risk we ran.

A dog began barking viciously from somewhere nearby, coming closer by the second accompanied by the thudding of big paws. Then the sleek, muscular dog was racing at us and launched itself at me.

I twisted to one side. Its muscular, furry bulk brushed past me close enough to for me to hear the wicked snap of teeth closing on air, its guttural snarl in my ear. The dog sailed right into the same bushes we had landed on, snarling, clawing to break free of the entangling branches. I drew the Colt and brought its barrel down across the animal's head.

The dog sagged, rallied for a moment as if it really wanted to recover, then collapsed, shivered with a little sound more like that of a cat, and did not move.

Angel gasped. "My God. Did you have to kill the poor dumb beast?"

I reached down, touched the dog's neck, felt the pulse. "He'll live."

"You wouldn't lie to me, would you, Soldier?"

"He's just taking an unexpected nap. He's in doggy dreamland probably chasing some fine bitches."

A pleasantly coarse chuckle. "You've got a naughty side too, don't you, mister?"

"Naughty? Haven't heard that word in years. Come on, let's do this ."

We advanced across the gentle upward slope of the property. The white Triumph was parked in front of a garage that was attached to the sprawling twin-level residence that dominated the property. An ugly, squat vehicle parked next to it looked like military surplus; a stripped-down Jeep painted OD green. We gained the side of a double garage, skirting the Triumph and the Jeep. The garage doors were closed but I could see the chrome of late model vehicles faintly through a line of glass windows.

The front door of the main house was further down. A door to the garage in this side of the house gave onto a walkway of individual octagonal stones along a path of gravel, bordered on either side by flower beds and tended lawn, a distance of several yards separating the house and the garage. There was no indication of a human presence anywhere except for the music thrumming relentlessly from inside the house, louder and recognizable now. Someone had a Jimi Hendrix album blaring on the stereo with the volume cranked to patent pending.

I said, "With the music booming in the house, they don't even know what happened with their dog."

"I see what you mean. No security."

"Let's hope that doesn't mean no Jimi."

"Stop being such a pessimist."

I nudged Angel with my elbow but she didn't need any encouragement. She was tense like a cat ready to spring. We hustled to the rear of the garage, where Angel crouched next to me.

I said, "Uh oh. Company."

A car, a Renault of recent vintage, had drawn to a stop before the wrought-iron front gate, clearly observed from our position although shrubbery near the garage would hopefully conceal us from anyone in the car. It paused, as the Triumph had, while the mechanized gate opened. The Renault tooled on through and came up the driveway to join the first two vehicles, blocked from our line of vision by the garage.

I gestured for Angel to hold her position, and then risked a squint around the corner.

A man strode purposefully from where he'd parked the Renault to the side door of the house.

I had seen him once before. The lobby of the sedate office building, just after he'd picked off Chet Daly and an unfortunate barmaid. His death defying leap from a second story window onto a double decker bus. The struggle on that bus, at each others' throat.

Yeah, I'd seen him before.

Mr. Brooks Brothers. He still wore the snappy black raincoat.

He reached the side door, opened a screen door, propped it open with a shoulder and gave the latch a try. Nothing. Locked. *So the idiots at least thought they had security covered.* My friend in the raincoat wasted about fourteen seconds, reaching for his keys. With a flick of his wrist, the door opened and he was inside.

Angel whispered, "Now what?"

I said, "Let's give it a ten count."

I had mentally clicked off eight when the music from inside stopped abruptly. The silence was startling.

Angel whispered, "Who the hell was that?"

"The guy I chased this morning. He's the shooter who killed Daly and that barmaid."

"Oh, my God…"

I said, "If Bandy works with Gearson, who does Gearson answer to?"

Angel shrugged. "Mike Jeffrey, maybe? This isn't exactly my circle of friends. Gearson is a lone wolf."

"My take is that your ex and Gearson are working this job for the CIA."

"You mean they brought Jimi here to set him up for the hit team?"

"I'm going into that house to find out. You stand clear."

"Soldier—"

I gestured with the .45. "Guns. They go off. People die."

"I grew up in Texas, dammit. I know when to duck."

What the hell was I supposed to do? I could have just KO-ed her with a sucker punch, but that didn't seem like a good idea. You can't always tell how long a person will remain unconscious. There were enough variables without someone semi-conscious stumbling into an armed confrontation.

I said, "Stay close to me then. If guns start going off, hit the deck and stay there."

"Hit the deck. Aye aye, captain."

"Sarcasm yet. Okay, set sail."

We broke cover from the garage and made for the side door of the house.

30

Despite his predicament, Jimi is having trouble taking his eyes off the girl they call Raven, who's down to a red satin slip and high heels, towering over the men from on top of the dining table, grinding sinuously to *Wild Thing.*

Then the dude with the black briefcase, wearing the black raincoat, storms into the room like the general catching a bunch of goldbricking privates. The ambiance changes as if a switch has been thrown.

Bandy does a double take right out of The Three Stooges, torn from watching Raven. He's more than half-drunk, so his reaction time is slow, stumbling a little in dragging himself off the couch where he's been slouched, sucking on a beer. The reaction of Gearson and Raven is equally comical except of course for the reality of Jimi remaining tied to a chair.

Gearson, the sharpie used to giving orders, scuttles to the stereo and lifts the phonograph needle from the album the instant the man in the black raincoat appears.

Raven continues dancing for several beats after the

music has ceased, her body undulating, suggestively carnal. When she realizes that the music has stopped, her eyes pop open. She spies the man in black.

"Who the hell are you?"

Gearson turns from the stereo.

"Button your lip, luv. Put some respect in your attitude. This is the boss man." He approaches the new arrival with a hand outstretched and a smile that is supposed to be welcoming but even from his vantage point, Jimi can see the queasy nervousness beneath Gearson's glibness. 'Welcome, Mr.—?"

The man ignores the outstretched hand.

"No names," he says between lips that do not seem to move, his voice pitched low and flat, more like the mechanized words of an automaton than of a living, breathing human. "I want this clean. No loose ends." Narrowed, cold eyes shift to Raven. "Who's she?"

Raven steps down from the table, retrieves the clothing she has discarded. Her eyes are wide orbs, her mouth a trembling crimson circle in features blanched albino white.

She says in a small, quavering little girl voice, "I don't know anything about this. I just tagged along." She looks hopefully at Gearson. "Really, I can go wait outside, G."

The man in black's narrowed eyes laser in on Gearson. "I'm asking you, numbnuts. Who is she?"

"She's nobody. She shakes her tail for tips at a club I run."

"Hey!" Raven's voice grew shrill with protest. "What do you mean, nobody? I thought you loved me."

Gearson ignored her. "I just brought her along for

some laughs to pass the time until you showed up. I thought that would be okay. She's just a dumb—"

"You were told to keep this quiet."

"I did keep the lid on tight, guvnor. Raven's the only one knows Jimi's being held here and she won't be telling nobody, will you, luv?"

Raven is hurriedly slipping back into her clothes. A frightened kid looking for a place to hide.

"I don't see nothing, I don't hear nothing, I don't know nothing. Honest!"

Jimi speaks up. "Well me, I'm seeing and I'm hearing plenty and if you're the boss man, dude, I want to know what's going on. Why am I here? This is kidnapping. Let me out of this damn chair."

The man in black says, "I'm afraid that will not be possible, Mr. Hendrix." He sets the briefcase on an end table next to a couch. He snaps open the briefcase, his back to them. When he turns, he holds a sealed bottle of Scotch in one hand and a small plastic orange bottle of pills in the other. He extends the whiskey bottle to Bandy. "You, get over here. I want you to pour this whiskey down his throat." He indicates Jimi.

Bandy blinks a couple of times and shakes his head once as if he hasn't heard correctly.

"You want me to *what?*" He lumbers over and takes the bottle and goes about breaking the seal.

The man in black hands Gearson the bottle of pills.

"Here. You pour these down his throat."

Gearson takes the pill bottle and reads the prescription label. He shakes the bottle, listens to the rattle with dawning confusion mixed with concern.

"Here now, wait a mo. The whole bottle, you say? Say

guvnor, what are we trying to do here exactly? I thought we was snagging Jimi because Mike Jeffrey wanted to stage his rescue or some such."

Jimi said, "There you go. I knew this was all about Mike Jeffrey being up to no good."

The man in the black raincoat spoke to Bandy and Gearson. "Mr. Jeffrey's plan was appropriated. Mr. Jeffrey was persuaded to step aside. Now do as you're told, both of you. You've been paid so get busy. Follow orders."

Gearson holds up the small orange bottle. "But this many pills, they'd kill a horse."

With the whiskey bottle uncapped, Bandy takes a long pull from it. Makes a face.

"Krikey, G. don't you get it? That's what the guvnor's paying us for. To kill Jimi Hendrix."

31

WE REACHED THE OUTSIDE DOOR TOGETHER. I GESTURED
for Angel to remain in place. I dodged to crouch on the
opposite side of the doorway. I gestured again. Angel
reached across and held the screen door open so I could
try the latch. The latecomer had left it unlocked. I nudged
the door inward.

Wooden steps led up to where I saw the bottom half of
a pantry and part of a kitchen table. The murmur of
conversation, not from the kitchen but from beyond it,
close by. We went up those steps and entered the kitchen.
Dirty dishes were stacked in the sink. A waste basket was
overflowing with empty beer bottles. More empties on
the table. We light-footed it across the kitchen and then
soundlessly started inching our way, side by side with our
backs to the wall, toward the conversation taking place at
the end of a short hallway.

There's a precognitive sixth sense quiver that can
wrinkle the psyche and make the hairs stand up on the
back of your neck. *I shouldn't have allowed Angel to accom-*

pany me. I thought of Sydney Blanchard. Nice kid. Nice and dead. Angel was a fine woman. She wasn't ready to join the real angels quite yet. I didn't like having a noncombatant shadow me into a situation no matter how good she was at knowing when to duck. I regretted my decision but it was too late now.

The voices were heating up. That the music had been abruptly silenced upon his arrival indicated that the late-comer was the one calling the shots.

Matters of import were being heatedly discussed.

32

_____

It was the strangest thing, thought Jimi. Reality was heightened with a crisp clarity because they were talking about killing *him*.

All his troubles, all of his pissing and moaning, but did he really want his life to end? They were talking about *him*. He heard every inflection of their voices, every nuance between them from Bandy's dawning awareness to the man in black, standing there with a presence that exuded complete authority and command.

Is this what it's like, just before you die? You remember every detail so clearly because they're the last images and sounds you won't remember at all but will leave behind. They were talking about *him!* He tried to speak but the words got tangled in his throat.

He cleared his throat. "Look, you fellas, I don't know what the hell is going on here but, dig, man, we can work this out, right? Get hip to that," he said to the man in black. "Don't do this. Make sure I *don't* die and I'll get you anything you want."

The man said to Gearson and Bandy, "When you're done, we'll moving the body to another location. It will look natural. Drug overdose, maybe a suicide. Everyone knows his situation. They're expecting it to happen."

Jimi couldn't understand why he should think of someone else at a time like this. He said to the man in black, "You killed Sydney Blanchard."

A sneer from tight lips that barely moved. "You're betting wrong right up to the end, loser," said the man in black. "I got blood on my hands today but I didn't kill that one." He snarled at Gearson and Bandy. "All right, you two. Do it."

Blind panic. Jimi glanced frantically from Bandy to Gearson.

"You guys aren't going to do this, are you? Come *on!* This can't be happening. You guys wouldn't do this to me. Look, turn on him. I'll make it worth your while. Bandy, we've partied together, man. Gearson, jeez, guy. This is murder. You'll never get away with it. They'll get you. Don't do it!"

The man in black said, "They'll do it." He spoke to Bandy and Gearson in a neutral tone. "And that will seal the deal between us, gentlemen. You will never divulge what happened here because you are a part of it."

Bandy said, with a hint of alcohol-fueled belligerence, "And if we don't?"

"Then you will not leave this house alive."

Jimi said, "Come on, you guys. It's me, Jimi." He knew he was pleading and he didn't care. "You're going to kill me for money, are you?"

Gearson said, in a strangely calm and rational voice, "I reckon that's the only reason we would kill you, Jimi. You heard the man. It's gone beyond us being mates. It's our survival, me and Bandy's."

"But what if he's lying? What if he's going to kill you right after you kill me?"

Bandy gulped audibly. "Sorry, Jimi. You see how it is. Okay, G. Let's get it over with."

Gearson braced his knee against Jimi's chest. In one hand he held the open bottle of pills. His other hand reached for Jimi's face.

"Now open wide, Jimi. It'll be like going to sleep. The best way to die."

Jimi clamped his mouth shut. Gearson's fingers tried to pry the mouth open.

"Come on, Bandy, help out!"

"I'm sorry, Jimi," said Bandy in a thick voice.

Holding the whiskey bottle in one hand, he used the other to grasp Jimi's long hair and yank his head back, trying to assist Gearson in prying open Jimi's mouth.

And the wild thing was that although Jimi's hold-onto-life reflex would not allow him to open his mouth no matter how roughly their grubby fingers pried, he could feel himself slipping into a strange sort of peaceful acceptance. Lucid thought weirdly possessed him. He had clawed his way through hard work and sacrifice to the top of the rock pile, and for what? To be drunk onstage, to be playing his music with contempt for those people who had paid to see him, with the buzzards fighting over everything he earned? Death was a release to be embraced, not feared.

A sudden anguished cry caught everyone's attention.

Bandy and Gearson reacted with a start. Whiskey

sloshed across Jimi's chest. Pills dribbled onto him from the prescription and then onto the floor.

Raven. Clothed, disheveled. Glazed eyes and gaping mouth, wild with comprehension and revulsion.

"Wait! You can't do this! You can't kill Jimi Hendrix!"

The man in black said, "Too bad you had to be here."

"But you can't just kill somebody! You've got to stop. You're all crazy!"

Raven started toward the front door.

The man in black drew from his briefcase a pistol that had been fitted with a bulbous silencer at the end of its muzzle. He fired once, twice, three times. Little spits of sound and flame lanced from the muzzle. Little splats as the bullets struck Raven and dropped her.

Stark silence.

Gearson whispered, "Holy mother of God."

The man faced Gearson and Bandy, not lowering the pistol.

"I said this had to be clean. She was a nobody, you said so yourself. You can dispose of her after you're done with him." He gestured with the pistol at Jimi. "Now get to work."

33

I stepped from the hallway and the movement itself caught the peripheral vision of the man in black. Gunsmoke fumes lingered in the air with the stink of something else; the smell of violent death, a sickly sweet, nauseous smell.

The body of a woman sprawled in a pool of spreading blood.

Gearson and a big lug who could only be Bandy McGuire, towering over a cringing Jimi, tied to a chair, twisting his head to avoid the whiskey and pills they were trying to force down him.

The man in the black raincoat pivoted, tracking his pistol toward me and Angel, who I knew would be right behind me.

I pumped one, two, three rounds into him. The boom of those three reports was loud. He stumbled back, landing face-up, his surprised eyes wide open, sprawled across Raven's body, their blood rapidly spreading together across the floor beneath them. The man in black did not move but to be on the safe side, I kicked the silenced revolver well away from him.

Bandy sidled away from Jimi. He held onto the whiskey bottle.

"Well if this don't beat all." His attention shifted from me to Angel, who stood at my side. "Woman, you pick the oddest times to show up. What the bloody hell—?"

Gearson dropped the pill bottle and hurled himself at my knees. He took me down. I heard a gasp of dismay from Angel. My head connected with the hardwood floor, right on the spot where I'd been sapped twice. A jolt of pain shot through me but this time I didn't lose consciousness. But Gearson had me down, a crazy, frenzied look in his eyes. We struggled over the gun, one of his hands at my throat, cutting off my wind, pinning me to the floor. I started seeing pinpoints of light and reality grew dim around the edges. His other hand wrestled with my wrist that kept trying to aim the .45 at him. My free hand clamped his throat in an attempt to crush his larynx.

Jimi shouted, "Watch your left! Your head!"

He could only be referring to Bandy. I jerked my head to the side just in time to miss a killing kick from Bandy's brogan that missed caving my skull in by inches.

Angel said, "Let him alone, you big stupid bully."

Scuffling from the direction of Bandy and Angel. A smashing of the whiskey bottle.

I had to make quick work of Gearson, who should have just backed off and walked away. I angled a knee and delivered him a short, sharp kick to the groin that made him gasp, weakening his grasp on my throat and on the wrist of my gun hand, allowing me to place the muzzle of the .45 under his jaw. I squeezed the trigger and blew his face all over the ceiling. I rolled away and came to my feet.

Jimi gave a nervous laugh, more than a hint of hysteria in his voice. "Well doggone if it ain't the cavalry to the rescue!"

Bandy had cornered his ex-wife. He had the broken whiskey bottle by its neck, waving its jagged edges in front of Angel's face.

Angel held herself erect before him, not backing down an inch.

She said, "Bandy, you're a fucking idiot."

I pointed the .45 at his head.

"Step back, idiot, and drop the bottle."

Angel said, "Do it, Bandy. He'll kill you, I swear to God he will. I know you're drunk but do this for me. I don't want to see you die. You can do that on your own damn time. Do what he said."

The tableau held like that for a handful of heartbeats. That razor edge moment of truth when any damn thing can happen.

Then he stepped away from Angel. But when he turned to me, he was holding onto the bottle like a weapon.

Jimi said, "Bandy, Jesus man, let it go. Put it down."

Bandy threw aside the bottle with a grunt of disgust.

"Soldier. What the bloody hell kind of name is that?" Bandy lurched over to where the body of the man in the black raincoat was splayed across the body of the woman. He said, "Poor Raven. She was a sweet kid, Angel."

Angel said, "I know she was, Bandy." A tender voice that sounded more motherly than ex-wifey.

Bandy gestured to me. "What about him? What's his next move?"

I hadn't lowered the .45 from its bead on his forehead.

"Did you kill Sydney?"

He blinked. "Not me, guvnor, I swear!"

Angel said, "Soldier, he's a dumb stupid oaf and I wish I'd never met him."

Bandy mumbled, "Gee, thanks a lot."

She concluded, "But please don't kill him."

Bandy said to Jimi, "Hey, I'm sorry, mate. I truly am. I don't know what came over me. I guess the kill lust was on me. Here, let me untie you from that chair."

Jimi said, "Fuck you, Bandy. You were going to kill me, you son of a bitch. Jesus man, you were going to *kill* me! Angel, get me loose from this damn chair."

"In a flash, Jimi."

She went to the kitchen, returned with a carving knife, and methodically went to work on the clothesline that bound Jimi to the chair.

Bandy said, "So what about me then? I fell in with bad company, I did. I didn't know any of this was going to happen. Honest, Angel. Honest, Jimi. God's truth."

I said, "I'm the one you've got to convince, not them. You were at Sydney's last night right before she was murdered."

"Right, but it wasn't me done her in! I was just luring Jimi out to the street so me and Gearson could trundle him away and I sure as bloody hell didn't know we had signed up to kill anybody. "

I lowered the pistol.

I said, "I don't think Gearson knew it either. He pulled a dumb play just now, going for me like he did."

"Then you're going to let me live?"

"For now. But I don't trust you, Bandy. You're too docile all of a sudden."

"That's because I want to cooperate. Make up for what I've done. You can trust me."

"From here on out, stay out of my way and stay away from Jimi."

I swung the .45 up and around, hard and fast. Its barrel cracked him upside the head. He made a funny nasal exhalation. His knees buckled and he collapsed. He started snoring.

Angel had finished untying Jimi. They joined me where I stood surrounded by fresh corpses.

Angel looked down at Bandy. "Did you have to do that?"

I bent down and revealed Bandy's ankle gun, another pistol worn at the small of his back and a knife hidden up his sleeve.

First she uttered a short snort of a laugh. Then she said to his unconscious form, "Ignoramus," and delivered Bandy a healthy kick in the ribs that did not interfere with his snoring.

34

LIGHT SHOWERS RESUMED. THE STREETS WERE SLICK BLACK mirrors reflecting countless headlights, the afternoon rush hour traffic growing heavier by the minute.

Angel backed the Toyota into a parking space at the curb, one block from the corner pharmacy where her place occupied the second floor. Not much had been said by any of us during the drive. I rode shotgun. Jimi sat in back.

Angel killed the engine. "Give me ten minutes to clear the place out. It's a crash pad but it's *my* crash pad and it's run to my mood. Hopefully no one will leave angry, but they do leave when I ask them to. The alley light will be on if it's all clear. If not, lay low, find a telephone and call me."

"Lay low," I repeated. "We've turned you into a gun moll." She touched my cheek with her fingertips and we traded a moist, warmly vibrant, intimate kiss. I said, "Be careful."

From the back seat, Jimi said in a quiet, shaky voice,

"And stay clear of the cops, especially that damn Hudberry."

Angel said, "It'll be okay." She caught my eye as she opened her car door and added, "Try not to kill anybody."

"I'll do my best."

We watched her walk away. She was worth watching, well-rounded poetry in motion. I lost sight of her for a moment among the flow of pedestrians hurrying along the sidewalk, then spotted her again when she entered the street door just short of the pharmacy. Jimi said, "We can't let anything happen to her."

I said, "We won't."

He'd mumbled the couple of times during the drive in when Angel inquired how he was doing, but he didn't look good. Jimi looked high, but for once not on drugs. Post-traumatic shock. I'd seen it plenty of times and hoped that this would be a minor case, so I was glad to hear him speak.

He gave one of his short, nervous laughs. "Damn brother, you were spectacular, what you did. Man, I about lost it in my pants."

I said, "I settle my debts. I've owed you ever since that night at Thelma Lou's pool hall."

"You think there's any way they can trace us to what just happened?"

"Bandy was a witness, but he'll have his reasons for not talking if the cops pick him up. My guess is that the house they used was leased under a false name or the residents weren't about so they just moved in and made themselves at home. It could be weeks or months before those bodies are found."

"I'm glad we left the gate open so that dog could get away."

I said, "It might be over for the dog but it's not over for us. There's questions that still need answers."

"I'm hip. Like who killed Sydney. Do you know the name of that guy in the black raincoat?"

"No."

"He shot that poor girl like he was swatting a fly. He said something about there was blood on his hands, but that he didn't kill Sydney."

"He killed a guy named Chet Daly; popped him this morning with a high-powered rifle."

Jimi said, "I never seen anyone die a violent death before, y'know?" The shock was wearing off, rendering him half-dazed, half-wired. "And seeing three go down in one fell swoop, boom boom, boom, well, holy shit is all I can say."

I felt edgy.

I said, "What about Mike Jeffrey?"

That sharpened his attention. "You think he killed Sydney?"

"Let's talk about this kidnapping first. Would Jeffrey be behind something like that?"

Jimi fumbled to get a cigarette lit. I reached over and steadied his wrist for him. When he got it going, he took a few nervous puffs.

"He had some PR stunt in mind that would make him look like a hero instead of like the thieving son of a bitch he is. From what they said before you showed up, Jeffrey set the deal up but neglected to tell Gearson and Bandy that the Brooks Brothers cat had taken over."

Up the street, ragtag hippie kids, singles and a few

couples started leaving the crash pad, straggling off in different directions.

Jimi said, "I sure hope Monika isn't up there, waiting on us at Angel's. She likes to know where I am and that ain't always such a good thing."

"When you see her, I'd just as soon you left out the part about me shooting two guys to death."

Jimi took a last drag on the cigarette like it was a joint and flipped the butt out the window. "Don't worry, my brother. I'll tell her I was shacked up with a broad."

"You don't think that might rile her up some?"

"Sure, it will but that's a fire I can put out. People dead from gunshot wounds, that's something else again, ain't it?"

Ten minutes elapsed. We left the car and hurried through the drizzling mist to the alley. I thought of happy, healthy, adventurous, alive Sydney Blanchard, squealing her sporty Austin Healy four-seater to a stop at the mouth of this alley yesterday to offer us a ride. The light was on over the second-story rear entrance.

Angel was waiting for us at the head of the outside stairs, standing inside with the door open for us.

"We're alone." She closed the door after us and latched the three deadbolt locks. "I've got some tea going. Herbal, to calm the nerves."

We shambled after her, into the dining area. Jimi and I sat at a large wooden table.

Jimi fumbled a cigarette into his mouth and this time managed to light it all by himself. "I'm mighty grateful to you, Angel. You put your life on the line for me when you busted in like that with Soldier."

Angel busied herself preparing the tea.

"Heck Jimi, we're just lucky that one of the three of us didn't stop a bullet. I'm sort of getting a soft spot in my heart for this Soldier friend of yours."

She was putting up a good front but breathing was shallow. Sometimes it takes awhile to sink in…

Jimi said, "Uh, Angel, uh, you got anything to smoke?"

Angel said, "Coming up," and reached into her purse.

Jimi said, "You get high, man?"

"Got nothing against it. Tried it a few times but never in a combat zone and until this mess is over, that's what London is for me."

So there we sat, sipping tea, listening to the traffic sounds drifting up from the street. Jimi and Angel smoked several bowls of what smelled like Grade A hash. I did my best not to inhale the fumes.

Jimi said, "I hope to never go through anything like today ever again."

Angel said, "That damn Bandy. Thanks for sparing him, Soldier."

"Let's hope we don't regret it."

She took a final toke on the glass pipe to confirm that the bowl was dead, and clinked it against the big glass ash tray that sat in the center of the table.

"So what about Sydney? Who killed her?"

I said, "I need to speak with Hudberry."

"That's no answer."

Jimi sat up straight in his chair. "It's plumb foolish, is what that is. Stay away from that copper, man, I'm telling you."

"Think about it," I said. "Am I supposed to report to my next duty station in Germany with Scotland Yard wanting me for murder? Soon as I show up they'll throw me in the brig and extradite me back here before I've eaten my first bratwurst. I can't just walk away from this."

Angel looked from one of us to the other.

"I can see why you two became friends."

"We both dig music," said Jimi. "Soldier's got soul to burn."

"I see that. It's also a case of opposites attract. Soldier and Jimi. Jimi and Soldier. You two represent the *yin* and *yang* of maleness."

I couldn't hold down a grin. "Hash brings out the psychoanalyst in you."

"Honey, I'm just getting started. I'd like each of you men to consider the other."

Jimi gave the tip of his cigarette a perplexed look. "What do you mean?"

She said, "Soldier and Jimi. A couple of souls as lost as any of the kids who end up on my doorstep looking for a safe harbor. Think about it. Each of you won't find in yourself what the other one has. Soldier, if it were within my power I would bring the peace and grace of Jimi's spirit to your consciousness. Jimi, I would bring to you the sense of self and the strength that is the core of your friend."

Jimi said, "You're right. I could damn straight use some strength. Soldier, you've been off fighting a real war where's it's kill or be killed. Me? My war is inside my head."

Angel said, "It's not just the inside of your head, Jimi. You're a force impacting the world around you. We all are. We have to break out of the prison of our past conditioning. That's going to require a real big shift in the collective consciousness. But if we can change ourselves, we can change the world."

Jimi spoke through a cloud of cigarette smoke. "There's a dark force that tries to hold the people of the planet down."

Angel nodded. "Music liberates the collective spirit, and that will liberate the people. Your enemies know this and so they see you as a threat."

"I want a world without war," said Jimi. "Not wars on the map or wars inside of people themselves. Eliminate the boundaries. Create harmony." He broke eye contact and ginned nervously. "Listen to me beat my gums. Angel, you're just what your name says. I can't believe a guy like Bandy McGuire landed someone like you."

"He landed me but he couldn't keep me. He couldn't keep himself together, much less a relationship that meant anything. Jimi, please don't go down that road. You need to straighten out, bro," she said, "and get your life together."

He looked down and squashed out his cigarette butt in the ashtray. "I know that, earth mother."

"The world needs your music to inspire and as a catharsis and well hell, just because it's so damn *good*. And by the way, it's not just you two. Look at the whole hippy thing. Sure, I think we may have a shot at changing the world…so long as we stay sensitive to embrace love and strong enough to take on our enemies when love doesn't work." She turned to me. "Soldier, what does it feel like to kill a man?"

I took another sip of tea.

"It feels okay. After awhile with guys like those punks today it gets to be like taking out the trash. You don't look forward to it but it feels good to know the trash is gone from the house."

She rested her chin on her hand and studied me. Her eyes carried a tender message. "Now say something sensitive. Go on, I dare you."

"Stop it."

She grinned a Texas grin. "Go on. I double dog dare you."

"Okay, okay. Something sensitive. What? Something like, you're a fine woman of courage and compassion, Angel McGuire, and I'm grateful that we met?"

"Well dang, that's a mighty good start."

Jimi pushed his chair back from the table and got to his feet.

"Uh Angel, thanks for the buzz, really, but hey you two, I've got to get gone. Only way I can shake this vibe I'm carrying is to play my guitar, so that's what I'm going to do. But first I'd better stop by Monika's. After what I've been through, I aim to round up that woman of mine and my guitar and hit the town tonight, do some jamming."

Angel said, "She's not going to be happy with you, Jimi, for running out on her last night with Sydney."

"Damn, that seems a lifetime ago. I need me a shower. I need a change of clothes. Then I'm heading out."

I said, "Jimi, just one thing, and this goes for both of you. What happened this afternoon . . . it never happened."

Angel nodded her agreement. "Bandy will keep his mouth shut and be glad he got out alive."

Jimi said, "It never happened. I'm good with that. Yeah, it never happened."

Angel said, "Jimi, do you want a ride? I can drive you to Monika's."

"Naw, I'm okay. I'll catch a cab." He scribbled an address on a pad of paper on the table between us. "Here's the address of a private club. There'll be some jamming tonight. I'll be there."

I said, "I should go with you now, Jimi."

"Naw, I don't think I have anything to worry about after this afternoon."

"You could be right."

"This club isn't open to the public so I'll leave your name on the guest list, all right? Come on down, Soldier. You too, Angel."

I said to Angel, "Are you free tonight?"

"I'm free, big man. But, Jimi, you don't look so good. Why don't you crash here for a couple of hours? As my Uncle Chester would say, you look like you've been et by a bear and shat off a cliff."

A grin without a trace of humor skidded across Jimi's countenance. "Uncle Chester would be right, and I'm feeling like I look. But Monika will take care of me."

"Just stay away from the ope-day, hear?" Angel arched her eyebrows, waiting for a response, more mama bear/mother hen than ever.

Jimi said, "Promise," but he avoided making eye contact with either of us. "See y'all tonight." A quick little wave and he was gone.

35

Do you remember the last time you saw your mother?

Maybe you're one of the lucky ones. You have a good mother and she's alive and healthy. The last time you saw her was a few hours, days or weeks ago and you've made plans to see her again soon.

Or maybe you're like me. The woman who gave you life is deceased, and the last time you saw her was more years ago than you want to count...

I'd spent my ten day leave at home and was catching the train prior to shipping out for my first tour in Nam. I wore my Class A uniform. I was green as a country apple.

We stood, Mom and me, on the station platform, waiting for the train. A fragment of time branded into my psyche forever, crystal-clear. An afternoon peaceful enough to hear the birds singing and the sounds of passing traffic on the two-lane county highway through town. We had the platform pretty much to ourselves.

Mom was 44 years old. Slender. Long chestnut hair

streaked with silver, worn back. A modest summer dress and sensible shoes. A country woman.

I was fumbling with my duffel bag. We had gone to Donna's Diner for lunch, and our small J.C. Penny outlet store caught Mom's eye on our walk back to the station. Against my mumbling protest, we made a detour and left Penny's ten minutes later with three packages of new boxer shorts, nicely shrink-wrapped in cellophane. I was going to Vietnam to kill Vietcong, but I couldn't stop my mother from buying me underwear I didn't need.

Such is the glory and power of motherhood.

So I'm standing there on the train platform, messing with a duffel bag that wouldn't fold shut properly, struggling manfully to position those three packages of underwear that defiantly resist my every attempt at packing them and clasping the bag shut. I'd been at it for a couple of minutes.

When the first toot of a train whistle carried from maybe a half mile away, Mom spoke up.

"Here, son." She politely shouldered her five-foot-three between me and my duffle bag. "Your mother's a packrat from way back."

An elbow lifted here. The other twitched there. She leaned her weight into the task. In the handful of seconds it took me to step around her, she had the duffel back nicely re-snapped, the extra added packages somehow tucked neatly away and no longer visible. She returned the duffel bag to me with a smile of affection tinged with sadness.

"Uh, thanks, Mom."

She blinked away whatever she was thinking. She gazed down the train track.

"Have you said goodbye to Connie?"

"A long time ago."

"Yes, but does she know you're going to," she hesitated, swallowed, "to Vietnam?"

"I'll be back, Mom. It isn't a death sentence. And Connie and I are though. She'd rather have a war protestor warming her bed than have to wait for a soldier gone to fight a war."

"Those hippies," my mother said in a quiet voice.

I said, "Connie's okay. We had a lot of long talks about the war. She's sincere in her feelings. And she fell for that guy after I was gone to Basic Training. Just got lonely, I guess. Reckon I can't blame her. I was the one who left. She's a good person."

"Well, she wasn't a good wife. I was glad when the divorce got final."

The train whistle hooted again, drawing closer. The railroad crossing signal next to the station started blinking and dinging. A few more passengers drifted out onto the platform.

I said, "How about you, Mom? I've done what I could to fix up what needed fixing around the house. You should be good when winter sets in."

She looked deep into my eyes. "You're a fine son, coming home when you could have been off cavorting. Your father would be proud."

We'd lost Dad to pulmonary fibrosis. Mom had nursed at home right up until the end. I should have done more.

I said, "I wish you weren't living alone."

She smiled. "Maybe I'll find myself a boyfriend. It's never too late, they say. Anyway, your Aunt Char and Uncle Dave live down the street. They can see our house from their place. They'll keep an eye on me. I'll be fine." She touched me on both shoulders. "You be careful, son, over there in that Vietnam. You're all I have left."

"I'll be home again, Mom," I said. "I promise. You'll see me again."

Those words to my mother were a lie.

Or should we be charitable and call it sharing a hope for what was not to be?

The train huffed and clanged and made its train noises as it slowed to a stop at the platform.

Mom tenderly cupped my chin and the side of my face with her curved palm.

"I'll pray for you every day, son."

She's the only person who ever said that to me.

The next and last time I went home was to bury her. Cancer.

After Mom died, I never seemed able to place total and unconditional trust in another person. Don't ask me why. Maybe it was being an only child and a born loner. I depended on the guys in my squad to cover my back the way I covered theirs so we could all get home before dark, but on an intimate, human-to-human level I'd lived my life never trusting, never depending on, anyone but myself.

Until now.

Until Angel.

Sitting alone with her at her kitchen table after Jimi left, I felt that in my gut with certainty.

I trusted this woman.

The wall phone rang.

Angel answered it, listened with a slight frown. A shrug, and she extended the receiver to me.

"Soldier, this is Klaus Mueller." He didn't have to identify himself. Even with the echo of background noise from his end of the connection, the clipped Teutonic accent came through loud and clear. Do I call at a convenient time?"

"Where are you?"

"That need not concern you. My friends and I are approximately twenty minutes from departing this charming country. I am afraid I have nothing to report on the matter you asked me to look into."

"You mean that there's no CIA hit team in London with Jimi as a target?"

"That is exactly what I mean. This is good news, is it not?" The clipped accent cooled with an uncertain tremor just below the surface. "We have an agreement. I made inquiries on your behalf, and you will cause me no trouble with the British authorities. The foundation for a working relationship when you are stationed in my country, yes?"

"No. Not even close."

A pause across the connection. The busy background noise of flights being announced.

"Soldier, I regret that I can provide no information for you."

"That's okay. It works better this way. *Auf Wiedersehen,* Klaus."

I broke the connection.

Angel had heard every word.

"What the hell are you up to, Soldier?"

36

I snagged the piece of paper on which Jimi had written the address.

"Think I'll invite a few acquaintances down to join us at that jam session tonight."

"But it's a private club." A frown of interest. "Anyone I know?"

"You'll see. It should make for an interesting party." I cradled the kitchen wall phone without releasing the receiver. "Things are falling together. The last act. I just need to get my details straight."

"What sort of details?"

"I'm trying to figure who might have had a key to Sydney's flat. You told me about you and Sydney being lovers."

"I told you that, yes. That's not going to be an issue between us, is it?"

"Hardly. Did she give you a key?"

"Yes. Yes, she did. I made sure she got it back when we

let that part of our friendship go. You already asked me if I killed her. Am I still under suspicion?"

I said, "I was hoping you wouldn't get testy. I told you I'm just trying to keep things lined up in my head. During the time when you had a key to her flat, could Bandy have snagged it from you without your knowledge, when you were in the shower or something; duck around the corner and have his own copy made?"

"I guess anything's possible."

"Do you know anyone else who she might have given a key to?"

"Not offhand. Why?"

"The cops, Inspector Hudberry, broke the door down after Sydney was murdered and I'd been stretched out next to her to make it look like I was her killer. But when I first woke up next to her body, there was no sign of forcible entry. I know I didn't kill her, so that means she let her killer in before she was murdered, or the killer had a key."

"Do you know who killed Sydney?"

"I've got some ideas. But it's been a rough twenty-four hours. A lot going on, coming at me fast with me trying to stay one step ahead of the cops and let's not forget jet lag thrown in for good measure."

"And that's all you're going to tell me?"

"For now."

She held her tea cup between her hands and stared down into it. "Why were you born, Soldier? Why are you alive?"

I said, "Woman, you ask some questions. Do I believe in God? Why am I here?"

"Well?"

"Why are we talking about this?"

"Easy," she said. "In Jimi you see a person in free fall who could benefit from some mental realignment."

"I guess that's one way of putting it."

"Well, that's what I see in you."

Knowing I was beat, I said, "Guess I'm like most people. Guess I haven't given that one much thought."

"In Vietnam you were otherwise occupied," she said wryly. "The basics of survival must always come first. I'm glad you survived. I'm glad you're alive."

"Well, thanks for that."

"And you and I are not of a culture much given to contemplating the spiritual realm. Religion answers most questions for most people."

"But not for you?"

"I believe there are grains of truth in every one of the world religions. We're all here, co-creating the world and our lives through our perceptions and our actions. Religion provides a framework for a culture to deal with things like mortality, each other and the universe itself."

I held up a hand as if I was stopping traffic. "Hold on. Can you see what you're doing?"

"Tell me."

"You've studied this stuff and you've memorized it and you try to live by it, and right now you're falling back on it because you need to embrace something comfortable instead of thinking about what you saw."

"So what's wrong with that? I don't study and memorize that stuff. Mister, I *am* that stuff."

I gave myself a couple of seconds. Took a breath and let it out. Sipped my tea.

"I know. Sorry. I'm more comfortable with conflict than I am with the spiritual realm."

Angel said, "We all have to work on that to one degree or another, every single one of us on the planet. See, I believe we're here to experience and evolve this physical universe and our place in it."

"And how do we go about doing that?"

"Having conversations like this with each other is where it starts."

"Maybe so. But in my experience, war isn't conducive to dialogue. Those basics of survival you were talking about. If you have to kill another human being in combat, you've got to believe that he's a piece of shit who deserves to die because he killed your brothers-in-arms and he wants to kill you."

Her expression was serene. Her eyes were sad.

She said, "I understand."

I said, "I've spent the last few years staying alive by killing as many of the sons of bitches as I could. I haven't seen much of London but what I have seen hasn't been that friendly, either. But okay, I see what you found here, Angel. Queen bee in a scene flourishing with enterprise and creativity."

She nodded. "A garden of contemplation in a world of chaos. Why shouldn't we, you and I and everyone alive, be the pebble tossed into the cosmic pond that starts the ripples in the collective consciousness?"

I returned her nod. "It sounds nice but there are barbarians slavering just outside the gate. I know. I've been on the front lines, holding them at bay."

She said, "Today, I was there. That man snuffed the life of an unarmed, defenseless woman before you snuffed him. You're one of the good guys. Damn, Soldier, after seeing you in action, you're the essence of every good man that ever lived. It is your dharma to be a warrior and you manifest your destiny magnificently."

"I like the sound of that."

"I'm serious. That garden we're talking about is where the soul retreats to reflect, to create and inspire and process the collective truths of our existence. Barbarians like Gearson and that creep in black and my creep of an ex-husband must not be allowed to violate the garden. Yes, I understand. The warrior stands guard at the gate."

"Well, I'm glad we got that settled."

"Settled? Nothing is ever settled, Soldier. It's an expanding universe."

I drew the receiver of the wall phone from its cradle. "Go do whatever girls do before they go out. Somewhere in this city there's a dinner waiting on us."

She laughed. "You," was her parting shot, "are a macho son of a bitch."

She had me there.

I dialed as soon as she was out of the kitchen. I expected to have trouble tracking Hudberry down but I got lucky and caught him at his desk.

When he picked up, I said, "Thought I should check in with the Yard."

He recognized my voice.

"Why not come in pay us a call in person?"

"I've got good news for your daughter."

"Leave my family out of this, you bastard."

"I thought she was a Jimi Hendrix fan."

"And you've located him?"

"I have."

"Alive or dead?"

"Oh, he's alive," I said. "There's going to be a little party tonight at a private club in Soho," and I read him the address Jimi had written down. "I was hoping you could make it, Inspector. How's about eight o'clock?"

His chuckle rattled across the line. "You're a ballsy one, you are. Unless this is just trying to get a rise out of me. Very well, I'll be there at eight with a squad and you'll be under arrest for the murder of Sydney Blanchard."

"And what about the rest of it? Those German thugs I told you about? Klaus Mueller. You get a squad out to Heathrow real fast; you can nab him and some of his pals before they catch their flight to Düsseldorf."

"Soldier, why are you telling me this?"

"Because I'd like Klaus to be present at our get-together. Tying this thing up in a tight package appeals to me."

He said, "You killed the Blanchard girl and you're going down for it."

"What about Bandy McGuire?"

"What about him? He's in custody. He was stopped for speeding about an hour ago. He put up a fight and is presently cooling his heels in a cell."

"Get anything out of him?" I hoped he couldn't tell across the connection that I held my breath.

"Nothing yet. He's a hardcase. Won't say a word."

Thanks, Bandy. He was paying me back for not killing him. There was a good chance that Hudberry didn't even know about those three fresh bodies inside that walled estate.

I said, "Maybe he'll have something to say under the right conditions. Bring him along too."

He cleared his throat. "As for your CIA business, Chet Daly was one of their ex-agents. We're working on that."

I didn't see any reason to tell him that I'd cancelled that CIA account; that Bandy had been speeding to put distance between him and three dead bodies. If Hudberry knew about me killing Gearson and the man in black, it was Bandy who would have told him.

I said, "Inspector, how badly do you want the killer of Sydney Blanchard?"

"That's my job, and I've hardly become so jaded that I could ever let pass lightly such a foul desecration of innocence."

"Hudberry, I'm about to help you do your job. I've got this thing in the bag. Give me ten minutes with you and these people and let me walk us through it and I'll bring this job to you on a plate."

"Who else besides us, Bandy and Mueller?"

"Jimi and his girlfriend, Monika Dannemann, will be there, and Angel McGuire. And if you can get your hands on Mike Jeffrey, he could really make it interesting though I've got a feeling he may be hard to find."

A lengthy silence ensued.

Then he said, "Very well. I will be there in exactly two hours with Bandy McGuire and Klaus Mueller, and each of them will be under the guard of one of my men. I will have the exits watched in case anyone in your party is crazy enough to think they can make a run for it. And you shall have ten minutes to prove to me that someone other than yourself murdered Sydney Blanchard. Failing to do that, you will be placed under arrest."

I said, "Fair enough. Two hours," and broke the connection.

Angel was back. She'd changed into a chic outfit of boots, leather trousers and a denim jacket with a turned-up color over a smart white blouse. The jacket boasted a little button with a peace sign on the left lapel.

She said, "I'm hungry. I crave sustenance."

I said, "Let's go find dinner."

37

SHE CHOSE THE SAME INDIAN RESTAURANT THAT SYDNEY had taken me to the night before. I mentioned this after we were seated and a waitress had taken our orders. The place was again busy and the seating was close so I pitched my voice for her ears alone.

Angel replied in kind. "I'm not surprised that Sydney would bring you here. This was our favorite place." She blinked away the emotion. "The butter chicken here is out of this world."

That's what I'd ordered and I was looking forward to having it a second time. It's always been one of my idiosyncrasies that when I'm at a restaurant and find a dish that I like, I never order anything else at that restaurant. There was a time when I could have walked into a score of diners between Reno and Ruidoso, ordered up "the usual" and the waitress would've known what I was talking about.

Except for a somber moment when we toasted Sydney,

we spoke of the food, other restaurants she knew that I must try next time I was in London; we spoke of things light and pleasant. The atmosphere of the place was pleasant and conducive to communication and at one point Angel initiated a conversation with an Indian gentleman seated next to us, a well-dressed, pleasantly plump, prematurely balding guy who was dining alone at the next table. Angel asked him about the dish he was having, one she had never tried, interrupted his solitude so gracefully that he appeared happy to yield it.

"This dish is Rogan Josh," he explained in that musical cadence of an Indian speaking English. "It is from Kashmir. The literal translation for the name is 'red lamb.' The color comes from the Kahsmiri dry chilies used in it." He chuckled pleasantly. "The name may sound fiery but the dish's heat is toned down by the cream that is added."

The three of us slipped into a rambling, pleasant conversation easily enough. Early on, Angel mentioned that I was fresh from Vietnam. I wished she hadn't but the guy remained friendly enough, so I soft-pedaled my admission with, "You're not going to call me a baby killer, are you?"

His expression grew serious without losing its warmth. "Hardly. You have about you, if I am not being presumptuous in saying so, the aura of a good and decent man. You are a soldier and you have been at war. Unspeakable things happen in war."

Angel realized her *faux pas*.

"Then let us not speak of them," she said gently.

She tactfully changed the subject by mentioning that she was halfway through reading a book on the Hindu influence on Buddhism.

"Ah yes," said our new friend, whose name was Aarush. "Those are religions I was raised in, and have recently found new meaning in." He looked at me. "You are on a journey, as are we all, but right now is a profound moment in your journey. You remain a soldier and yet, unless we are overrun by the communist menace or the Nazis return to life, your days of combat are over. One phase of your life has ended and another is about to begin. I am on a journey too, you see, and not only from New Dehli to here in London where I am privileged to serve my clinical internship. My father is a very prominent Indian cardiologist in New Dehli and I was raised with every expectation that I too will become a man of medicine. My sister and I were thoroughly indoctrinated in the Hindu faith. When I came of age, I rejected religious dogma, much to my father's chagrin. But I embraced the medical profession." A self-conscious chuckle. "Now I find myself deviating from mainstream medical practice as I rediscover ancient truths that are most relevant to our modern-day world. This transformation I speak of, which you and I are experiencing, is not always easy."

Angel sighed. "Amen to that."

Aarush said, "But as the caterpillar dies, the butterfly is born."

I had to crack a grin. "I'd make a hell of a butterfly, doc."

Angel gave me a look. "He's speaking metaphorically and you dang well know it."

Aarush said, "With our words, we prophesize the future for ourselves and for the world we live in."

I said, "After listening to you and Angel, I sure hope that's true. You both imagine a better world."

"It is true, my friend. These are the ways in which I deviate from standard medical practice. It was in observing the placebo effect that got me thinking in this direction. The power of the mind over the body. Think of it! Ridding oneself of negative emotions, developing intuition by listening to signals from the body, improves our health, and from a collective well-being can spring a healthier world consciousness. These are the truths revealed in the ancient texts of my father's faith. The power of faith to manifest a better reality. "

I half-seriously asked the Indian guy, "Did she pay you to show up here and talk this stuff to me, because she was talking it to me before we left for dinner."

He chuckled pleasantly. "I only hope that I have brought unity to any divergence of opinion." He dabbed at his mouth with his napkin and nodded his thanks to the waitress who handed him his bill. "It has been a pleasure speaking with both of you. I trust you will accept my apology if I have overstepped any social bounds."

Angel was quick to say, "It's been great talking to you," and she kicked me gently under the table.

She didn't have to.

"Yes, thank you, Aarush," I said, meaning it.

He was beaming as he laid out a generous tip, snagged the bill and reached for his hat.

"In that case I will leave you with a final thought, for I have determined that my dharma is to spread this knowledge rather than being only one more well-meaning drone practicing standard medicine. Love, health and happiness are possible without war, without killing. Ultimately the universe is a friendly and benevolent place where orthodoxies old and new can meet and make peace with one another. Good evening to you both. *Namaste.*"

And he was gone.

I never saw him again.

It was time for our get together with Hudberry.

38

THE PRIVATE CLUB WAS A MODEST SECOND-FLOOR establishment. Comfortable ambiance. Bare wood dance floor. The place about half full, but it was early. A four-piece band played mellow, tasteful instrumental jazz from the bandstand.

Jimi and Monika sat together, of course. There was a strain to Monika's manner and expression. Jimi smelled of beer, alcohol, cigarettes and marijuana. I had called him after finishing with Hudberry, told him about meeting the cop. He hadn't wanted to come. I explained that this could settle his troubles with the Inspector. He finally agreed and promised to go easy on the dope and drink. This apparently was the best he could do.

There wasn't a police uniform in the place but at nearby tables burly, ruddy-cheeked fellows with short haircuts sat in pairs or alone. They might as well have had the words *undercover police* tattooed on their foreheads.

The manager of the place, a smartly dressed, corpulent

guy with slicked-back hair, hovered on the periphery, exuding anxious displeasure.

Hudberry saved his appearance for last, accompanied by two hulking men who each led in a man wearing handcuffs. Hudberry didn't look much improved. A new, bright strip of white tape crossed the bridge of his nose. His black eyes had lost some of their swelling.

Klaus Mueller held himself erect with that innate regal grace as if he was Count von something or other; as if his handcuffs did not exist.

Bandy McGuire shambled in behind Mueller. He avoided looking at Angel and everyone else present except me. His eyes caught mine for the fraction of a second and he gave me an unmistakable eye twitch of a wink that was brief enough to escape the notice of anyone else.

Hudberry sat at the head of the table. The prisoners remained standing with their guards. This brought a turning of heads from the club's patrons. Cops in a nightspot will always put a damper on things but none of the customers got up to leave. Conversations dropped in volume, nothing more.

At our table, Monika fidgeted, toying with her martini glass.

She said to Hudberry, "Jimi and I should not be here. What is this about? Is this a police inquiry? Jimi, we should leave."

Hudberry said, "I understand that except for *Herr* Mueller, everyone here knows everyone else. Only Mike Jeffrey seems to have eluded our net."

Angel glared at Bandy. "I know this big lout too damn well."

Hudberry said, "My men are present to witness these proceedings. There are questions that need to be answered. To be precise, who killed Sydney Blanchard in her flat last night and who killed a man named Chet Daly this morning in a pub? Anyone want to confess?" He panned the unresponsive faces assembled before him. "I didn't think so. Nonetheless, I will be making an arrest before I leave here tonight."

I said, "Uh, Inspector, you said I could have ten minutes. It may not even take that long to run a few things past everyone here."

His stiff upper lip trembled with indignation. "This man," he said to the others, indicating me, "has requested that he be allowed to make a statement with those present as witnesses. I have granted him that request." He nodded. "Very well. You may proceed."

Klaus Mueller looked down his aristocratic nose at me. "Excuse me. Before this goes any further, I should like to speak to the German consulate."

Hudberry said, "You're under arrest as a person of interest in a murder investigation. Be glad you're out of your cell."

Jimi said, with one of his little humorless chuckles, "Wait a minute, Soldier. Are you saying that someone at this table killed Sydney?"

"That's exactly what I'm saying. The Chet Daly kill is something else. Daly was part of a hit team authorized by the US government to kill you, Jimi."

Jimi started to say something, thought better of it and busied himself with lighting a cigarette.

Angel said, "Daly was part of the hit squad? He's the one who got in touch with us to blow the whistle. He's the one who told us about a CIA hit team. You're saying his own team got him?"

"His conscience got the best of him. Killing off popular entertainers; the idea's as stupid as it is evil. Daly was the spotter. The setup man. It's the only way he could have known so much about it. His partner did not have a guilty conscience. I sensed that Angel and I were being tailed when we went to that pub to meet Daly. Daly's partner got suspicious, followed Daly to Angel's and then followed Angel when she left to meet me. That took him full circle, back to Daly. An innocent barmaid was collateral damage."

Hudberry said, "And what happened to this partner, the one you're saying shot Daly and the barmaid? He's still at large."

Everyone had their eyes on me. I could almost hear their collective sigh when I said, "Consider him out of the picture. His sort don't get caught by the authorities."

Hudberry's eyes narrowed. "Watch the mouth, Yank. If there's a killer like that at large, I want him and Scotland Yard will get him."

"Whatever you say, Inspector. But for now, though, let's set him aside because he had nothing to do with the Blanchard murder."

Jimi said, "Well then, who did? I hate to say it, Soldier brother, but damn dude, you're taking your time."

Monika said, "Jimi is right. If you know who is the killer here, tell us."

I said, "Patience. I want to be thorough and show everyone how there's only one way it plays. I intend to clear my name here tonight. Let's look at motive and opportunity. Bandy, by any chance did you have a key to Sydney's flat?"

Bandy's features darkened. "Now mate, don't you be trying to put me in hot water. There's things I could say, y'know."

Hudberry said, "Really, Bandy? Like what?"

Bandy looked down at his handcuffs and muttered, "Just things."

Angel said, "You made a copy of that key back when I had a key to Sydney's place, damn your horny soul."

Bandy couldn't make eye contact with her. "Aw don't be cross with me, luv. So I wanted a little taste of what that chickie was doling out. I didn't get it but not for lack of trying. Blazes. You was getting it from her so what's wrong with old Bandy snooping around?"

Hudberry sad, "What's this about Miss McGuire and the murdered woman?"

"Aw nothing," said Bandy. "Angel and Sydney was friends. Me, I only used the key once. I sneaked in and, uh, sort of surprised Sydney coming out of the shower. I just did it to fun with her, didn't mean no harm. Guess I was a little drunk."

Angel said, "As a matter of fact, I know about that. Sydney told me and I figured to let sleeping dogs lie so I never threw it in your face. She said you were pathetic, Bandy. She threw you out."

Bandy said somewhat sheepishly, "Yeah well, I reckon she did."

I looked at Angel. "Did Sydney ever mention if anyone else had a key?"

She said, "As a matter of fact, after the Bandy incident,

she got a little paranoid. She told me that she was never going to give her key out to anyone again."

Jimi said, "But even if Bandy had a motive to kill Sydney, him and me were together after we left her flat."

"Yeah," said Bandy. "Me and Jimi was together, so we're each other's alibi, ain't we, Jimi? Ain't that something?"

"Uh huh," Jimi mumbled with no show of enthusiasm.

"So that lets Bandy and Jimi off the list of suspects. Thorough, like I said. Okay, let's consider our German friends, Klaus and Monika."

Monika gasped. "Me?" She laid a hand on Jimi's arm. "Jimi, you know I would never hurt anyone."

He mumbled, "I know that, baby."

"Then why does your friend say such a thing? I barely knew Miss Blanchard."

I said, "Maybe you did, maybe you didn't, but you knew that Jimi was spending time with her and I've seen you in action, Monika. You're the real, *real* jealous type. Who knows how far you'd go to cancel out the competition."

Monika said, "I did not kill that person."

"I know that. So okay, let's drop you off the list. Then there's Klaus Mueller's motive."

Mueller bristled, exuding arrogant belligerence even while wearing a pair of handcuffs.

"Me? Motive? What motive could I have to murder this young woman of whom you speak? I did not even know her."

I said, "You wanted to ruin Jimi. Framing him for a rough-sex drug murder would be a damn good way of getting him out of Monika's life."

Monika's eyes widened. "Ruin Jimi? But why?" She stared at Mueller. "I know nothing of this!"

Hudberry said, "I'm prepared to believe that."

"And that's why Klaus is in the clear on Sydney's murder. He didn't do it because he was following Monika home, and he has a chauffer to back up his alibi."

Mueller appealed to Hudberry. "Then I should be allowed to leave, is that not so, Inspector? Why am I being held?"

Hudberry said, "I don't like the cut of your jib, but we can do better than that. You were armed with a concealed weapon, I'm told, when you were picked up at the airport."

I said, "And there's the little matter of ordering Jimi thrown off a roof."

Mueller's eyes narrowed. "I thought we had a deal."

"Uh uh. My head still hurts where one of your goons sapped me. And tell your chauffer that I don't like people pointing guns at me."

Hudberry eyed Angel. "That leaves the queen bee, Miss McGuire, and though I'm still mad about the way she deceived me this morning, luring me into that trap you two set for me, I have difficulty imaging her as a cold-blooded killer."

Angel smiled demurely. "Why thank you, Inspector."

Hudberry turned to me. Gloating smugness. Indulgent smile. "And so there you are, my soldier friend. You seem to have used up your ten minutes and accomplished nothing but to clear everyone else and further implicate yourself. Nice work. Who else is left?"

I said, "You, Inspector. You killed Sydney Blanchard."

39

Hudberry said, "Well that is a good one, that is. Why don't we go around to Buckingham Palace and interrogate the Queen? She had just as much to do with Sydney Blanchard's murder as I."

"Something occurred to me," I said, "and when I set it alongside everything I've just run through, the puzzle started straightening itself. For me, this all started with you bird-dogging Jimi for a handle on Tobe Gearson."

"And where is Mr. Gearson, by the way?"

So the bodies at the estate had not yet been found...

I continued as if I hadn't heard the question.

I said, "But after I took you down in the alley behind Angel McGuire's, it became personal, didn't it, Inspector?"

Hudberry's nod was stiff. "That's where it started between me and you, Soldier, right enough. I told you this was my town. Nobody takes me down like you did, not even a baby-killer for the US Government."

Angel said, "Oooh, that was uncalled for."

"No, it wasn't," said Hudberry. "This man is a

murderer. I have no respect for a killer of women. Who knows what barbarous acts he committed under cover of war?"

I said, "There's a long answer to that, unfortunately. But let's get back to the issue at hand. Inspector, you killed Sydney Blanchard. I don't know about the similarities between her and your daughter. Maybe there's a Freudian angle your defense team can work when this gets to court."

His meaty, pockmarked face reddened. His fists clenched. "Shut your filthy mouth, damn you."

I said, "You followed me last night from Ronnie Scott's Club when I followed Jimi and Sydney to her flat."

Monika pouted. Under her breath she said, "That slut."

I said to Hudberry, "You saw Bandy drive off with Jimi. You had seen me position myself outside Sydney's flat. You circled around and got lucky and KO-ed me. You made up your plan on the spot. That would get the word out on the street, wouldn't it? Inspector Hudberry is not a man to be trifled with."

Hudberry snarled at a pair of nearby plainclothesmen. "Take this man into custody."

The plainclothesmen started to rise and advance. Patrons at adjacent tables drew away apprehensively from this escalating confrontation.

I said, "The fact that there was no forcible entry at the murder scene is what tipped your hand, Hudberry. When Jimi left her flat with Bandy, I clearly heard him tell Sydney specifically not to let anyone in. She wouldn't have, either...except for a cop. She'd have opened the door for an officer of the law. She'd have let you in, Inspector."

He said, "This is outlandish. You're trying to muddy

the water and divert from your own guilt. And you're leaving out the details, Soldier, that will nail your coffin shut."

"Such as?"

Two of his men stood, one to either side of me. One held handcuffs. Hudberry raised a hand to them. He was enjoying himself.

He said, "You mentioned Gearson awhile ago and then dismissed him rather offhandedly. Gearson ties in with this and I daresay more than a little. Perhaps there's another killing to be laid at your feet."

Bandy McGuire chimed in on cue. "I don't see how, Inspector. Tobe Gearson wasn't with me when I went to fetch Jimi from Sydney's flat. Eh, Jimi?"

Jimi stayed busy with his cigarette. "That's right, Bandy. You were alone. I don't know where Gearson was but he wasn't with us."

"Bloody right," said Bandy. "Me and Jimi went out and had ourselves a high time, yes sir."

Monika glared at Jimi. Angel sent a moue of disgust in Bandy's direction. But none of them said anything. We were as thick as thieves.

Hudberry said, "Bandy's lying and so is Hendrix. Jimi, you're lying through your teeth. This man who calls himself Soldier is right about me tailing him from the club last night to the woman's flat. I saw Bandy and Gearson hustle Hendrix into a waiting car and they sped off. That's when I called for backup. It looked like a kidnapping."

Bandy's eyes were glazed but he held his head high and said as if swearing on a Bible, "You saw no such thing. I've got no bloody idea what happened to Gearson. He could be anywhere. He could be nowhere. But he weren't with me when I went to Sydney's flat to fetch Jimi for a night on the town."

I said, "It doesn't matter about Gearson. It doesn't matter who left with Jimi. The point is, Inspector, you saw them leave. That establishes opportunity. After they left, you took me out. Then you dragged me into Sydney's building. At that time of the night, or morning, there wasn't a soul to get in your way or stop you. You knocked on her door, identified yourself as a police officer and told her you needed to speak with her. She opened the door for you. You would have had to work fast because she would see me there, unconscious. You silenced her before she could raise a ruckus. You dragged me inside and set things up. Then you let yourself out, wiping away your fingerprints. Did you rape Sydney and then kill her, or the other way around? Like I said, Freud is your best bet on that angle."

Hudberry leapt to his feet, his fingers curled into claws. His eyes said he wanted to tear me apart.

"Enough." He snapped his fingers and gestured at the hovering plainclothesmen. "Escort this lunatic out of my sight."

His men rested their beefy hands on me. I resisted the impulse that twenty-four hours ago would have had me putting them down and half-dead.

I said, "You had motive and opportunity, Inspector, and I've got the proof."

That stopped everyone, including the plainclothes men. I had everyone's attention."

Surprise flared again in Hudberry's eyes. He would be

a damn good poker player, but so was I and I was riding this bluff all the way to the finish line.

I tensed, ready for anything. The plainclothes cops must have felt me hunch up. Each tightened a steel-like grip on one of my shoulders.

"Proof?" Hudberry sneered. "Very well, what is your "proof" that *I* killed that poor girl?"

I said, "My proof isn't a what, it's a who. Sydney's neighbors. Glenn and Bruce. Glenn was having stomach trouble so Bruce was starting out to visit an all-night pharmacy, but he pulled up short when he heard movement and he waited and watched a man leave Sydney's apartment. He's ready to come forward, Inspector. He's identified a picture of you, Hudberry. That's the proof. An eyewitness to your presence at the murder scene before you called in for backup."

Everything I'd just said about poor Glenn and Bruce was a complete fabrication. That's the bluff I was putting my money on.

Hudberry spent a few seconds considering the doubt that animated the expressions of everyone around him, including the cops within earshot. He could have done three things at that point. He could have knocked me silly to shut me up and ordered me hauled off and chances were I'd be found dead in my cell before morning. Or he could simply disavow my ranting as that of a justly accused man, and have me hauled off. Instead, he opted for choice number three.

He pivoted and bolted for the nearest exit.

I gave into impulse, leaping out of my seat like a jack-in-the-box and throwing the plainclothes men off me and onto their backsides.

I shouted, "Don't let him get away!"

I started after Hudberry.

Club patrons scattered as he barreled past them.

The nearest exit suddenly became filled with a pair of his own men who looked determined to stop him.

Hudberry drew a pistol and opened fire on the officers in the doorway. Shouts and screams filled the air. The music from the bandstand tapered off. Patrons hugged the floor to avoid the line of fire.

I dodged and weaved as if I were chasing a VC through a crowded marketplace in Saigon. I made it to where Hudberry was running across the length of the bandstand, seeking an escape by that route. I raced after him, brushing by the onstage band's stunned guitarist. Jimi's guitar was on a guitar stand behind him. Without slowing, I grabbed that guitar by its neck. Narrowing the distanced between myself and Hudberry, I twirled the guitar above my head like a war club and let fly.

Hudberry flung a glance over his shoulder as he reached the far end of the stage. The sailing, rounded body of the electric guitar caught him full-force in the forehead. He spun half-way around and pitched from the stage, already unconscious when he landed on the dance floor.

40

———

TEN MINUTES AFTER THE LAST OF THE POLICE HAD departed the private club, after Hudberry had been revived and led away with Bandy and Klaus, after statements had been taken, the club more or less returned to normal although anyone walking in fresh, without knowledge of what had just happened, might find the atmosphere and the patrons somewhat reserved. The combo onstage had resumed playing. The club manager looked like his breathing had returned to normal.

Alongside the stage, Angel and I stood with Jimi and Monika. The house band had invited Jimi to sit in and he hadn't hesitated in accepting the invitation. His guitar was restored to its guitar stand. The group opened with a mid-tempo number as an effort to restore a semblance of normalcy to the club.

Jimi looked worn out, his features ashen. His eyes held no luster.

He said, "You sure you two can't stick around. I feel like laying down some good music tonight."

Monika's features were drawn. She was a little drunk. She leaned against Jimi to help her remain upright.

I said, "Thanks, Jimi. I'm flat worn out. I'm stopping to pick up my duffel bag from the cops, and then I'm catching up on my sack time and a flight to Germany."

Angel stood with an arm linked through mine. Her nearness, as always it seemed, titillated my senses. She squeezed her self closer to me and whispered impishly in my ear, "I'm looking forward to sack time with you, fella."

"Soldier," said Jimi, "I've gotta say you took care of my street business like I hoped you would. Thanks for putting it on the line for me."

"Yes," slurred Monika, "we appreciate what you have done very much."

I gave her a smile but figured it best not to say anything to her. I didn't know what Jimi told her about his time in captivity. I doubted he'd told her anything. I doubted that she would be with him next week on the flight to New York.

I said, "Can I give you some advice, Jimi?"

"Of course, man. You can say whatever you want with me, you know that."

"Okay. Here it is from someone who cares. Buddy, get yourself some rest. Take a break. Clean up."

He gave me the old Jimi chuckle. Shy. Modest. Hip.

"Aw, maybe tomorrow, man. We're making the rounds tonight. I'm playing me some music, some jamming. Wish you were staying, bro. So damn many vultures, how am I gonna stop them all?"

"One at a time," was the best I could offer. "One at a time."

He said, "That was some slick trick you pulled tonight.

Glenn and Bruce. They didn't see a thing but that sure was bluff enough to pop Hudberry's cork. I like that."

The number ended onstage. The leader of the group spoke into the mic.

"Uh, as if tonight hasn't been exciting enough, we've got one more surprise in store for you. Hey everybody, let's give Jimi Hendrix a round of applause and bring him on up."

The crowd came to life with resounding applause.

Jimi released Monika. She managed to remain standing. Enthusiasm shone in Jimi's eyes.

"Well, it's time to do what I do."

He and Angel exchanged a brief hug and touched cheeks.

She said, "Please do what Soldier says. I thought I was going to have to leave the UK but the way things are turning out, with Hudberry behind bars, reckon I'll stay where I am. You come on by the pad if there's ever anything I can do."

"You know I will, Angel. Thanks."

Monika stared icily at nothing.

I said, "Watch your back, Jimi. Take care of yourself, buddy. I'll buy your next album."

"Buy, hell. You stay in touch, soldier man. I'll see that you get a free copy. Until next time, brother."

"Until next time, Jimi."

We embraced. Not that spindly, loose-limbed semi-embrace that I'd seen him reluctantly dole out if circumstance warranted, but a full-on chest-to-chest, manly bear hug. *Abrazo*, the Hispanics call it. Masculine friendship. Camaraderie. A bond deeper than words.

Angel and I made our way to the back of the club

while Jimi joined the band onstage. He strapped on his guitar. When we reached the door, Angel sensed that I was hesitant to leave, so we stood there together for a minute or so.

The group deferred to the star. Jimi counted off a slow blues and played a quiet, extended solo of licks effortlessly coaxed from the fret board by those exquisitely long fingers.

The last time I saw Jimi Hendrix, he was standing at the microphone, still as a post, his eyes closed, playing those deep blues as if his life depended on it.

Singing about a red house over yonder.

EPILOGUE

"The Jimi Hendrix Experience is over. The acid rock musician was pronounced dead this morning in a London hospital, apparently from an overdose of drugs. He was 26."

We heard the news on the car radio, on the way to the airport, the next afternoon. Angel had again insisted on driving and was again doing a fair job of negotiating the rainy day traffic.

We'd gone back to her place the night before and found the crash pad still clear of crashers, or whatever the hell they were called. Nature took its course and before long we were on the big fluffy bed in her bedroom with pillows and candles and incense. We indulged in heavy petting (or at least that's what they called it when I was a kid), and then a funny thing happened. Everything caught up with both of us at once before anything serious could get started. We fell asleep, fully clothed, in each other's arms.

We made love in the morning. Good. Very good. So

good that I'd missed a scheduled morning flight and was hoping I could catch an afternoon flight out on military standby.

She flicked off the radio once the announcer's voice began droning something about politics. For a minute or so, heavy silence settled between us. The only sound in the car was the back-and-forth *flap-flap* of the windshield wipers.

She said, "Oh, my God. Poor Jimi. They got him."

I said, "It could have happened that way. A third man on the hit team. A backup replacement in case something went wrong, the way it did."

She read something in my voice. "But you don't think so."

"I don't know what to think. It could be what they're saying. Too many sleeping pills. Too much booze. If I was a betting man, that would be my bet. Hit teams on jobs like this work in pairs, spotter and shooter. And you saw the condition Jimi was in last night when he left your place. What do you think, Angel?"

"I think it's a fucking waste." She tapped the brakes and brought us down to a reasonable speed. "Should we go back? Do you want to check to see what—"

"No. There's nothing I can do for him now. It's over. Jimi's gone. And so am I. Just get me to the fucking airport."

Emotions rolled over and through me almost too fast to track. My first reaction was to be angry at him. Goddammit, Jimi. You had it all. Talent. Success. And you had to be a fuckup, so damn sensitive that all you could do right was play that guitar, with a need to anesthetize everything else to keep the pain out. You couldn't listen to

Angel at that kitchen table last night or even to common sense. Dies in his puke because he couldn't control his appetites. I'd spent the past years in hell, fighting to stay alive, and here's a guy who's got it all and it's like he wants to die. Then there was just that sense of loss. But you can't stay angry at the dead for long. Emptiness ached inside my heart.

Or was there more than there seemed to the death of Jimi Hendrix?

In the years following his death, nearly everyone who knew Jimi personally wrote a book about their relationship with and impressions of Jimi. While such books varied in quality and viewpoint, the constant among them was skepticism that something wasn't right about Jimi's death; that foul play was a possibility.

Could I have done more to help Jimi? And if so…what? Hell, ask yourself. What would you have done? If it was today, Jimi would have gone into rehab. But those days were different. And Death comes when it's your time, whether your name is Sergeant Chug Brown in Vietnam or Jimi Hendrix in London. Or Sydney Blanchard. At least her killer was behind bars.

I caught a flight that was boarding as we walked up to the reservation desk. I scored the last vacant seat. I had police clearance and my duffel bag. I would be expected to cooperate at the appropriate time in Hudberry's prosecution.

Time restraints made for a hasty goodbye.

Angel said, "I wondered if I would ever say this again but…I'm back on the team, Soldier. You're in my heart, deep. You damn well better stay in touch."

I promised her that I would, having every intention of

doing so. That's how goodbyes are in airports. But I meant it. Our goodbye kiss was lingering, delicious with promise. And then it was time for me to go.

Details were made public in the days that followed. On their return to her flat, Monika had taken a sleeping pill, that powerful German brand called Vesperex, about 4:00 AM and slept through whatever happened next. She awoke a few hours later and realized that Jimi was in a coma. He had vomited. She called an ambulance. When Jimi was wheeled into the Emergency Room at St. Mary Abbots Hospital at 12:45, it was determined that he had been dead for several hours. He had ingested at least nine Vesperex. The prescription called for one-half to one pill. The inquest would rule the cause of death as asphyxiation through inhalation of vomit due to barbiturate intoxication.

Angel wrote me later that within hours after Jimi's death, all of the flats he had rented in London, or was known to visit, were thoroughly searched and looted of his clothes, instruments, writings and recordings.

Michael Jeffrey remained a secretive and controversial figure until he was killed in 1973 in a mid-air collision over Nantes, France while aboard an Iberia Airlines DC-9.

Monika Dannemann committed suicide in 1996.

I returned to London to say my piece in court. Hudberry got life in prison. I missed connecting with Angel on that trip, for reasons too complicated to go into here. We did encounter each other again some years later in Texas, but that's another story.

On that rainy September day in 1970, I left London as surely as Jimi Hendrix had, if not as permanently.

I was en route to my next duty station.
Call me Soldier.

AFTERWORD

Movies often claim to be "Based on a True Story."

Jimi After Dark may or may not be based on the truth.

The real-life characters in this narrative include the late Monika Dannemann, the late Michael Jeffrey, and the immortal Little Richard and Jimi Hendrix. Soldier and all of the others are figments of my imagination.

The novel was inspired by Jimi's assertion, made to associates and his inner circle on more than one occasion, that he had been kidnapped in England by armed thugs in October, 1969 and held captive until *other* armed thugs came to his rescue. Jimi claimed that Mike Jeffrey was involved.

Literary license was invoked in shifting this alleged incident to Jimi's final days.

I refer to the "alleged incident" because no such kidnapping was ever reported to the authorities. The skepticism Jimi's claims invoked among those he told prompted him to soon refrain from mentioning it. Jimi's "kidnapping" is much debated among Hendrix scholars.

Debunkers have, over the years, unearthed convincing evidence that the whole scenario could well have been a drug-addled fabrication by Jimi intended to further cloud his legal problems.

I visited London three times during 1966-1967, each time on a ten-day leave pass as a US soldier. Most of that time in very Swinging London was spent pursuing hot music and romance, both of which proved to be in abundant supply. The air was alive. My portrayal of the London rock club scene of that era is drawn in large part from personal experience.

In writing this novel, two Hendrix biographies, the anecdotal and compelling *'Scuse Me While I Kiss the Sky* by David Henderson and *Room Full of Mirrors*, a slick, thorough compendium of data by Charles R. Cross, each provided information and insight, as did the memoir, *Are You Experienced?* by Hendrix sideman, Noel Redding.

The notion of the Nixon administration sending out hit teams to silence rock stars like Jimi, Janis Joplin and Jim Morrison has been around for decades, and is vigorously investigated in depth and at length by Alex Constantine both on-line and in his book, *The Covert War Against Rock*.

A LOOK AT HANK & MUDDY

In steamy Shreveport, Louisiana, two musical legends-in-the-making come together: a whiskey-soaked country singer named Hank Williams and blues artist Muddy Waters. What they've got in common over several hectic days of drinking, singing and whoring is an interest in staying alive despite local mobsters, bent cops, and a truckload of Ku Klux Klansmen. Then there's the bank robber's daughter...

Available Now

ALSO BY STEPHEN MERTZ

Dragon Games

Night Wind

Devil Creek

Blood Red Sun

Hank & Muddy

ABOUT THE AUTHOR

Stephen Mertz is an American fiction author who is best known for his mainstream thrillers and novels of suspense. His work covers a wide variety of styles from paranormal dark suspense (*Night Wind* and *Devil Creek*) to historical speculative thrillers (*Blood Red Sun*) and hard-boiled noir (*Fade to Tomorrow*). Mertz is also a popular lecturer on the craft of writing and has appeared as a guest speaker before writer's groups and at universities.

Steve's writing output increased dramatically when he emerged as one of the country's most in-demand writers of adventure paperback novels, averaging four books per year for ten years. His work on Don Pendleton's Mack Bolan series is regarded by fans as some of the best in that series. He also created the Mark Stone: MIA Hunter and Cody's Army series, written under the pseudonyms Jack Buchanan and Jim Case respectively.

Stephen Mertz lives in the American Southwest, and he is always at work on a new book.

www.ingramcontent.com/pod-product-compliance
Lightning Source LLC
Chambersburg PA
CBHW060552030726
47498CB00005B/1359